Katrijn van der Caab, freed slave and wigmaker's apprentice, travels with her eccentric employer from Cape Town to Vogelzang, a remote farm where a hairless girl needs their services. The year is 1794, it is the age of enlightenment, and on Vogelzang the master is conducting strange experiments in human breeding and classi-fication. It is also here that Trijn falls in love.

Two hundred years later and a thousand miles away, Sister Vergilius, a nun at a mission hospital, wants to free herself from an austere order. It is 1961 and her life intertwines with that of a gentleman farmer – an Englishman and suspected Communist – who collects and studies insects and lives a solitary life. While a group of Americans arrive in a cavalcade of caravans and a new republic is about to be born, desire is unfurling slowly.

In Claire Robertson's majestic debut novel, two stories echo across centuries to expose that which binds us and sets us free.

PRAISE FOR *THE SPIRAL HOUSE*

'An astonishingly adept and richly imagined novel, a layered, subtle story that resonates with important ideas about history. We applaud the sensuous quality of the writing and were amazed by its remarkable language.' – *Sunday Times* Fiction Prize

'With *The Spiral House*, Claire Robertson has lifted the bar of South African literature in one stroke. An unsettling, unforgettable work.' – Michele Magwood, *Sunday Times Lifestyle*

'*The Spiral House* is set apart by its language: sometimes sparse and hard as exposed rock, but more often given to vivid, detailed descriptive passages like poetry ... This complex, persuasive novel rewards an attentive reader with a wealth of experience and sensation.' – *Cape Times*

'Subtle yet mesmerising ... The stories twist together to reflect on a violent history, freedom and salvation.' – *Essentials*

'Claire Robertson is a rare master ... she is confident and deft enough to let her beguiling characters, acute observation and finely crafted language do their work ... It is understatedly beautiful and a real pleasure to read.' – Kate Sidley, *Sunday Times Lifestyle*

'A breathtaking novel of extraordinary strength and originality.' – *Woman & Home*

THE SPIRAL HOUSE

CLAIRE ROBERTSON

UMUZI

Published by Umuzi
an imprint of Penguin Random House (Pty) Ltd
Company Reg No 1953/000441/07
Estuaries No 4, Oxbow Crescent, Century Avenue,
Century City, 7441, South Africa
PO Box 1144, Cape Town, 8000, South Africa
umuzi@penguinrandomhouse.co.za

First edition, first printing 2013
First edition, second printing 2013
This edition, first printing 2014
This edition, second printing 2015
This edition, third printing 2016
3 5 7 9 8 6 4

ISBN 978-1-4152-0752-9 (Print)
ISBN 978-1-4152-0522-8 (ePub)
ISBN 978-1-4152-0523-5 (PDF)

Cover design by Joey Hi-Fi
Text design by Monique Oberholzer
Set in Adobe Caslon

Printed and bound by Novus Print, a Novus Holdings company

To my family

BEFORE

IT IS HOURS BEFORE THE HOUSE BEYOND THIS ROOM WILL wake, but in the lordlingshouse and workshop that are the neighbouring buildings they keep kitchen hours, and now there's the creak of a hand cart as Melt hauls wood up the avenue. In the kitchen, a deep room lit at one end by the dripping pre-morning, a charred log settles at the hearth, adding its shuffle to the flatus leaking from a mound on the floor, to the burp of the beer barrel and sigh as meat rolls in brine.

Morning: a rogue bantam (from Bantam) confirms it from a patch under the gooseberry bush at the end of the stairs; by the third note the cook is on her feet, piss pot in hand and scratching her breast and a kick for the rump under the table. Morning. No need to tell her twice. At the hearth, the kindling catches and the last log from the basket is balanced, ready to burn. A conserve pan picks up the yellow light and an orange tom toasts its back side.

The cook uncovers dough in the baking trough and drives her fist into it to let out its sour breath.

'It was the black ship again,' she says.

She is addressing a girl who has left her nest of sacking, splashed her face at the rain barrel beside the kitchen door and emptied the piss pot into its twin.

'Nay, Ma?'

The cook's report on her dream and the girl's response to it are as much part of the pattern as the thump of Melt stacking wood next to

7

the fire place. The dream is most often prophetic and frightening – black ships in full shivering sail or mountains rent.

'Ja, that black ship,' the cook says. She tucks dough in rounds and covers them again. A boy enters with a bucket of milk, splashing some as he moves around the table to the larder, earning a push on his shoulder on his way past her and a jar of small beer and yesterday's heel when he returns. Derde Susann. Third Susan. That is the cook's given name, though not by her parents. The men and boys, when they enter her kitchen, lift their hats; the women defer to her; she is chief among the household and on all this outpost estate only Melt would fetch more.

Derde Susann collects chops from the cool room, closes the oven door on the loaves, swings a griddle over the fire, flicks the cat from her path. She moves smooth as a priest's boy, stoked by her own pity for her lot. Now she lifts her head: horses on the approach to the house. She slides more cuts to the griddle, tells the girl to gather extra bowls: guests to break fast. But the riders are not guests; they live here. They are the son and daughter of the house who left not three days ago for a fortnight at their cousins' farm, now suddenly returned, he in a sulk, she in tears, running to her mother's room like a child.

Probably the mother does not shriek so loudly as to reach the kitchen with the sound, but unease travels to it and throughout the house. The tom bolts into the morning.

Admit only your victories until you have hooked their interest, then you draw them closer and admit the sort of failings that reflect well on a fellow, sentimental failings: that was the theory of courtship the young master had formulated on the ride there, only to have his chance of putting it to the proof snatched by his sister's insistence that they return home at once, last night, with her turbaned and muffled like a night watch man, not saying two words on the ride but none the less driving him ahead of her with her will.

His mother is in the front room in her cap and night gown, clutching her front and staring at him in a way that makes him feel blameworthy. Now she turns at the sound of her husband entering from the other end of the room, a small rock of sugar and the key to the sugar box in his hand, and transfers the awful look to him. She steps backwards, her eyes on the men of her house to block their approach. She closes the door to her room. Son and master hear the snap of the key.

In the kitchen the women widen their eyes and purse their mouths. It is so quiet they hear an onion settle in its string. Later, orders come from deep in the house: bring goat's milk. Goat's blood. Bruise leaves of mallow and gather dung, wild and from the heap. Apricot kernels, but crush them in sweet oil. Lard and muslin and mastic and vinegar, calomel, vitriol, nostrums, other nostrums. The kitchen women make a bed for Master in a room among the sugar and tea. Madam's door is locked all night, part of the day.

Word comes back to the kitchen: young mistress's night waters are not for the lant barrel. The girl who has that office must take her pot to the muckheap behind the stables and empty it there and be sure and cover that over.

The young mistress is barely seen about the house, never on the farm. Something is wrong, but no one will say what.

This, at least, is what I surmise.

1

AS YOU KNOW, A HEAD IS A DEAL HEAVIER THAN IT LOOKS. That is one reason you do not want to drop it anywhere near your feet. Another is that it takes a long age to push it back in shape if it should fall on its sides or on the back. The face matters less but the sides and the back take an age to put right and he almost all ways could tell if you had gone and dropped it while he was out.

He was out when they came so sudden to the door and I stumbled and let the thing fall but held on at the last and spared it and my toes and set it on the sill of the street side window, where there was light to see by. At their end of the shop the man blocked light from the door and the woman who walked before him moved under a dull cloud. She stopped three steps in and spoke to her man without a look at him or me, or anywhere but at her hands in finger gloves held at her stomach, pressing the dark stuff against her. She said:

'Melt. Ask after the master.'

The man Melt moved from the door, and light followed him into the shop. He looked at the blank faces on the shelf, then at me, his expression the same for me as for the wood and wax, yet under his eyes I felt my shoulders drop and a stillness settle in me, I recall it as that sudden and thorough, the effect of his looking. Though she had not spoken to me I answered her that my master was at the barracks for a fitting as he taught me to say, and so of course he straight ways made me a liar by arriving on the threshold in his bare feet with his shoes and stockings in one hand and haarder fish in the other and him shouting: 'Trijn! Onions!'

We were in the front room of the shop on Low Street. It is a baker's now, and its street is cobbled, but then it was all sand and stones around us.

I moved to meet him and he spun where he was, handing the fish to me as he came around with a lift of his brows, then stepping into his shoes and ending bowed over the lady's hand to give to her a press of his lips and a share of fish reek, by which I knew he had bought them (and those not lately from the sea) and not caught them as he was likely to boast.

With him engaging her I was free to look and saw a packed party, not tall, with hair, where it showed beyond her cap, that jinked and swept over her forehead in matching lines, a regular series that did not move independent of her head and being fair but not clean wore the several colours of an oyster. A sweet jasmine pomade compounded this. Still, she rode low in the water, her silk and the silver of her reticule saying she was heavy with goods. I saw that he saw this too, had likely marked it on the instant he stepped in to the shop.

'Crispin le Voir, my lady.'

She made no answer but lifted her chin and I noticed that her nostrils tended to the vertical to give her a greedy aspect. She twitched her head at her man and Le Voir turned so that only I could see the face he pulled. The tall man held the door for me and I passed close by his body with its arm stretched wide. He did not linger near the shop but walked off towards the square with not a word and I was left with a boy guarding the cart and with the sound of her lofty speech and Le Voir's answers, though I could not hear the words. He was using his best voice on a country woman, the voice he kept for castle men.

On the street a gust lifted my skirts and put the boy in a crouch to take shelter next to the cart. The brown mare closed her eyes against the sand. She snorted and shifted in the traces, lifting now this hoof, now that in irritation. In this season the wind was all but ceaseless. I think I would not have minded a lashing gale but this hissing, snatching on and off noise that bit at the corners of the house and made every window bump without rhythm in its frame … 'It is illogical to attribute wicked intent to the displacement of vapours,' Le Voir would say when I muttered about it, though when a day broke still and warm I saw his mood was lifted same as mine.

At last Le Voir showed her out and the tall man came and handed her up to the cart, though I had not seen his return. For a moment I hoped Le Voir would see her off with one of his company bows: a leg stuck out in front, one arm straight up at the back and a deep bend of the waist − a bow that made me laugh; but he only dropped his chin to his chest in the manner of one affirming an arrangement. I burned to know her business. Measuring for a wig would have taken longer and messed her own hair, so it was not that. As she settled and shifted her back side in the cart she gave me a direct look, taking my measure, and for a plunging moment I thought she might have asked after me; I was not in play, but you ever feel you may be again if once you were.

They left. A pair of boys chased the cart until it turned the corner and gained the paved road.

'So, Trijn,' said Le Voir. 'Here is a thing.'

I followed him within. He cleaned the fish and I sliced an onion and while we worked he told me that seven days from today the tall, silent man would return with a wagon and we would pack into it the goods and trade tools of C le Voir, Peruker and Surgeon, and leave this town for the far country.

Well.

Le Voir wanted most in this life to be like the naturalists who blew through the town with presses and guns and barrels of brandy, but he had fled his homeland with only his hooks and lace and the skills from his father and here slowly fashioned the prop roots of a small enterprise weaving goats' hair to wigs for such as could bear to wear them in this hot place; there was no money or spare time for expeditions to the ever-receding interior, and no patron. I could see by the way he now set about wrapping his books and a new pot of ink that, whatever else it was, this journey was also his chance.

He said that I ought to consult my mother and father; there for after our meal I left the house of reason for the humours at the home of my family four streets away towards the castle gardens. There, among other fancies, my mother held and my father conspired to hold that our family had been under a curse for fifty years, and that now due to end in weeks or months. There would be three signs, my mother said, and two of these had made themselves known. When I was at Le Voir's shop I did not believe in curses but my mother nursed an old flame, and on the streets between his house and hers I kept a sharp eye all the same.

At our home I pressed through the tangle of brothers and sisters to reach her. She had borne only my brother and me in twelve years then, after we all four were bequeathed our selves, had burst into flower and free born children, birthing one a year, and each one sound and set to live past weaning. As dark as her previsions were, my mother in person was scented and soft, and careless of her children clamouring for her lap; I had seen her tip them to the floor as she stood to reach for a sharper needle and this only made them want her more.

Now she cleared a space beside her on the bench and sat me there and took my face in her hands.

'Kattie Katrijn,' she said in her gentle mother voice. She had taken to doing this since I was sent to live at Le Voir's place; each time I came back she would look over my eyes, my mouth, seeking something, I have a good idea what. There was no change to see. Le Voir would have fled on a ship before he would use me that way – heavy, loose Le Voir, his untidy body and over large head bending to the fine work of knotting lace and weaving hair. 'I am not good at this,' I would hear him say as he worked and, looking out to the sandy streets, conclude, 'But then I do not need to be.'

I gave my news. My move to the country was not the determinate sign that the curse had been lifted, Ma said without much thought over it. This journey would be the farthest I had travelled, but for my brothers and sisters and parents it was merely what would happen Tuesday next.

When I returned to the shop Le Voir was all but packed, a week before we would go, and telling the row of heads on the sill, 'Goodbye, Calcott!' I should explain that this was in reference to Arthur Calcott, our rival in peruking in that place.

For the first hours of the journey the man Melt barely spoke, so that we came to disregard him along with the boy walking at the head of the eight span. The wagon was smaller within than you might think. Its size taken as a whole, and the train of beasts, seemed a fearsome lot for moving a few trunks and two people but there we were, wedged and perched under the knocking canvas. Our progress was slow enough on the flats that I thought at times the oxen were stamping in place, kneading the sand with their hooves; my middle body hurt from pulling with them in the salty heat.

Le Voir lay himself across the baggage and slept, waking when we reached the first river. When we were on our way again, he sat straight and looked around him. 'Now, Trijn,' he began, and I saw he was about his best-loved game.

'Attend me: a man leaves his home. As he steps onto the street, he decides from the heat of the sun that he had better wear a hat (we will say that he is a rough fellow and does not follow fashion). Back into the house he goes, rummaging and so on, and five minutes later he is on the street once more, with his hat on his head, and he sets off. Not forty steps down the road he passes a smith and as he passes a piece of molten metal from the forge flies out! It is going to hit the man's head! Perhaps it will blind him! But at the deciding moment it is knocked away by the brim of his hat, surely sparing his sight.'

Le Voir fanned his face with his hand, rolled his eyes.

'Now, tell me: was our walking man *put* in danger by the wearing of the hat whose fetching so delayed his journey that it placed him in the path of the metal at the exact moment, or was he *saved* from danger by the fact of the hat itself being on his head?'

He shot his cuffs. 'Do not hurry to answer. You must be ready with your explication when your man here allows us onto the ground again.' And Le Voir settled against the baggage, contemplating the unfamiliar mountains.

It was his intention to teach me to reason as much as it was my mother's to have me attend to the signs of unreason. Ours was the age of enlightenment, he said, when the battle cry was, 'We must know, we shall know!', and reason would depose superstition and we be liberated by it. To this end for a few hours every day in the shop we had set aside our lace work and hair knots for the books and slate. Then, though I could not all ways make out the sense of the arguments, I made sure I learned the new words so they hooked in my thinking, and I knew the reward when one came that exactly named the thing that was before me, or the thing in me, and also had the delight when I could use it to one of them, dropping 'axiom' so easily as 'cabbage' to see the new reckoning in their eyes. Le Voir relied on me to learn their spoken language, and I on him for every other learning thing, among them these games of logique.

I wondered what the man Melt made of it. From where I sat I could see the side of his head. He faced forward but I could feel him listening to Le Voir. He did not hold himself like a slave, this one, but then only the meanest slaves did, my mother said. It seemed to me that part of her rusted ire at having been one herself was directed at those still held in bondage. As for the class of person who had owned us – who yet owned those like us – her response was a profitable revenge, though it hurt them not: she studied them and put us, her children, to work to meet their needs; the younger rinsed gut for sheaths to sell and re-sell to the sailors waiting at the Lodge, the elder ground soapstone for face powder, shells for tooth powder, flaked lead into acid to make them lovely, to make them whiter. We lived by serving them and not their better selves either, and when I had learned the wigmaker's trade our family would profit off them crotch to head.

The wagon left the sand flats for harder and thus easier ground, flanked on our left by mountains that rose blue and steep above their hills. The air was cooler. Melt called a halt and the boy ran down the span slapping them to stop. For hours we had seen farms and homesteads showing white among the trees but though we had heard about town how hospitable were the country folk, our wagon passed by the gates, did not even slow, and we were stopped out of sight of any farm. Did he do this to spare me sleeping like a slave that night? It is true that there were too few of my type to easily place between the front rooms and the floor of the kitchen, but such niceness on his part did not come to me then.

Whatever the reasoning, we out spanned before sunset beside a stream, by a stand of oaks. The boy led his unyoked team to drink, Melt flung a length of carpet to the ground and tossed out blankets, showing Le Voir that he must make his bed beneath the wagon. On the bed he pushed and pulled Le Voir's boxes to one side and lined the space with a blanket and showed it to me with a tilt of his head. Then he was quickly away, fetching rocks and firewood, building and stoking a fire, boiling water and making coffee and a supper of a chicken's eggs and wine, and bread and salt meat.

Le Voir stood to one side, observing Melt and the land about us with ease but starting like a girl at the sound of the boy and his beasts coming from the stream. He laughed at himself for this and lay back on the carpet, a cup of wine in one hand and a cooked egg in the other.

'Well, Trijn?'

It was time for the lesson. I cleared my throat, conscious of Melt and the boy.

'Had the man left when he intended, without his hat, he would have been well past the smith by the time the gobbet flew out from the forge,' I began. 'Unless ... unless it was his approaching footsteps that somehow forced a moment of inattention on the part of the blacksmith, and his approach, *whenever* it happened, would be met by the flung steel ... as it were ...' I seemed, for these explications, to follow Le Voir in acting the frosted scholar. I thought more and, warmed by Le Voir's eyes on me, brought my argument around.

'In which case, the hat was a necessary defence whatever time he left the house. But if he had no effect on the, ah, the launching of the hot gobbet, then the hat *did* place him in danger, at least, his going back to fetch it did so.'

'Ah ha! You have stumbled right up to the essential inquiry!' Le Voir was on his feet, slopping wine. 'Does everything influence everything else? Or is there a set path for each phenomenon and we either intersect or do not? Do you see, Trijn?'

I hoped I did, but my answer was not expected. Philosophy done, food followed. I had not thought to see how the resolution of our game was received by Melt, and soon I was in a smoke-scented bed, listening to the fire. On the point of sleep I heard Melt say this to Le Voir: 'The man was never going to pass the smith later or earlier than he did pass it. The matter of the hat, all that, was the only thing that was going to happen because it was the only thing that did happen. There is no "what if". Only in stories.' This came with a fierce hiss as he damped the fire. His words, by some magnitudes the most we had heard from him until that moment, put an end to argument.

The boy had tied the oxen to the wagon; the sound of their breathing and the odd musical clacking of their horns soon sent me to sleep.

I would decide for myself where I would spend the next night.

We arrived at noon. The white buildings cast no shadow and the trees stood each in a blue pool. Fallow dogs leapt from the veranda to catch our wagon, scattering geese as they came. The house's windows and great door seemed to hold thicker air than we breathed, air that would keep its shape and stillness no matter how the vapours blew without. I had only a moment to see these things; in that time we had passed in a wide sweep from the front of the house with its China jars of flowers and were halted at the rear and there were women come to meet us.

The goods on the wagon held most interest for them but, when it grew clear that we had brought luggage for a long stay, that we were no overnighters on our way across the plain between the mountains, the burble of voices dipped and the women looked us over. Le Voir turned his back on the servants and said to me in a low tone: 'I believe we may be expected only by the mistress of this house. None the less, a man who has stared down a ducal mistress over a second stuffed tit—' He was working to encourage us; this was how he did it in those days, calling up the fantastical creatures who had visited his father's shop. He watched, an eyebrow cocked, for my smile, and when I gave it he turned, arms wide, and presented his most ridiculous bow to the large woman among those there. Puckering and pressing forward his lips as though to sip from her he introduced us in the formal language of the place, its round, half-swallowed sounds, as now, never less than absurd in his mouth: 'Crispin le Voir, peruker to the gentry of the town such as they are and on this day also to parts beyond, and my apprentice, Miss Katrijn van de Caab.'

My shod feet and his way with my name made me as a freed person though I were black the same as them, and on seeing these things and hearing them the women watched me with new interest or darkened brows. But at least now they could place us, even if it was as being from that half world between garrison and estate, jetsam from the port come to ordained Vogelzang.

The house women numbered three. There was the cook, Derde Susann, fat. There was a yellow girl, Jansie, who moved with a twitch of her bottom, and the last was Meerem, tall for a woman, who hunched her shoulders and held her head low to lose her height. They were engaged in some mutual task, all with their sleeves rolled above the elbow and in heavy aprons. The three of them turned back to the kitchen, the younger women hefting sacks and parcels. Melt shouldered a trunk and led Le Voir towards the lordlingshouse. Other men followed with other baggage and I would have been left with the dogs sniffing my skirts had Derde Susann not looked back and lifted a hand from her hip, opening the way for me to follow.

In the kitchen they were about rendering. A brass kettle of such dimensions as to seat a dog was on a trivet over the fire and rolling in it clear fat and browning dumplings of fat. At the table Meerem took a cleaver and swung it at a pile of rosy bones. Jansie, with a smaller knife, pared at ox kidneys, adding to a heap on the table. The wagon goods were in a corner beside a row of scoured boxes.

Derde Susann straight off asked for my story though that took few words to tell; the truth was that I did not know that afternoon why Le Voir and I were there; by that night I would (and still not tell it). Then Derde Susann leaned back from the rendering kettle and told me theirs, and Meerem and Jansie gave her the hungry looks of dogs at table while she listed each's history and faults, and the virtues she allowed.

'Meerem is from up there and were not so high before she was on the ship and off it and here. She is not clever but strong as a man, and sweet.' Dark as roasted coffee, with wide-set eyes, Meerem had a broad face with something of a night jar or frog about it, some creature that frowns shyly from under its brows. Her wide mouth closed over teeth that had been sharpened to points, her arms swung forward as though to hide her breasts. Dark as a coffee bean as I have writ, and rough husked, she was the household's heavy lifter.

'Now Jansie's people is from my land – in the least, her mam was but you do not get this' – and she leaned across the table and pinched the arm of the pretty yellow girl – 'without a pa that was the other thing.' She kept hold of the girl's silken pale skin and said in a warning manner, 'Jansie is a foolish girl that has caught the eye of one she did not ought to have invited to consider her in that way.' Jansie giggled even as she made a face at being pinched. Her free hand moved to her throat where hung a thread with a small bow of red ribbon tied on it.

A scraping of feet at the door. Melt was standing back to allow Le Voir to enter and Derde Susann turned at his throat clearing noises, pushing out her lower lip to see him in the kitchen. He took it as a challenge to be charming again and came to the kettle, ignoring the elbows Derde Susann raised against him, and looked in.

'Ah, graisse à friture, kidney fat from the ox, the marvellous fat, very pure.'

It was comical to watch the looks chase one another across her face and to see the advance of Le Voir and the retreat of Susann, flustering her arms and apron to make herself grow. Jansie stared at him where she stood, jaw slack and knife in suspense above a purple kidney. Meerem paid them no mind, chopped at the bones.

'How so ever Mesdames,' Le Voir said when he tired of teasing the cook, 'I come not to disturb your useful work but to fetch my girl prentice. We go, Trijn.'

Melt had carried in Le Voir's net box. I picked it up from the floor and followed the wigmaker, not out to the day but through another kitchen door and into the house proper. It was dim and quiet; we were in a long hall with the front door at the far end. Light from the door laid a path the length of the hall on the polished floor. Half way down the room tall screens of wood and window stood folded against the wall; a table, and chairs that matched one to the other, filled part of the place. I followed Le Voir past these into the front room that met the hall like the cross bar upon the letter T. This front room had a door at either side, a fine bench against the wall and a cupboard with grand plates and silver jugs.

The door to our left was open. Le Voir knocked and a madam's voice called him to enter. It was the packed party from the shop, sat over a foot stove, winding a handkerchief between her fingers. Her eyes flicked over me and the box and her mouth tightened.

'My daughter is through that door. She knows you are here. Wait!' she said as Le Voir turned towards a door that led to an inner room. 'What about this girl?'

'Madame, I will not speak of this. Trijn like wise. A peruker would not hold custom if he could not keep his client's affairs private. You must not worry.'

The door opened inward to the adjoining room and as he pushed it he said in a low voice, 'Crispin le Voir and his apprentice.'

The windows were to, the curtains also, and the room lit on this bright afternoon by a lamp of oil. I could see a girl seated at a table, her back to us, watching us in a glass. There was a bitterness in the air. Le Voir approached her; she did not turn to meet him but bent her turbaned head and waited, hands in her lap. He stopped behind her. After a moment she raised her head and met his eyes in the mirror. He lifted his hands and held them on either side of the turban and tipped his head as one who asks permission. The girl closed her eyes and opened them, to give it.

It was my task at this part of the business to hand Le Voir the calliper and tape, or sometimes lace and a threaded needle, and I bent over the box to find these and set them in order. I heard a sharp sound from him as he unfolded the last layer of cloth and laid her scalp bare. The bitter smell was stronger.

'Miss, I must examine you in proper light. Trijn, curtains.'

The light showed a head naked of hair. It was crusted with scabs that lay over and around blisters and broken skin. Green matter, part of a compress, clung there. The girl had bowed her head again, her inflamed scalp supported on a pale nape and neck, these clear of blemish. Le Voir let me know with a frown and flick of his hand that I should pack away the measuring gear. He turned to a chest by the table and looked over the bottles there, making suckings of disgust, then he found me again, and told me in a low voice to fetch cold butter from the cook and these herbs, and these, from the garden if they were to be had. Also hot water and what clean spare linen there was.

I hurried out, skirting with some fright Madam who had risen and stood, breathing hard and glaring at her daughter's room. In the kitchen Derde Susann gave a box of butter, a basin and jug of water from the steady kettle, all with a tight mouth, refusing to ask why. Jansie she sent without for lavender and comfrey, and bucku from the fields. I made two trips to the back room where Le Voir had drawn open the other curtain and moved the girl's chair nearer to a window. The turban cloth he had unfolded and laid across her shoulders to protect her gown, and from somewhere had produced a small bottle of spermaceti in which were specks of dark matter. This he placed in her hands, bidding her roll it to warm and bring alive; I could see it was a piece of kindness from him in that room, to make her feel part of us three and not some piece to be done unto.

He had me stand at his side, the basin against my stomach and held there with straight arms, and here he poured warmed water. He tore lavender and scattered the flower heads over this, closing us in sharp steam; he reached in his coat pocket for his kerchief, and wet and wrung this, and addressed himself to the head.

The sun moved in squares across my feet; I changed the water thrice, moving quickly through the kitchen to the grounds to keep private the pink slops, and Le Voir yet worked on her skin, pressing the cloth to dissolve a bloody or a herbal scab, and switching lavender for salt.

In the weeks since the girl had fled home in horror at the handfuls of hair that slid from her scalp at a touch, we learned, her mother had tried many things, nostrums and scalding and rubbing with canvas and packing with a green poultice, menacing the hair to grow again. She had tried many things and this in secret, surely to spare the estate the shame of it; by the look of that scalp she had done this with a force that was also punishment, for what could cause such a thing but the pox, and the pox gave the lie to the girl's virgin state, and if she were no maid she were not fit to be a bride and bring a new master or stitch the estate's fields of cattle and vine to those of another, and then what of her? She was daughter, yes, but also chattel, and now lessened, now lesser.

She made no sound as we worked to cure her mother's cure.

After my final trip with the bowl of blood and water I returned to the room to see Le Voir lean over and fetch the small bottle from her hands. He pulled the cork with his teeth and poured a share on his palm, then set the bottle aside and rubbed his hands together. He placed them on her head and she caught her breath at this blessing that, mild though it was, yet stung.

He made no movement with his hands, bringing to this business of healing only the oily stuff, and the heat of his flesh.

2

SHE WOKE BECAUSE THEY HAD STOPPED. AND THERE WAS something else – a conversation with the steward, through the door and apparently in her sleep. Coffee. And fifteen minutes to disembark. That was how she arrived at Bandolier a decade ago, when the train from Cape Town stopped at the siding at the northern border of the farm.

She was twenty-six and from Ireland, and tall. The train left, heading for Southern Rhodesia; she waited on the siding in the still heat, felt it ease her shoulder muscles and warm her stomach, breathed in scents of chitin and wild sage and steel. A sister found her next to the shed where the agent keeps his paperwork – Sister Patrick, come to collect ah Sister Vergilius, is it? In a borrowed Bedford they travelled on the Great North Road, going south for a mile or so, to Mannamead Mission. There the Immaculate who had driven her from the railway siding showed her into the parlour in the nuns' quarters behind the hospital, where the woman in charge – it was Mother Rose back then, too – had gathered the others. Three of them crowded on a low bench; sunlight flared the colours on the holy pictures and termites chewed the furniture and shat it out, building a sour scent in the room.

'Sister Virginia. There you are. At long last.'

'God be with you, Sister. It's ahm Vergilius, actually.'

'Yes, well, God be with you and it's ahm Mother. Actually. Mother Rose, mind the thorns. Hmm hmm.' It was a kind of laughter.

Rose patted the seat of an upright chair next to her, across from the other sisters. Tea was poured and passed. The sisters rustled in their seats, bobbed their veiled heads as Rose named them. She indicated that they might speak; they said: to cope with the heat she would swap her woollen habit for cotton garments and fewer of them. The sisters wore open-toed sandals over their white wool stockings and their wimples were of muslin, though still starched. They bathed almost every day and had an arrangement with the hotel in the village to use its swimming pool, after dark, if there were no guests. By these measures and by the construction of mission buildings to create shade and hold on to it, sisters wearing habits designed for the northern hemisphere survived in the southern. Thrived. They broke the Rule with each accommodation, of course, but the bishop was in Pietersburg and his diocese the size of Wales.

One of the women on the bench across from Vergilius was a heavy-browed, yellow-complexioned woman who slumped into torpor when she was not being addressed. Every so often the ripple of a smile lifted a corner of her mouth. This was accompanied by a snuffling sigh as though she had laughed or almost laughed. The slow convulsion was repeated every few minutes and when it was, the Immaculate alongside patted her hand and murmured to her without moving her lips. She caught Vergilius staring and Vergilius, flustered, looked down at her cup and said: 'Like Moslem women, all in black in a hot country. But we can feel the breeze on our faces, at least.'

Mother Rose turned her mouth down and lifted her brows and said: 'O ho, what is this that has arrived on the Thursday train?' She spoke as though to herself but loud enough for her sisters to hear. Vergilius flushed. The others stole looks at her from lowered faces as Patrick slid her hand over the plate and palmed the last Marie biscuit.

With the new young sister, the Immaculates at Mannamead Mission numbered seven. Only three had taken the names of female saints when they left off the names their parents had given them; of those, slight Mary Margaret would slip away before two months had passed and be buried in a child's coffin in the mission grounds. Xavier was the sister with the eerie smile.

Vergilius was given a cloister cell opening onto the rear veranda. She was allowed to fall asleep, and woke after dark when this Xavier brought more tea and a sandwich on a tin tray and stood in the door-way of Vergilius's cell, her mouth agape, her eyes cast up and to the side, and said: 'The others have gone after supper that you missed to swim Mother says you must join them if you want if you don't if you don't if you DON'T you must come to lauds at six o clock.' She spoke in a watery voice that was split, at unnerving intervals, by an insane bark. Now something or nothing in the corridor outside the cell caught Xavier's attention. She sniffed and turned towards it, then placed the tray and a hurricane lamp and box of matches on the floor inside the doorway of the cell, and said with her hiccup-ping emphasis, 'I gave you here HERE this for when the generator does not go.' She turned a loose hand towards the lamp and left the new sister.

While the generator still ran, the cell and the rest of the mission were lit by light bulbs that buzzed like trapped beetles as the power ebbed and surged. Vergilius put on the nearly new lightweight habit she found in the clothing alcove, ate the peppery tomato sandwich, stepped out of the cell. She found the dispensary, where she set down the unlit lantern, and moved through a silent theatre, past a bed, an autoclave, a table with a tray of instruments. She adjusted her stride as she passed through the wards where five men and a dozen women shifted in their high beds. The lighter cloth of the habit slid against her body; her stockinged toes flexed in the sandals, groping for shoe leather. The lightness of the clothing left her feeling curiously un-tethered, a feeling compounded when she stepped off the veranda and walked away from the mission buildings.

The night was warm. In the distance she could make out strained, echoing grunts from throats stretched above water. Splashing, a yelp and other sounds came from where lights shifted through the thorn scrub. Here in the mission grounds her footsteps had silenced the night creatures. Vergilius could hear her own breathing and then, as she tipped her head and faced the stars, her own intake of breath. They were sharp against a dry sky and resisted their known patterns. At home Vergilius could read the constellations like the psalms but here were random, scattered stars. She narrowed her eyes to find the familiar groups: not much of a Milky Way, an upside-down Orion and, most wondrous of all, a rampant Southern Cross. For all her reading about the Union of South Africa on the great ship that brought her here, Vergilius had not anticipated this. She swivelled to find more she would recognise.

After a while she became aware that the noises from the pool had dropped to a murmur. She heard a wheeze of effort as a body left the water. Natural night sounds started up. From far away came a rill of icy yelps, rising higher and dying suddenly, and the groan of a truck on the road.

Vergilius was about to turn back to the mission buildings when she saw torchlight rocking through the blackness towards her. She stepped backwards into the deeper dark of an acacia's night shadow and held her breath as her new sisters filed by, their wet hair cooling the air when they passed close by her hiding place.

Soon it was nine o'clock and the light in the mission windows flickered and dimmed and the generator motor puttered to a stop. She left her tree and picked her way back to where the lights had been, grey thorns crackling under her sandals.

The next morning Vergilius came upon six-year-old Jacob, who had arrived at Mannamead a day before she did. He was watching the hens in the cage behind the handyman's room at the back of the mission. She stood alongside him and studied the curves of his nape and skull, the walnut folds of his ear, his knees grey from a day without his grandmother rubbing Vaseline into his skin. Vergilius was forbidden to touch him and did not in any event have an instinct to do so; as for Jacob, he was by that time less alarmed by the nuns' swooping shadows and was not troubled at all by this new young sister; he exhaled and shifted closer to her. The hens bobbed on the other side of the chicken wire, their drowsy popping noises confirming that they, too, were unafraid.

For years, after that day, it would seem to the farmer on whose land the train stopped a remarkable thing, a break in logic, that he had not known of her arrival in the moment of its happening. Once he even hunted through his diaries and cross-checked the date against the labels on a dry-season Precis octavia he pinned that day, looking for a clue to where he was, what he was doing, when she came: had he, at the moment she stepped off the train and shook the dust from her habit, looked up from his collecting box and listened for her beyond the veld sounds and the breathing of the dogs? How had he not?

3

MADAM'S SECRECY ABOUT HER PLANS FOR LE VOIR AND HER
suspicions about how her daughter had lost her hair – suspicions
that had come to rest, after what I would not call a thoroughgoing
audit of the potentialities, on her husband – made life at Vogelzang
difficult for the wigmaker at the start.

By the time he left the women's rooms and re-entered the front
room that first day it was dusk and Master, who had been told on
his return from the fields that a French stranger had moved into
the lordlingshouse, was on hand to see such a one emerge from his
wife's room, and her pale with tears and disarrayed and with only a
sour look for her husband. Master was somewhat younger than his
wife. In those days, when a healthy woman could get through four
husbands in her span, there were many masters who, like the holder
of the office on this estate, had first come on loan from the castle as
an overseer. There was usually one such on hand should the husband
succumb to toothache or abscess or take his own life or have his life
taken by debtor, gunpowder, leopard or whatever of a thousand
whatevers, and so it had come about here. No woman could man-
age an estate the size of Vogelzang alone and nor would she want
to with a new man on hand to flatter and fetch for her and join her
in the heavens bed.

But, they told me in the kitchen, he had lately been banished to
a cot in the room across the way. There he had no heavenly canopy
to shield him from the reed and clay above and there, his dreams
interrupted by the sifting grit, he must have spent his nights flinching

or hiding his face beneath the blankets. He knew he was suspected of laying a hand on his step daughter, but without he was accused he could not claim innocence, and how to claim innocence any way when, I have not one doubt, he had thought in fond and cruel detail of so doing.

Was the big fellow his replacement? I do not believe Master thought that exactly, but being out of favour himself he set his heart against who had gained it.

Master was slack; his thighs did not fill his breeches with muscle, and a round belly hung over his belt. They said these had been fat years for Vogelzang; the new wine, beeves and corn had become dollars of empire and those more slaves to tend it, and left less for him to do. He ordered pamphlets from the academies and affected a wig like the men in town. We must know, we will know – the cry was heard here too, in that time when every heresy was aired, every daemon tempted because science was divine and philosophy our fluent dogma and we were about gaining perfect dominion over nature – the planet's nature and our own, and no fungous rites tolerated. Two years behind the old countries and somewhat bent by the sea journey, the age of enquiry and illumination had reached even this half caldera of fields and transplanted trees: on this estate the master and his children's tutor pored over such maps as there were and plotted the constellation of the Southern Cross upon the land below – there son, there holy ghost, here Paternoster; on that, they kept two savages from beyond the next river as gentlemen (but one of them sickened and died).

That first night on Vogelzang, Master took Le Voir's catechism at the dining table, a dizzy trade when he sought new ideas from town but only to try to best these with his own cleverness, and answered each new thing not with 'Yes, I see,' but with 'Yes, I know.' The chief thing Le Voir learned was that Master was pulled between wanting to impress him and wanting him gone from the estate. As a newer arrival from the homeland, or at least the home continent, Le Voir was both to be begged for his impressions and lectured on how things were – and to be made to concede that in the backwoods of the world, on the far edge of this place, the cult of science yet had its ordained priests.

We worked on the fiction upon which Le Voir and Madam had settled: Le Voir was the estate's answer to rumours of a music master on the next estate along – a peruker and surgeon for Vogelzang, at least for a season; it followed from this that the first to receive our services should be the master, so Le Voir, tired out from our journey and from the afternoon in the daughter's room, none the less called me again from the kitchen to fetch the box and join him.

The mirror in Master's room was smaller than that which had shown us his step daughter's misery but other wise the symmetry was close: he was seated before it, Le Voir behind, unwinding the turban from his head. He next took up a flat grey pelt from a stand before the mirror and set it upon Master's head. It was too dark in that room for even the illusion of taking measurements (for in any event we would make the new piece on the old) but the low light from the candle and lamp helped Le Voir as he used Master's own vanity to head off suspicion.

From the box I set at the floor by his side Le Voir drew a hank of combed and coloured sheep's wool worked to the stage where it is ready to be spun; it was half a hand's breadth wide and a few feet long. He gave it a few turns and laid it on Master's stubble, twisted here and folded there until the image in the mirror was wearing a full head, sweeping in a steep foreland at the brow, retreating to keep the temples cool, a double roll over each ear. Whereas a moment before he had called himself a man of science, now Master was credulous as a girl before the glass. He trailed on for a few sentences about phlogiston and such but he was caught in his returned beauty and clutched for it when Le Voir muttered some specificities of fit and style to me – the private nonsense we used to fatten the worth of it – and whipped the wool away. In the mirror Master shrank from his naked head.

Doubly wearied we came at last to bed, in a room in the lordlingshouse for Le Voir, serried in a noisome warm heap on the kitchen floor with Jansie and Meerem for me. The finer details of my place in the household were yet to be settled, but at least I knew in which camp I would spend the night.

No free black had set foot on the estate of Vogelzang before me, without you count the first people who roamed there and they never were enslaved so never called free nor treated with, but trapped and shot and at times kept on these estates as trackers or sod turners and the rest feral in ragged skins in the mountains. But of one shod and in skirt and shirt and head cloth, none 'til myself. I could have stood upon my station, not bound to work the kitchen, but neither would I be free to sit over a foot stove and smoke a pipe when I was done with my lace work. I elected to cast in with the women of the kitchen, with nothing said on either side. Derde Susann was dainty in her steering of this and did not order me to the unliked work of wood and gross butchery but told me as a mother would to lend a hand with this dish or that, or these house jobs. Indoors, I left off the shoes.

On our third day she placed me in a line of the three of us girls and set us to work on larks. The birds in their hundreds came every day to the corn and vines where boys trapped them or brought them down with hand catapults; now Meerem plucked and drew them, Jansie pressed force meat in their bodies and pulled the thin grey skin to cover this and I wrapped each in sage leaves and placed it in a crock with spek between it and its sister.

Mid way in the morning Derde Susann sent me to the forward rooms of the house to fetch coffee there and Jansie a bucket of coals for the foot stove, and to bring away linens from the heavens bed. Madam's stove was in the front room today and she was sat over it by a cage suspended from a stand. Within were two red-cheeked small birds resembling no bird of this place; these were Madam's darlings and surely about some clever act when Jansie and I came to the room, for Madam's face was against the cage as one leans on a lover's chest and she making damp clicking sounds, her brows lifted and eyes almost shut. Jansie knelt by her, pulled the stove away from Madam's skirts and changed lit coals for ashes and slid the stove close again, lifting Madam's feet onto it one by one, and tucked the skirts there. Her thanks for this was to have the seed bowl from the cage shaked in her face, which Jansie took as meaning that she must fill it and she left the room to so do. I had set the coffee by Madam's side and she now bade me, grotesquely enough through the same pursed lips and with a sweetheart's high tone, to offer some to Le Voir.

I went into her room. The door to the annexed room was ajar and I pushed it open with no noise. There the young mistress was seated before a window, her head bare and her eyes closed. There stood Le Voir behind her and as I watched he poured oil on his hands, warmed it there and laid them on her. Her body lost some of its tightness at his touch and so, I thought, did his. I made no offer of coffee to disturb them.

With the larks baking in a slow fire and Derde Susann standing over the bread trough, I left to explore the estate. The family house was the central and the grandest building but it did not over shadow its neighbours by much. A short way off from it was the lordlings-house and alongside that, workshops. Next was the pigeon house and then the cellar and wine pressing room; there was a smithy hard by though the forge was cold. These buildings and the homestead were within what they called the werf of the farm, and the thick, low, whitewashed wall enclosed as well a kitchen garden and herb patch. Under the trees, the bell.

I met Allaman, hard as an ox's hoof, quite bald, a grey nebula clouding one eye. He was the oldest person on the estate but not the oldest creature as he told me in a practised introduction, saying that honour, your honour, went to Old Haarlem. Allaman leaned into a peach tree and pulled out a few over-soft fruit, then walked me to the wall of the werf. Here he made a curious sound directed to the area the wall kept out, the less kempt part of the farm, sounding, 'Pers ke ke ke! pers ke ke ke!', ending the word for peach with a sound like the call of a big bird or crane. At first, no effect on the land and on our side a still wait, then a boulder in the shadow of an oak rose and tilted towards us. It had back swept, squamous feet and an angulated face, stretched forward haughty as one of Le Voir's duchesses but with a contented look. It made heavy work of the distance and then was hard up against the wall and Allaman and I laying over that on our stomachs, pushing fingers into the peach flesh and pressing bits of this to the hard mouth 'til drool and juice ran down its neck.

Allaman giggled in a high register. 'He likes them fresh and he likes them long in the grass; Old Haarlem, he just likes a peach,' he said.

The creature angled its shell to lie alongside the wall and I could reach it and scrabble my finger nails on the waved ridges. I looked forward to telling Le Voir about the giant, for if there was a focus to his study of creatures volatile et reptile, as he called them, it was tortoises. In town, many were the Sundays spent tracking them on the peak and over the Saddle. We had never found one even close to this size and age; Old Haarlem had more than ninety years, Allaman said.

The old man showed me his garden, where he had slaved for almost twenty years and which he knew as a woman knows a pattern she has made from all types of stuff. He was, of course, half blind, and listed as he walked as though he were loosely joined at the middle and in danger of falling on a bed. Allaman fed the farm from this plot and now he loaded a trug with leeks and herbs for Derde Susann and was so boldened by having a messenger that he added a white peach and some apricots for that lady and tell her it is from Allaman.

I left him with the full trug against my hip and made my way. The garden's loam and the scent of the herbs were covered by a stronger smell as I came to the workshops. A joiner's part used a third of a long room shared with a wagoner and wheelmaker. Each of these commanded a high barn door opening onto the avenue that ran from smithy to kitchen stairs, but within were no walls dividing them. Windows along the far wall and the door apiece lit the room. At one end was the outline, the skeleton if you see it that way, of a wagon. There were no men at the wagonwright's nor the next area, where rough elbows of wood were set out to be shaped to a rim.

I had thought I was alone also in the part where I stood. It was given over to work of a fine sort; here were shaped lines and smoothed wood, this last the source of the porridge scent that drew me. A table was being made and was almost done. Six legs of grey wood supported a frame; the table top leaned in three broad lengths to one side. The design called for drawers set in the carcase, and something else, a nest of angles at the rear of one of the exposed drawers. It drew me forward – only to be brought short by a shirt and brown breeches stepping into my side vision. It was Melt, his body blocking my view of the table. He stood at ease, regarding me, my basket of leeks and fruit, my startlement when I had thought I was alone. He said: 'I had no thought of surprising you, Sister. I will show you what is here, if you say I can trust you.'

It took a moment to realise he was asking for my word. I was unsure of my footing and may have turned on my heel rather than risk looking foolish by being drawn into a confederacy over furniture but I was held there by the dusty light, his voice, the wood scent. He reached out his hand and took the vegetables from me and brought me to the table.

'Each piece made here has its own one of these,' he said, and leaned over the table and pressed the left side of the midmost drawer and thereby released a panel at the back to show a snug box hid there. With the workings bare like this I could see the sprung mechanism that operated the false back. When the assembly was complete you would not be able to tell this drawer from its lieutenants. I smiled at the cleverness of it and he, watching my face, eased his mouth – almost a smile.

'As you are here, you may advise me,' he said. 'Star,' and he held up a fillet of wood bearing a lean four-pointed compass rose, 'or shell?' and in his other hand another pattern, this of a fanned shell. I chose the latter; to this day you will see the little fan shapes on the drawer fronts of a long table in a parsonage in the far country and know by whose choice they are thus (though you may guess better than I what the dominie hides there).

Melt let me stay to watch him lay out the patterns, but before he took up his chisel and mallet to mark them he made reference to the vegetables being wanted in the kitchen. I yet stood a while on the avenue and listened to the twin taps as he cut into the wood.

At the smith a man by the name of Caspar was helping one Apollo. They were honing a ploughshare. I chose the opposite way, making for the kitchen and there enjoying Derde Susann's face at Allaman's gifts – a tightened mouth and a glance at me, who showed by my look that I knew nothing of apricots or white peaches – until a humour drew me back to the door to seek out what puzzled me of what I had seen, but not seen, as I came to the house: in the distance, near a grove of trees and slightly up the slope of the mountain, Master and his knecht were pacing out a shape on the ground, consulting a piece of paper in the master's hand.

I shook my head at the fancies that drew me to look out again, and thought no more of it then.

Goat would do for Master Gottlieb Calcoen, but for his step daughter Le Voir planned a wig of another sort. In the two years I had been with him we had worked with human hair only a few times and those all for whores of the dock streets. Subtlety was not their aim; we had turned out massively curled dark and auburn wigs, using slave hair for the former and other wise, just once, hair that Le Voir said was the finest we would find in this place. This was the crop of a pair of daughters of a Zacharias de Buys, one of the wild men who farmed the farthest country, those men who chafed at the sight of other men and at any law beyond what Moses carried down the mountain – chafed for chafing's sake, I believed of the rawhide visitors who stalked about the town with irritation at our prattle and noise when they made their annual trip to sell butter and soap and pay their loan rent and stock up on needles and gunpowder.

On Zacharias's visit to the town two years before he had happened to pass by our shop with his daughters. Le Voir chased after them on the street and used every effacement and bluff construction to get them to return with him to the shop. An hour and a mug of brandy later De Buys agreed to sell his daughters' hair to the wigmaker for more than the fetch of the family's soap yield.

Two years on, and the heads would be ready for harvest again. Le Voir sent word with a tinker that De Buys should find him at the estate when he passed this way. While we waited for him to find us we would work lace into a cap and heal her scalp.

It was given out at the estate that she was ill. Le Voir, deciding that her healing would be helped by the sun, devised a bed cap with wisps of wool escaping and had four men carry her on a bench, a narrow thong-strung affair, to Allaman's garden. There I stood watch and she bared her head when we judged it safe. From my post at the house end of the herbs the two of them were framed by pomegranate trees, he sketching Old Haarlem bribed to come near, she laying back, and about them a remote air as if they were coupled above Vogelzang in the sky.

The girl's own mother, she that the kitchen women also called 'Mother', had already bought herself Le Voir's dislike by her disgustful look at the sight of him touching her daughter's scalp; in her alarm she had convinced herself it was a contagion. Fearing her own child and hardened against her husband, and not daring to open her heart to any person, she tilted more every day while she brooded in the front room with her birds.

Her cast-off husband suspected nothing of our real purpose, I was sure. In any way, duly measured for his goats' hair and then discounted, he was in the grip of a nervous enthusiasm that kept his mind from us.

I had come by then to be conscious of this aspect of slave lives: at one and the same time the masters held contrary beliefs about those they bought into their homes, viz., It did not matter what a slave saw and so behaviour that the masters would be ashamed to even have rumoured about them was carried forward unchecked in front of their slaves; and at the same time they protested: how dare you, a slave, look at us as we do thus or thus? This last made me think they were not so hardened to the witnessing eyes. In the usual course the surface unconcern for being observed meant there were few secrets that were not shared by at least the kitchen women, if not the field men and trained men as well, but on Vogelzang at that time this was not so; here the mistress hid her daughter from the household, and it had become apparent that the master hid something, too.

None of us four working together in the homestead had more than the merest gleaning of what he was about. At the grove, new men with sacks of lime or a load of bricks passed the kitchen door on the way there, but they knew or would say nothing of their business. One dinner time Jansie stole to the place, avoiding by a whisker being caught in the act and able to report only nonsense when she made a safe return to the kitchen. It was, she said, a fancy garden laid in a spiralling shape, though with not enough turns to be interesting. A folly so far from the main house? None credited her, but as the master had put a terrible man, a daemon of a slave they called Doof Hendrik, to guard the place and we were all much afraid of him, we could come no closer to a satisfactory explication. Something for his plants, I thought, or to do with the measuring.

O the measuring! I had thought Le Voir's methods of making a lace cap for a new peruke a weary process – ear to ear, the cap line, peak to nape &c – as much as I liked that lines and numbers could describe a natural shape. But I had not known you could set out a whole person thus. Within days of our coming to Vogelzang Master had us both in his room barefoot and bareheaded and him with calliper and line, bobbing from us to a bound sheaf of papers marked with columns for height, cranium, angle of jaw, facial angle, distance between ear and eye, eye and hairline, nostril and nostril, as though he needed numbers to cover the whole of a body and, like lighter and darker marks from a pen, describe the person beneath.

He forgot me while he was measuring Le Voir and surely did not guess I could read letters so I looked undisturbed into his book. I found myself in the leftmost column: *Katrijn van de Caab, H Asiaticus, (?) 17, female, grey, black, medium*, and the rod of numbers. My place in the book was succeeded by an entry on Le Voir; Master had filled in this much of him after his name: *H Europeanus, 32, male, green, brown, fair, French*. Le Voir was a category to the good, I saw.

He leaned into Le Voir's face with the calliper and breathed on him, holding forth on this new science of which calibration was the test; these measurements would describe classes of being and we who had provided the parameters would be fit within them. To hear him tell it, this classification of species was the hope of Man. The measurements were part only; much could be known else wise: Homo sapiens Asiaticus, I would learn, is thus (should you ever need to adduce that this person is that person): *yellow, melancholy and greedy. Hair black, eyes dark. Severe, haughty, desirous. Covered by loose garments, ruled by opinion*, if I have remembered right. Homo sapiens Europeanus was *white, serious and strong. Hair blond and flowing. Eyes blue. Active, very clever, inventive. Covered by light clothing, ruled by laws.* I liked him already though we had never met. Melt was *H Afer*, I found by silently paging back, and Afer *black, impassive, lazy. Hair kinked, skin silky. Nose flat. Lips thick. Crafty, slow, foolish. Anoints himself with grease. Ruled by caprice.* Though it was foolish stuff I could not smile at it, this last.

But my mind was none the less gripped by this way of seeing the world. It went beyond people (or peoples, I should say), and in truth the least interesting part of it was the delineations in which I am sure none but the blue-eyed inventive man would recognise his person and humours. No, H Afer and so on were the dull end of a cunning system – a way of sorting the jumbled everything. It had to do with species, orders, classes and more, and went to show what all creatures or plants or animalcules shared in common and where they diverged. That is how I understood it from Le Voir, and it was as satisfying and solidly correct an explication of the world as to soothe the brain, like taking up a tangled sewing basket and smoothing, bundling and sorting skeins until they followed a logic that pleased the eye, and you knew where to find a particular one or put it, and doing so like wise with the needles and so on.

Le Voir said he admired the system because it made the boundless here and now a degree less ungraspable, less fearful – a gloomy thought from him that made me wonder at the change when I had all ways known him to be ready to take this world in great swallows. Before Vogelzang, on our walks out of the town, he had made me laugh with his tipsy praise for the place and his place in it, calling himself a god in dominion over nature as he stood on high ground over the bay, the next moment saying in seriousness that we needed God Himself – do you know why, Trijn? For a destination for the gratitude we feel for this our world.

Now he had been shaken and cast down and a slim girl was the reason, who had cut him and there inserted a slip of herself. Some time after he began his healing work I found him walking in agitation on the avenue between the lordlingshouse and the house. He said to me, as though to continue a conversation, 'She asked me, Will any one love me like this?' and he took me by the elbow and said: 'Trijn, how am I supposed to know a thing like that?'

Such a little thing she was, her head naked as a babe's on that slim neck.

It was not too long before the young mistress was well enough, in our play act, to join the household for some of the day. She sat on the stone bench on the front veranda, her sewing box by her. She wore a japan robe and cap, like a man. Derde Susann and Meerem and Jansie sat on the floor and I found a place on the lip of the veranda a couple of feet above the ground. I was about relining Master's coat, tedious work of peeling sweat-worn cloth from the sleeve holes and neck, stripping out the whole and stitching in fresh. There was gossip from the sheltered plain, who had wed, who died. The kitchen women were heedful of the young mistress's illness. She was working buttonholes on a pinafore; Jansie was letting out a skirt band for her belly and for a while the talk drifted around childbearing, with the two orphans much absorbed, but like wise young mistress and myself, in what Derde Susann promised in the way of swollen bosoms and dreams of birthing cats. Jansie stretched and arched her back, making more of the small mound under her apron and sighing at becoming a woman among mere girls.

Meerem handed her scissors, their hands meeting in the exchange in front of my eyes and for a moment touching, and I paid notice to the colours they made in the autumn air – cream and rich brown and the metal's glint. I laid down my work and fetched up from the sandy walk at my feet two stones of those exact hues; the darker was the harder to find. Then a yellower brown for Derde Susann, and one with less yellow and paler for me, and almost the same for the young mistress. Every one of us had many colours but if you took, for ease, the back of each one's hand, every one had a colour I could take as theirs and match to stone.

The veranda was of dark red ballast tiles, each with a shallow cup or belly, and the pebbles looked fine against that ground. I set them in the centre of a tile, pushed them into order. Jansie was lightest, Meerem at the far end from her, and not much to tell among the young mistress, me and Derde Susann in between; our colours graded one into the other. I was pleased our match was so easily made in the natural world – that animal's colour was also mineral's. I picked up a last, darkest, stone for Melt but here smooth cool stone could not match up. It was a pebble the size of a plum pit; I put it between my lips and set it by mine. Wet from my mouth, it came closer to him.

I took up my work again. Derde Susann leaned over and inspected it, turning her mouth to a line of approval. It was a fine seam, even and true, and laid down fast under my fingers. I was not in the usual course much of a needle woman but today – for a few days – I was filled with clear purpose, a sort of optimism that reached to my penetralia. I was cleverer, taller, more sure footed than I had been heretofore. I recall a breath-held sense as though listening for some one long missed and thinking every moment that you hear their wagon on the road.

Every day the walls of Master's folly were builded higher and our guessing about it was a rote thing. Then it dropped from our fore minds because the grape harvest was on us. All was busyness and quick movement; neighbours lent their people and we in the kitchen baked every day and tended Derde Susann's biggest pans. Not even Meerem could lift one of those on her own and we had to call Caspar to take a side and carry it with her to the vine yard. I followed with a basket of loaves on my head. The air was sharp, the sun and shadows on the avenue seeming to have been cut out of the day like piercings in a lantern.

Above Caspar's grunts I could hear cheerful sounds, growing louder as the pickers moved from the vines to a shady area where we had set jugs of last year's wine. I saw Melt among the jostling men, his face tipped back and mouth loose with laughter, and I stopped and watched until Meerem set down the cauldron and came to take the bread from me.

She and I stood behind the stew. I tore round loaves into quarters and handed to her pieces that she split, and ladled into each a heaping spoon and passed it to a harvester. They settled under trees and ate, and drank from jugs passed among them. Some tucked themselves to sleep, others leaned against the trees and nodded to their neighbours and shared drowsy chat. Allaman hobbled among them to bring wine and straight away his loose gait was imitated by a boy from another farm. Allaman laughed sourly and the boy's fellows spurred him on and he started a guessing game: who is this, and he leaned back, tucked his jaw into his neck to add chins, brought his lower lip almost to his nose and cried in a strangled voice, 'Hendrik! Hendriiik!' at which one of the boy's fellows shouted, 'Wretched boy!', and a certain grandmother stood there.

'More!' they said, and so he stepped dainty as an egret bird from person to person, peering over spectacles at their crusts and jugs: 'This can surely stretch another day ... you will not drink that whole jug ... Dollars do not grow in the field, you know.' A few hooted and called out 'Aunt Anna!'

Our own master in turn pored and peered and stretched imagined string across the bosoms of the handsomest girls. We rocked with laughter, the shared thing, and were loud with it so missed the bell and suddenly the Vogelzang knecht was among us with the dogs and his habitual slender whip to call them back to work. The boy, careless on wine or praise, planted his legs wide to grow fat and lowered his head 'til it swung like a stone between his shoulders, and he piped in a fond voice at his fellows, 'Come, dogs,' and the laughter died. The knecht made two strides to the boy and cut him down with his small whip. We watched him cringe and heard him plead, 'My little boss! My master!' where we had not heard the bell.

Allaman walked with Meerem and me as we took our bodies back to the vines and kitchen; he held the basket and we the empty cauldron. I wanted to close my eyes on the day's gifts that burned like citrus. In the kitchen another batch of dough was hardening into loaves in the oven and Jansie was tending the fire. The year before she had helped bring in the harvest and taken her turn trampling out the grapes, and was explaining to Derde Susann, who surely needed no telling, how grape juice and soap would turn the merest scratch black and leave hands with a lattice of lines and the only help for it was to wash with the juice again and rinse with water. As she spoke she turned her golden hands in the afternoon light. Neither Meerem nor I mentioned what had happened with the whip and the boy.

I had lace to knot and left the kitchen for the inner house. Madam was in the front room at an accounts book. I bowed my head as I passed and she raised her eyes, blurred with the wine she drank all the time, and slurred some unfriendly words; without stopping to consider I hissed back at her, knowing in my inner mind I was safe to do so. I knocked at the young mistress's door and entered the room. She was smiling with high colour at something Le Voir had said while he sketched her portrait. He nodded at me and I settled at my station at the window and went on with hooking fine lace for her cap; I used the thought of Melt laughing to chase out of my mind the picture of the boy at the knecht's feet, beseeching him.

I had borrowed Derde Susann's scissors and after supper that night crept through the house to fetch them back from the young mistress's room. I spoke for a moment to her and when I left her room and came again into Madam's it was to see Melt with his arms about her waist, tugging her towards the bed. He spoke to her in a parent's voice, yet calling her 'Mother', and asked her gently to go to bed, recaught her attention when she remembered some urgent task or imagined it in the way a drunken person will, blocked her way as she lurched towards the front room, wildered as a moth. She knocked a candle in her tumbling wretchedness and I rushed forward and set it right, then took his directions to draw back the curtain of the heavens bed and open the covers. Together we got her in and trapped her there with rough tucking, and doused the other candle and left the room.

In the front room Melt asked me in sober tones to keep what I had seen to myself.

'We would be troubled if we were her,' was how he excused it.

4

IN THE STILL OF THIS WEDNESDAY AFTERNOON, ALMOST TO the month a decade since she arrived in this place, Vergilius is the largest moving thing, she and her bicycle, pedalling the quarter mile to Gupta's general store in the village of Slagterskop with a box of eggs in the basket in front of the handlebars. The macadam of the Great North Road creaks as the day's heat seeps away. Vergilius nears the store and brakes; free-wheeling parallel with the high veranda at the front of the building, she swings her legs over the side of the bicycle, slides from the saddle and patters to a stop. She leans the machine against the porch, mounts the shallow steps with the box held before her and enters a deep room smelling of Lifebuoy soap and Native cloth and cheap, violet-scented sweets of a flavour known hereabouts as musk.

In the village are: this general store, which has on its shelves grey and brown blankets, milk powder and nests of safety pins; one modern tearoom squatting like a cooling coal behind orange Sun Filter curtains rancid with frying fumes and clogged with greasy lint; one police station with two flagpoles but, this week, no flag (the policeman in charge is pretending that he has mislaid the Union Jack, and his wife is mending the second flag that usually flies there); one ten-bedroom, three-bathroom hotel with doomed Amphimallon solstitiale paddling in its spit-warm pool; a petrol station. There are half a dozen houses for Europeans on the only street, each with a shack in the back garden for the house servants. Most gardens have a fig tree, a peach tree and a trellis of Catawba grapes.

Down the Great North Road, which is to say, due south, a slaughterhouse and butchery hunker behind fly screens, and all about the mission and village are farms. The sunburned soil looks too thin to support even sheep, but Bonsmara cattle and white maize survive amid the thorn trees and koppies. Deep in the bush, deeper even than the farms, are the Tribal Trust Lands, where Natives live in villages of adobe and zinc and where white men may not go without a permit.

Vergilius has lately befriended the owner of the general store, the mission's near neighbour for the ten years she has been here, and has taken to visiting him most days; small journeys beyond the confines of the mission are part of her fledging. She returns each night to the convent cells, but each day's foray lasts a little longer, takes her a little further, and each pretext is less credible. She startles herself with how close she comes to forcing a reckoning, then forgets her fright and flexes again against her life.

As Vergilius enters the wide room, a crone behind the counter looks up from a magazine to screech at the ceiling: 'Vikram!' In a moment the bead curtain at the rear of the shop parts around a man dapper in a waistcoat. He carries a spanner in each hand and chides Vergilius as he approaches: 'My goodness, Sister, you are catching me in sleeves.'

He reaches over the counter to take the eggs from her and confides something innocent about tightening his sprockets. He is referring to the unreliable movie projector that dominates the small sitting room behind the store. Gupta leans over the box, flicks a piece of fluff from a shell and counts the eggs, circling a pencil over them. He thumbs open a school notebook labelled *Mannamead Mission Hospital* and writes a number in the credit column, then raises one hand and rotates it as though he is about to dance: 'Mughal-e-Azam! Don't ask how, don't ask who! But it's on its way. From Bombay. Any day.' He twitches his shoulders to the rhythm of his sudden doggerel. As Gupta speaks he lifts the eggs and packs them wooden tray fetched from beneath the counter.

'Krauna Kolhapur ti aweh,' Gupta's mother mutters, weaving towards them with glasses of chai, 'Sandal Agra ti aweh!'

'Sandals from Agra, crowns coming especially from Kolhapur,' Gupta translates.

Gupta has arranged with a long-haul truck driver to drop off parcels of newspapers on his way north. He hauls out a fresh pile and thumps it on the counter and he and Vergilius work through the stack, reading to one another about the world beyond the village.

Soon two girls from the Reserve come out of the sun. They shuffle up to the counter on the side marked 'Non-European', separated by plywood and chicken wire from Gupta and Vergilius, and place their order in whispers, keeping their eyes downcast. Mrs Gupta flips up a section of the counter on the Native side, grips an ear of a sack in each arthritic claw and walks it off its stack. One of the girls takes it from her and, leaning the sack against her leg, lifts her head and ventures a hand on the counter and says, 'Please a beads.' The old lady fetches a box crammed with small packets, slides it across and sets on either side of it a thin arm weighted with bracelets and glossy with petroleum jelly. She keeps her tender thumbs off the counter top, sprays spittle on the packets as she names the price of the strings of tiny glass beads they hold up. Except to give prices, Mrs Gupta has spoken no English since 1947; shillings and pennies are all she will concede. The girls select a few strings, pay over their coins. One hefts the sack onto the head of the other and Mrs Gupta encourages them to quit the store with a tremble of her knuckles.

Vergilius notices everything about these trips into the world.

This one ends when Prakash Gupta pushes through the curtain to call his father and grandmother to supper. He greets Vergilius with an Americanised 'Hi there, Sister Vee.' His father shoos him

out of the store ahead of Old Mrs Gupta, who chatters to her grandson in Gujerati as he holds the strands aside for her. Gupta shoves
the papers into a stack and puts this back under the counter, where
it will be kept ready to wrap parcels of beads and pins and keep dust
from bright cloth on the way back to the kraal, there to be torn into
squares and, as Gupta once startled his mother by saying, used to
wipe Native arses.

Once a week women appear in ones and twos out of the bush with
babies strapped to their backs. They converge on Mannamead for
the infant clinic, and within the first hour after prayers the hospital
veranda is host to a dozen flat-footed mothers from the Native Reserve. They sit on the polished cement floor, their legs and ridged
yellow soles in front of them, and crochet blankets or keep busy
with bead work and give half an ear to Sister Benedict's hectoring.

In a room set aside for the clinic the sisters heft the solid baby
bodies and peer into the infants' faces in anticipation of a smile as
they get on with polio shots and measles vaccines, with weighing
and measuring and spreading dimpled fists to admire palms, fingernails, the satiny plumpness enfolding wrists. Simple Xavier confides
that when the babies rest against her body she feels as though a hand
is cupping her own head and someone is saying the name she had
when she was a little girl.

Today the babies' mothers wait out the lecture, then share news
of their chief, who is gravely ill. Jacob passes among the women with
a pitcher of barley water and brewer's yeast powder. They admire his
tall form and tease him as he steps among their legs.

As the heat of the day peaks the women reclaim their babies,
bind them with blankets to their backs and thread their way into the
bush in twos and threes. The sisters move on to their adult patients,
and the most pious of them, plump Perpetua, sidles off to her cell,
and leaves the cloistered area again when she judges it safe, steals

across the garth and finds a patch of blackjacks whose seed heads she snaps off and tucks into her sleeves.

The farmer of Bandolier drives to Slagterskop on Mondays for the post and supplies; every second Wednesday afternoon he spends an hour at the police station with the new policeman from Pretoria. Today they conclude the formalities as they have done each fortnight for the past three months, then the Special Branch man puts down the file on the 'named' in his area – he hopes in time to have more than just this one name, Francis Shone – and takes up a file of a different colour.

Slagterskop lies a few dozen miles as the crow flies from the country's northernmost border, and is a way station for those seeking to cross into or out of the Union without formalities. This fact inflates the village's importance beyond that of a mere dorp, which is a source of pride to its Sergeant Okkie Louw but has also caused to be stationed there this professional man from the capital, a source of disquiet. The man from Pretoria is an irritation to more than just Louw and Shone; Shone's fellow farmers prefer to draw seasonal labour from across the border where the men and women are unsure of their footing so far from home, and will work for less and leave afterwards without murmur or demand. It is the new policeman's job, Shone's neighbours guess, to tighten the border controls.

But it is not fruit-pickers he is after: for forty minutes or more he probes the farmer for the revolutionary passions of the several families who live in the kraals among Bandolier's koppies.

On Bandolier, a mile from Slagterskop, Jacob's grandmother, Mariah Kobe, a dark, grand woman of almost seventy, takes care of Shone. He has been the master of the koppies, two ploughed fields and several fine grazing camps – and of Mrs Kobe, it must be supposed, for that is how she addresses him – for nineteen years this autumn, ever since a typhoon of whiskey and bare-chested pioneering spun him out with sun-damaged skin and an intolerance for alcohol to show for it, and a careless episode up north left him with a slight limp.

A farmer who does not farm in the accepted sense, and the only English-speaking rancher in these parts, Francis Shone is cited as evidence by his Afrikaans neighbours that they don't know how to, you know, the English. They shake their heads at the hopeless things he does: he does not slaughter his own cattle or know how to help the swayback girls deliver their calves, they tell one another. He sends away to other countries for books, gadgets, turkey pullets. He plants different things, and at different times, to the rest of the district. That he preserves and studies what ought only to be sprayed or crushed under a heel is beneath comment.

His neighbours visit to lecture him on the timetable of sowing, baling and cattle-dipping that he is always behind on, their flat gazes seeking out the latest foolishness – a wood lathe in the workshop or, in the garden, a straw target for a tall bow and many arrows, imported as much to have an untaxing new sport as for the chance to use some fine old words: toxikon, chrysal, fletch. Shone makes a ceremony, on his neighbours' visits, of requesting tea from Chief Henry Kobe's terrifying big sister. Everyone – this should be understood to mean every white one – has three or four house servants except for the poorest of poor whites who beat and bully just one at a time until he or she fails to appear one morning and the boss boy is sent to the kraal to pick out a new one. But the novelty at Bandolier is that the master addresses his housekeeper as 'Mrs Kobe'. He does this even when his neighbours are not present – there is something in the upright backbone of Mariah Kobe that forbids a more familiar address; he is aware, however, that it rankles his guests and so he makes a point of treating her like an adult woman as she moves among them.

Each spring he drives along the perimeter of Bandolier on the side bordered by the Great North Road, with the boss boy clinging to the roll bar in the back of the war-surplus jeep. It is Daniel's job to scoop a tin mug into a bag of cosmos seed and sow it over the veld so that by winter the farmer will have something fresh to look at when he drives out. To hide the shame of planting flowers, the farmer tells the district that they are spreading something for weeds.

The men hold him in contempt, but their wives and sisters like to visit; their faces patterned with tension against drought or farm accident or their husband's fists, they come to him as dour as the resurrection plants his boys bring from the veld, black twigs to be revived for mercy's sake and curiosity's.

And actually, he is more than competent at calving, which calls for careful timing in the matter of when to be compassionate and when ruthless with the beseeching, bellowing cow. He has entertained the thought that his neighbours like having one of him in the district, having their own Englishman, although he will insist that he is as South African as they are. But perhaps his presence is more in the nature of a provocation, and his actions: he pretends ignorance but he knows what those spindly pink and white flowers mean to men who still punish themselves with every detail of their war, picking at it like the scab of the miniature Union Jack in the middle of the flag.

A chrysal is a crack in a bow, a particular flaw. Shone uses the word to describe the policeman across the desk from him, although not to his face. The bow, in this analogy, is the volk; the crack that will prevent it from shooting true is this new strain. Half an hour ago he was amused by his interrogation, then resigned, but he is a lip curl away from open rudeness when the banging door in the next room announces the return to his station of Okkie Louw. Shone leans back in his chair to look through to the other room; Louw surges into his charge office, stamping his feet at the threshold, rumbling with amusement. Crashing about, he sets his leather-covered baton, peaked cap and pistol on a shelf behind the counter, eases off his shoulder harness and belt and allows his stomach to find its own level.

'Snaakse jong!' the farmer and the other man in the inner office hear him grunt, 'Strange lad.' The Special Branch policeman across from Shone, one Valentine Teichert, takes up the file, slides in the forms he has been using to quiz him and replaces the folder – that there are forms and a folder sickens the farmer – and joins his pale hands at the fingertips, elbows on the desk.

'O ja?' says Teichert in the rising tones of a stage duchess, tilting his head. Louw's shoulders slump as he turns towards Teichert's voice.

'No, it's nothing, only … O, uh, hullo Meneer Shone … You know that boy that lives there by the mission?' Louw switches back to Afrikaans. 'I say to you, the bloody boy just now tried to race the car! I come from making arrangements with them there about the Americans, and I am already on the main road, then I see the kid running along next to the car but he looks damned serious, as if he really wants to chase the car. He makes a bloody good job of it, too … I have really to put foot to shake him off. Cheeky bugger …'

Louw trails off. Valentine Teichert is apparently not going to smile at the thought of the mission boy racing a police car. Indeed, although Louw does not mention this, there was something disturbing about the boy's pumping elbows and set jaw, the tears he thought he saw.

'So. The Bantu chases the car of a policeman? The one always with that Roman sister?'

Teichert looks into middle distance as he speaks, and purses his lips, divining layers of meaning that lie beyond ordinary comprehension. Louw describes this habit of his colleague, but not to his face, as 'speaking through his teeth like some sort of bliksemse bioscope captain in the Battle of Britain'. Teichert is altogether not what Louw can tolerate in a policeman. The captain is a slim man of thirty years. The skin over his skull is drying out where the hair is clipped from the sides of his head; the rest of his thin crop runs straight back from his forehead, above yellow eyebrows, in brittle strands, a mango pip sucked dry. His mouth is puckered as though it has tasted some of what the nostrils above are finding so offensive. Teichert's long hands flutter there, hiding his mossy teeth.

Massive Louw, with almost twice Teichert's years, his low-slung, nodding head sporting a ratel's thatch of thick hair and a jutting jaw beneath his moustache, habitually stands too close to those to whom he speaks, and will, in the course of a conversation, make lunges with his chin as though to catch their scent. Something he sniffs in Teichert he does not trust, but man proposes and Pretoria disposes and three months ago Louw cleared away boxes and old police saddles to make an office for his guest, and who knows what he gets up to in there. Louw does not want to know. He tries to ignore Teichert in the way a mastiff, after his initial investigation has found the thing wanting in irredeemable ways, will disregard, say, a goat.

Louw trusts that the Special Branch policeman will confine himself to the lone local English Communist and to the passers-by who flit through in the night, and leave the running of Slagterskop to him. Legally speaking, speaking in terms of his classification, Gupta ought not to live behind his general store with New Mrs Gupta and Old Mrs Gupta and their boy, Slagterskop having been a white Group Area these ten years or more. Strictly speaking, Gerrie Saayman of the deep tan, pointed cheekbones and tight black curls should not work as a mechanic nor buy and sell a strategic material such as petroleum, and definitely not share a bed with his pretty, pale wife, not if you looked into his family background, asked sharp questions of the Office for Race Classification about where he ought to be entered in the population register ...

Louw would get a headache if he tried to add up the laws Saayman broke every day as the man paid his bills, kissed his kids good morning, fixed any bicycle that came his way for free because 'two wheels don't count, man', locked the pumps each night and saw the nightwatchman off on his rounds, as befitted the manager of such a Strategic Key Point in the nation's arsenal as the Slagterskop Verre Noord/Far North Dienssentrum/Service Station. Everyone knows, and has always known, says Louw, what is a crime. But the matter of breaking the law, the ever-changing law that streams north in new addenda to Butterworth's every week while Parliament is sitting in Cape Town, and in a Greek chorus of Government Gazettes when Parliament has risen, that sort of thing is addressed on Louw's patch only if it sticks up its head and makes a nuisance. The village has seen the nun with that boy ever since he was a piccanin and she a wide-eyed newcomer. Louw knows Jacob's grandmother and great-uncle, and even knew his mother although that one was rubbish, and if they had given their jongetjie over to the Roomse to be taught, there was no law against the sister and the boy being always in each other's company, whatever their classification. Or not yet. Maybe his guest can send a letter about it to Pretoria.

Louw's face has soured. He nods to Shone, picks up his baton, jams his cap on his head and crashes back into the day, leaving the security policeman to his attempts to calibrate the exact degree of resentment of his sort harboured by the Bandolier men and women who milk the Jersey herd, muck out the barn and bring interesting insects to the farmer's study window in their cupped hands or the folds of a lappie.

Teichert sucks his teeth, picks up another file and reads out a question he finds there: 'Are you now or have you ever been a member of the Communist Party?'

In answer, the farmer lies. The policeman makes a mark on the page.

'Are you a member of any organisation to which you pay dues, or whose materials you receive or disseminate? If yes, list the organisation slash organisations.'

Shone stretches his face between eyebrows and mouth, looks to one side. He says, slowly, 'I have been a member, since its inception, of the Witwatersrand Arachnid Society.'

Teichert makes it as far as 'Witwatersrand' before he catches on and puts down his pen, and looks at Shone with disgust.

Evening comes. On the veranda at Bandolier, the farmer lights a hurricane lamp, and sucks on his pipe to keep the insects away. He turns from the irritations and disappointments of the day to the more vivid past, opening the book on his lap to admire the prim self-certain girl whose story he has before him in the pages of a brown cloth edition from the Van Riebeeck Society.

The girl's story is marked at odd intervals by a crabbed commentary, but Shone takes her side when the editor of her narrative seizes on an assumption about who made the furniture, or who built the house – when a footnote tries to slap down the particular because in this place, always and forever, the particular is the universal, and if one slave made one table, then all tables were thus, and extra virtue goes to them at our cost. Shone notes the editor's petty ways with Trijn's story, recognises the attempt to tell his own by stealing bits of hers. He will ignore the footnotes, he thinks. It's the story he is after, not what we think we have decided about it since it was lived or first described. Here, where history is either fable or tribal anthropology or a cold wall of begats, he will ignore these attempts to borrow the credentials of the forebears; he will read her tale as that of a girl he might know. He thinks: I side with her, but how can she love me in return, and knows he is no longer thinking of the freed slave, or not only of her.

These women who move through this landscape, holding themselves safe amid the terrible and sudden dangers, holding their limbs close to their bodies to lessen their profile, to lessen the places life can catch at them, and still maintaining movement, and still attending to men even when they elect to live a life apart from them, we can rely, he thinks, on having these women among us, rely on their courage to keep us brave.

On the outskirts of Slagterskop, in the house behind the abattoir, the butcher's wife and her sister set one another's thin ginger hair in curlers, growing sleepy under the comb's touch. They part from each other when the butcher snaps on a blue porch light and crosses the passage behind the shop to bring his smell of cold air and blood into the house. Mr and Young Mrs Gupta, Old Mrs Gupta and Prakash run a movie on a wall of the living room and doze in armchairs by its light. In a cottage attached to the police station Louw's wife welcomes his heavy sidling and nudges him deeper against her. Teichert lies alone in his hotel room, playing out conversations and confrontations in his head.

At Mannamead, in a pool of light at the far end of the men's ward, Chief Henry Kobe, rigid against the pain in his gut, tries to concentrate on Jacob's voice as the boy reads to him in a low drone. Outside the chief's window Vergilius leans against the wall and listens. When the boy stumbles, the chief corrects him with a grumble.

And the lights dim and die at nine o'clock as the generators fall silent, and the day ends, much as it always does.

To someone watching from outside the convent, the sisters – most of them – seem to be women whose urges are not so fierce they cannot be damped down with a sodden weep or a sisterly embrace or by finding release writhing in a vest strewn with prickles; a faint fennel astringency clings to Perpetua's habit, but, apart from the one who wears weeds under her clothes, they mostly smell only of nun – some sour, some of violets, some of stone. From one of them rises a thermal of clean female skin.

5

THE VINES WERE PICKED CLEAN. OUR FIELD PEOPLE LEFT before daybreak to walk to other farms, swinging lanterns and clapping their hands to warn off the leopard. Meerem and Derde Susann went with them to help feed the harvesters, and the knecht left for the town. The family remained, and Le Voir, Jansie and I; when in the usual course there were thirty or more people coming and going, now we were six.

The dogs padded to the kitchen door and whined there 'til Jansie chased them off. We had been set to work on the copper and I went at a kettle with lemon and salt, working this into the places where the rolled seam met the body. There came a scratching at the door and Jansie, whose feelings were high these days, screeched for the hounds to get away but it was Allaman. I had forgotten him in my inventory of who was too old or too child-heavy to use at another harvest. He was quite as injured as the dogs and slunk into the kitchen with a suffering air and parlayed Jansie's bad feeling about shouting at him into a cup of beer and some bread. For a moment he sniffed and muttered about 'Allaman taken for a dog' but his heart was not in it and he left off.

Allaman had been born on the estate and given when he was six to Madam, then about two years old, as a body slave. She was just Cornelia then, underfoot on the farm, and Allaman her guardian and companion to hold her sunshade or her pony's head, and hold her back, once, when her foot came within a blink of stepping on an adder. He would make her smile with clever whistling that could call a bird and keep it in the branches about them, prepared to woo or fight the bird that really was this boy; when she was nine years of age she was the alchemist and he the assistant fetching pomegranates to be rubies. Cornelia thereafter became Little Mistress and then Madam; he stayed Allaman, unalloyed, moving to the fields, then the garden, lying with women, making children with them, stepping in place like those oxen on the flats.

Now he sat in the kitchen of her house, listening hard at what we told him of how she was these days, and he spoke about the important little girl and the fine woman who could make anything grow, flowers or fruiting trees, who made the estate fatten and extended its vines and fields up steeper slopes than anyone on this side of the mountain, she who now moaned all the day to her cagebirds.

Le Voir entered the kitchen; Allaman scuttled out. The Frenchman took a seat at the table and made faces at his reflection in the copper, his nature tugging at his new melancholy like a child wanting to play. He hummed a country song, stood and paced about lifting this and that and setting it down, sliding the tom's ears between thumb and finger, setting a haunch of cured meat swinging at its rafter. He fetched up back at the table. Jansie followed him with her eyes. Their men were rarely seen in the kitchen; Master was never here; but here was a large one, touching things and with no knowledge of what right manners there were.

He sat himself across from Jansie and pushed his jaw towards her until she met his eyes and gave an uncertain giggle. He asked her about my contribution to the household – I was not much of a cook but I could sew well enough, she said. He asked her opinion of the young mistress and she had none but she hoped her health would return and she would be there to give direction in the matter of preserving, for the kitchen might run low and she had a good touch in the matter of preserving.

Le Voir let out his breath at the effort of getting conversation from her. I would have told him that the sole matter of interest to Jansie was Jansie had I not enjoyed hearing him try to rub a spark from such soft metal. But talk will come in the end to questions about the other, and his did and at these she came alive. Yes, she had been to the town, more than once a season, where she was the one to walk behind Mother though that would not be possible now for a time given her, Jansie's, condition. Her first, just so, and yesterday Master hinted that he would send to town for a midwife from the old country for the birth, a white one, though such a thing had never been heard of on the estate, where Derde Susann had all ways attended what births there had been, but this was not an ordinary matter and clearly regarded as greater than such if there really was to be this trouble taken. This was fresh knowledge to me, a midwife from town to come this long way for a babe, and that not born free.

She weened with pride and I recalled Derde Susann speaking of Jansie having made a match she ought not to have. The knecht? But not even Jansie would preen at the thought of that, and it was in any event the common practice on these farms for the master to all but pen his white servants with the ready girls to bring him new slaves and these of a lighter colour as is favoured for house use, so there would have been nothing worth the remarking in such a breeding. Derde Susann had guessed the truth and barred it from her kitchen, I believe to keep something dangerous from being spoken aloud, but also because of how impossible it was for one slave to abide airs in another. Jansie answered all attempts at finding her out with an annoying smile.

She interrupted herself to take hold of my hand and direct it to a spot I had missed. You would suppose it was her own ware we were about cleaning, I thought. All those attached to these households took pride in their place all be it they were themselves the chief assets of it, but her air was even out of the usual way. Now she blinked at Le Voir, having found him suitable for flirtation, and pitched her voice to a child's piping. I regarded Le Voir to see how he would receive this, he who was so sceptical of affectedness, who could mimic a courtesan pouting and not forget how she scratched her head or a worser part when she judged no one was looking, and the way she adjusted her bosom like one twitching pillows on a bed. And indeed he was not captured by Jansie – but nor was he secretly laughing at her with that tightened mouth and brightened eye with which he met much of the world's foolishness. He was regarding her almost fondly, and I was puzzled by this for I had thought I could have set down his amusement as guaranteed.

There was an impulse that ran through me in those days, a question, a quest, that coloured how I saw myself and other people, other women and girls in particular, and it was this: how to be. I cannot say for certain if this was the product of having been, some seven years before, at the age of nine, old enough to understand bondage and manumission and to feel my place in human society alter in a matter of weeks. The shivering happiness of my mother and father after days of whispering, and their small sounds of delight as word leaked of what might be in the old lady's testament, the fear that some cousin of hers or an official from the castle or dark ship and sjambok or the turning passage of the stars themselves would prevent it – and the day they brought home shoes for themselves and for Tobias and me. I sweated in mine, the first I had ever stepped into and out in, but I walked a circle into the ground in the back yard watching my own feet and the pale track I made, then walked into the street and imagined or saw that now I was paid notice, me with the other thing they had brought to our daily life: a name to add to our names, a name to share, we four now creatures of two names apiece, and for my brother and me the prospect of adulthood one day. But what did they see who saw me? There was no one to answer the question: am I pretty? Ma would never allow such talk and less still volunteer the opinion and it is not a matter one can know objectively, as Le Voir would frame the matter. Ma had been enslaved for years longer than I and she was living a life begun again since that strange week when we were released to humanity. She was more free woman than mother, and yet intent on breeding free children, living over again the life she had so far lived as though, if she could just retrace the steps, the light would cancel out the dark, press it back to the far end of the cave until the shadow crept away all together. What did prettiness matter against so important a thing as freedom? Who could waste a moment on finding out how to be a mere girl when one was now a free girl? The daughter of a freewoman? Great things had visited my family, but when they had moved to the next, the small questions remained, undigested, at least with me. There for I watched people. As they were, so would I know to be. Even Jansie was worth watching.

She piled kettle on bowl on platter and carried them into the main house. Alone in the kitchen Le Voir and I did not straight away speak but sat easily among the tom and the fire. We had seldom been thus since coming to Vogelzang though it had been often just we two in town. There we had each learned the other's humours, had almost a language apart wherein we told our progress and plans for the work, our new thoughts about the world. Measured against the place we now found ourselves, our town life seemed to have been one of Le Voir's experiments, the proof of a new manner of living, after the manner of the dreams spun by children and new married people, and new freed. At Vogelzang the world was snatching at our heels, mine and his, to attach its weighty parts.

Without my speaking of it he picked up the thought and began to worry at the matter of Calcoen's particular science, how it depressed his spirits and did not rouse them as the harmony and formal effort of a new theory did in the usual course. If this was science, said Le Voir, why did he himself meet it like a doubter when confronted by a true believer, or even, less nobly, why did he feel such an impulse to retreat to instinct? In the face of such vigorous claims about mankind, such a call to reason, he could offer only vague feelings that Calcoen was astray. But he could not speak it out sensibly, not when Calcoen was all statistical pronouncements and binomial nomenclature and appeals to the evidence of the eyes.

'He leaves me to argue all ways in the negative. He is so heated in his enthusiasms and forceful. Mine is overwatered ink when I speak to counter him. And really, Trijn, if we are able to perfect humanity, would it not be wrong to abstain from trying to so do?'

It was not a real question, or so I thought, and any way Jansie was back and had pulled out the sewing basket and a pile of night shirts and pushed half to me along the table top. Le Voir slapped his knees and stood, made a silly bow to Jansie, with a side glance to enjoy my smile at this, and went into the day's wet air.

Rain clouds came so low they risked a piercing on the vine stock standing in lines naked and black as stitches on a cut. The harvest was well over, the vine juice working against itself in barrels. I passed the cellar, saw Allaman and Caspar lifting a scoop from one of them, tipping that into a bowl by the light of a lantern.

In town I had been regularly oppressed by winter, our season of mud and drizzle, with ships hunched on the rain-flat swell of the roadstead, sodden flags stuck to their masts. I felt myself turn grey in those cold days, turn ashen and diminished, though Le Voir had tried all ways to shake the endless drip from his shoulders. He kept the stove in the shop's front room lit day and night and set on it a roiling kettle of spice wine for us to come in from the street to a warm room and the scent of mace and cinnamon, and dip a cup where the orange rolled in its thin broth. We spent weeks weakly drunk, then a crystalline day would break the weather and send us blinking with sore heads out to the blue air of the town.

But out here on the avenue above the vine yard I liked the cold wind on my cheek and the secretive feeling within the blanket over my head. I sought at one moment to bundle against the wind and the next to spread myself wide, let it blow into my mouth, through my hair and spread fingers. I hurried, pulled by an impulse to escape the over full household. In the three endmost parts of the T shape in which the Vogelzang homestead was formed were three tableaux, each of such fullness as to fill a house alone. In the kitchen at the foot of the T Jansie drove Derde Susann to a frenzy of worry and irritation over her boasts about the child in her belly. Derde Susann knew the Fates might not look often on a slave but they would not ignore one who openly showed the forbidden emotion, and to hope in their situation was to want more than there was to go around for, in the balance of a slave's lot, if one had more another went without. Derde Susann knew survival depended on them keeping their heads down and exercising only the play allowed in the narrow channel they walked. My story – free, so free as to be paying one of them to teach me, enjoying the prospect of a good and various future, was in the nature of a traveller's fable, of interest but no credible meaning.

At one end of the T's crossbar Le Voir and the young mistress maintained the careful conversation of surgeon and patient they had adopted since she had shaken him with what she said about being loved. But cool as was their talk, his hands, slick with spermaceti, daily found her scalp, his warm palms covered her skull and his fingers slid into the channel between ear and head, slid down to and pressed her neck and shoulders. Daily she loosed her chemise and he could see her bosoms as he worked, and she closed her eyes to allow him to look and listened to his breathing and her own.

At the other end of the crossbar Calcoen waded through drifts of paper, books held open with stones, pages of loose paper covered in his calculations, letters in mid draft – to a donkey breeder near the town, to a man who kept goats, or rather, to an agent about the man's goats for the man did not read, letters to the castle about a midwife from the mother country and to the chandler about sheets and lime wash. Should you knock to request sugar he would hardly glance up, flicking a hand towards the sugar box, the key, while he pored over a text – once, I saw, on child birth – his mouth moving with the angular Latin.

At the crux of the household, dark Madam, whom all left alone in her indurate misery so that now she was a fixture of the room like the cupboard built in to the wall and the portrait of her father. She stayed hunched over her stove, the passage of the day marked by Melt helping her to the chair in the morning and bringing her to bed at night, and one of us wiping the mess she left and not too nice to show that we cursed her for it.

These things left me with an impulse to shout into the wind or effect some other small freedom.

I kept up my tramp towards the slopes behind the estate. The avenue ran out a small distance from a low pondok; this the men and women of the estate used when they needed to be alone together; in the mountains were caves where better privacy was to be had and where, from time to time, two might even play at being married. The road way of the avenue became a rough path cut more by the winter streams than by a hand. In contrast, the low round bushes to either side of the path looked like the topiary work Le Voir spoke of from his home. This neat verdure was the wild veldt, beyond the ragged planted oaks and chestnuts. I was higher now and moving on a slant that had me bent. I stopped and looked back over the farm. From this height I could see over the lordlingshouse and the cellars and workshop to the main house. I saw the T from an angle as though, were it on a page, I was the end stop on the sentence before it, but further away by many magnitudes. This aspect showed me the window to the young mistress's room and a candle that burned there. I could see the kitchen door, which opened as I watched. Jansie, by the rolling step and shape of her, came out with a bowl, lifted the lid off the lant barrel and dipped into it, carried this indoors.

The wind dropped. Smoke rose from the house's only chimney, set in the kitchen wall, and from another at the end of the lordlings-house. There was not a sound to be heard. We were warned often about tygers in these hills – Le Voir never heard this without muttering 'leopard cat' under his breath – but the day felt too cold and still for anything to be afield but myself. I followed the track along a contour, moving in parallel to the Vogelzang avenue, wet bushes soaking my skirts. Not a bird, nor the slightest movement of a shrub, nor in it. I heard my breathing within the blanket and then the bell. I made out a male figure tugging at the chain under the solitary arch to the side of the house; now shapes moved along the avenue towards the end of the lordlingshouse where the open kitchen was and where a meal of bread and hot paste would be dished. A movement to my right caught my eye: a child was preceding Doof Hendrik on the path down from the grove. Of course, he would not hear the bell; they would send a boy for him. With no clear thought I broke into a run, moving opposite to the way the boy and man took, heading for the white wall I could see through the naked branches of the woodlet.

I came upon it from above, a most curious building and not entirely unlike Jansie had described: a maze built in one spiral (and there for, I must say, not a maze, for you could move only to the centre and away from the centre however confounded you might be between) but with walls as tall as any other farm building. There was yet no roof – work had stopped for the wet season – and as I came down the slope towards it I could look down into it where it lay like a broke open shell, a tight-curving wall running inward to a central place. High set windows pierced the wall.

I could not guess its purpose but at least my walk had gained me my own sight of it and the intelligence that Doof Hendrik deserted his post when, I suppose he would have reasoned, all creatures on the estate – and most of all Master – were like wise at the trough. I resolved: when the weather cleared and work recommenced I would watch as I chose and glean the purpose of Calcoen's curious building.

My time in the cold gained me a fever too. It began that night with a creeping ache in my knees and hips that told Derde Susann it could be the ague and she chopped and sprinkled and boiled a brew accordingly. I can not say it helped because I shivered and entertained a delirium where I walked the spiral over and again, never reaching the centre and all ways tensed for my next step to bring me there and fearing it. They placed me on a cord-strung cot in the kitchen, a pail near by for I could not even walk so far as the corner pot. Nor could I eat but only lie and shake in misery and sleep with no rest. After four days or five it broke, in the morning, and I left the cot feeling like I had been soaked and wrung and yet left unclean with old sweat and foulness, and wanting, more than to eat or drink, to be fresh.

Le Voir made me a gift of a bath by charming and teasing the kitchen women to fill one of the cut-down vats with kettles of hot water and the boys to meet these with buckets of fresh from the stream until I almost could be covered over. At the suggestion of Le Voir from where he stood behind the door, Jansie poured pitchers of water over my head and soaped my hair with soap and lant, then rinsed that with vinegar. I had been abed through a wash day and Derde Susann brought a clean skirt and chemise and my old shawl.

After this I felt new born to the day, weak and coddled, and in this spirit walked out to the thin sun to feel it make me strong again.

At the door to Melt's workshop I stood listening to the whistle and bump of the foot lathe and the hum as a chisel touched wood. Then a curse and a clatter and the lathe winding down. I looked in to see Melt sucking the knuckle of his forefinger and guessed he had let it wander too near the spinning stock. He looked up and I saw drawn cheeks and reddened eyes. Derde Susann had said that my forehead had been kept cool and my body covered day and night – this by the kitchen women while it was light but by another once the household was asleep, she did not say who, and now I guessed by Melt's face who it had been.

I had not an idea how to broach it or thank him. Instead I stepped forward and reached for his hurt hand and took it between mine and blew on the knuckle. The power of my daring, the feel of his dry, warm hand as he let me hold it, my clean body – wood scent from the heated lathe stock, my breath and his breathing … to recognise contentment when it finds you, that is the thing.

6

AFTERNOON SHADOWS SLIDE UNDER THE LAST OF THE DAY'S
heat. Vergilius watches Jacob from the kitchen window. He is helping the convent handyman clear more space for the chief's people,
who are also Jacob's people, on the lawn between the building and
the vegetable plots that run along the property's fence.

Like his uncle before him, Jacob was born on Bandolier. The day
after she gave birth to him in her room in the servants' compound
at the back of the cattle shed, Jacob's mother had risen from her bed
and bound her breasts with strips of cloth and walked off the farm
to catch the train to Johannesburg. Her name was Gracie; she was
Mariah Kobe's youngest child. Mrs Kobe had watched from the
farmhouse veranda as her daughter walked away, then put down
a tin of floor polish and crossed the back yard to the compound,
worked out what she had taken and who was left behind. Then she
wrapped him and handed him to Daniel's wife to watch over, marched
off the farm and an hour or so later was home again with a family-
size tin of milk powder, a baby's bottle, rubber teats. She made a
pad of clean mielie meal sacks, lined a box with these and set it in
a corner of the farmhouse kitchen, near the coal stove that kept the
room at blood heat throughout the year, and there the baby slept for
a few hours each day swaddled into a smooth pupa. For most of the
time, though, he went wherever his grandmother went. At a sound
from the basket she would lean over and swing him onto her back in
a smooth arc, flick a bath towel around them both and pin it over
her bosom. Mrs Kobe was in her fifties when Jacob was born but if

she thought there was any loss of dignity in having a baby strapped to her back at that age she did not acknowledge it, and the farmer would have drunk cattle dip before suggesting there was anything untoward. The baby was in the house, nothing said or asked.

The baby made cries in a register that set Francis Shone's hand trembling over a carapace or the moth cage and sometimes brought him out of the study with his hands held before him to help, but Mrs Kobe only turned a bony shoulder and performed a manoeuvre with lappie and water that stopped the sound. Later, the baby made other sounds – chortles, and a particular noise that was interrogative and more human. He unfurled his creases, grew fatter, focused. His smells added to the household mix of paraffin wax and starch from Mrs Kobe, acetone from the killing jars, the gravy tang of the mastiffs. He acquired a name.

There was a day after Jacob learned to crawl when he escaped from his grandmother and found Shone in his study. The farmer heard the smacking of palms on the linoleum of the hallway, then the baby appeared in the doorway and crawled into the room and to the desk where he was at work. Jacob tilted himself back onto his bottom and regarded the man, who weighed whether to pick him up with an idea of seating him on his lap; before he could make a move Jacob tipped forward, clutched his trouser leg and toppled upright. Shone braced his leg to keep tension with Jacob's fistful of cloth and keep him standing for as long as he could; he hovered his hands about the baby's shoulders but, unsettled by the female softness as his hand brushed his hair, did not touch him. After Mrs Kobe slapped in on her flat feet and picked up the child, the farmer slapped his trousers as if to remove a mark.

With Jacob on the loose there was at least a ceasefire in the farmer's battle with Mrs Kobe over the matter of what was allowed to live in the farmhouse and what must die by ant powder, cockroach powder, or in gusts of fly spray pushed out of the red pump that she snatched up at the first mutter. Shone had declared a free zone in rooms where he housed moth and beetle bodies and gave shelter to the flat, fawn-coloured rain spiders who hunted along the cornices, but even these had been under threat from Mrs Kobe's campaigns to tame or terminate that which came into her clean house, until her grandson breathed the same air.

Jacob grew teeth; to stop his grizzling Shone gave him biltong to gnaw. He made vague plans for his schooling, his prospects, but did not speak of these to Mrs Kobe. In imitation of his grandmother, the child, when he learned to speak, called the farmer 'Master' and tried to echo with his voice the tunes Shone whistled.

Jacob was with him the day a rare party gathered in the garden. He was four. Mrs Kobe had placed the kitchen table next to the jacaranda tree and laid it with yellow damask and gin and Marsala, plates and cakes. Daniel set up a target against bales of lucerne at one end of the garden and lined up bows and arrows. Men in blazers and open-necked shirts, women in frocks, took turns with the bow. They were in the main exiled Englishmen and women from higher up the mountain beyond Louis Trichardt, ex-India, ex-Malaya. They cupped Jacob's head, fondled the dogs' ears.

'… no but your average munt now, he's not going to stay put, no matter how deep in the bundu they shove him.'

'… so he stops whatever he's doing, him and the umfaan, and they just stand there watching me trying to rescue the damn frog with the thing, you know, the pool scoop, and the frog is trying to get away, huge bloody thing …'

'… the power of the chiefs? No, there's not enough left there to tell the young bucks to stay put. Bit of a chance when there was at least a bloody hope of land for his own couple of cattle …'

'… and you can see it's tired and it's about to drown and stink up the place and these two jokers are just standing there, shtum, watching the madam struggle with it. So I get it out but the bloody thing takes two hops and jumps right back into the pool. I just screamed for Harold. I tell you, they jumped too. What a palaver!'

One woman sat in a camp chair, sipping her drink and not moving into the groups of guests. Later, she took up the bow. Shone told her that she had a good stance, to which she replied, 'No, man, but I didn't want to have my go while the others were looking. I'm worried not to make them feel bad, hey.' She was the daughter of the woman who ran the café and tearoom in Slagterskop, a decade younger than the next youngest woman there that day. By habit she was an aggrieved girl, as though her yellow hair ought to have brought better treatment from life than she had received. It was her relative youth she meant when she spoke about not showing up the other women.

Jacob wove his way among the adults with a mangled rose in one fist, trailing a ribbon one of the women had given him. He offered these to one or two of Bandolier's guests but would not give them up. The men played along, making a show of being dashed by Jacob's refusal to part with his toys. When the boy was done with his game he found Shone among the seated adults and settled between his legs; the farmer shuffled his boots to make room for Jacob's body and the boy wiggled against his shins and watched from there. After a while he leaned forward and set out his petals and ribbon on the lawn and began to load them into a blue tin truck that had arrived in the Sears, Roebuck crate in time for his birthday.

There was a lull in the talk; the adults watched the boy, the care with which he placed the petals from the smashed rose in the toy, one by one, counting in solemn, light English. Then the younger woman's flat vowels cut across Jacob's voice, as she stepped into the circle:

'Hey, watch this,' she said.

She leaned over the boy and rattled the ice in her glass, her smallest finger sticking straight out, her lacquered hair and stiff, cocked head calling to mind that spiky flower, the strelitzia.

'Hey, little muntu! Just top up the madam's drink, hey.'

Jacob smiled and reached up for the tinkling glass.

'Hang, Francis but that's a clever piccanin, man. You train this one and you'll end up with a good houseboy in a couple of years.'

She looked around her at the circle of men and women.

'You got to catch your kaffir young, hey?'

A man chuckled. The woman shook the glass again but before Jacob's hand could touch it, Shone leant over and pulled him into his lap. Mrs Kobe, crossing the lawn with a saucer of lemon slices, heard the café owner's daughter's assumption about her perfect and only grandson.

Two summers later she packed his shorts and sandals, storybooks and trucks in paper bags and walked him down the farm road and to the mission and gave him to the Immaculate sisters to raise. She did not consult Shone in this, nor mention Jacob on Bandolier much after that. Every Sunday she walked to the mission with a parcel of clean or new clothing and spent half an hour with her grandson after Mass, feeling him need her less each week as she and the tall sister weaned him from his family.

At Mannamead, a decade on, a pair of bantams, clutch sisters from the previous autumn, scratch and fuss about Jacob's feet, one of the hens with a brood of her own darting between her feathered ankles. There are four other chicks, weightless as dandelion heads, batted about amid the martial self-importance of their elders. The little party is easy around Jacob. Many animals are, and most of these he raised himself – them and their parents and great-great aunts, one of whom he helped to hatch out, having stowed her, still in her shell, on a shelf behind the convent's coal stove. He was a dreamy boy but he never once forgot to turn her after supper. He christened his first hatchling 'Jewel' after the brand name of the oven set in an arc on the door. It became 'Julie', which sounded enough like 'Sister Gilly', Jacob's name for Vergilius, to cause confusion.

This did not matter to him; he needed, in those early years as the only child at Mannamead Mission, sleeping alone in a room behind the main buildings, to know where both were at any moment of the day. His need to be around his creatures is undiminished now, when he is almost seventeen years old, his body a groaning, stretched thing with huge hands and feet, nose and ears, the whole bending without grace to scoop up his hens to take them to their hutch each night, or to cup one of the convent rabbits as it bites into a carrot and chews, deadpan, in his lap.

As Amos and Jacob move mielie sacks and the wheelbarrow, the chicks are in danger; Jacob chases the group around the corner with flapping motions. He passes close to the kitchen window as he does so, and Vergilius catches his eye. She smiles at him and he lifts his chin to acknowledge her.

She fetches a folder of stationery and settles at the kitchen table to write letters: one to a scholarship fund in London on behalf of her pupil, one to a Jesuit fund for secular scholarships in Rome, reminding them that Jacob, whose education they have funded for years, is now of an age to be considered for study in Rome itself. The third will need no postage: it is her weekly formal letter to Mother Rose to ask, in ritual, permission to wear the robes she wears and to use the convent's soap, toilet paper, pencils and paper, sanitary towels. Vergilius lays this last letter in a tray outside Mother Rose's study with more of its kind; she leaves the other two, addressed and unsealed, on the hall table for Rose to read and approve for mailing. To have even an impersonal letter read by Rose by fiat has turned correspondence into another test of will.

The bell rings again, once. The sound hangs in the air. Vergilius fetches a clean shift and a towel and joins the line of sisters on the veranda. They wait at the door to a windowless room, the last in the row of cells. The line moves forward. She enters a dim, damp space. It is divided by a head-high partition into two stalls. She takes the furthest one, where a galvanised iron bathtub sits beneath a tap protruding from the wall. Cold water is dribbling into it. She crosses the wet floor to a shelf high on the wall and feels for the foot-long chunk of soap and blunt knife there, cuts a slice, halves this, sets it and the clean clothing on a footstool next to the tub and strips down to her shift. Vergilius is trying to keep her movements quiet, and the sister in the next stall is similarly trying to make no sound, but every susurration and sucking footstep echoes. They hear one another gasp as they lower their bodies into the hip-high water and screw the taps closed.

The size of the tub does not permit reclining. Chill water laps at the tops of Vergilius's thighs when she straightens her legs and, manoeuvring beneath the shift that has wicked water as high as her ribcage, bathes. She distracts herself with a ritual of her own devising: she chooses from her small store of sensory pleasures (but it is growing every day now) and invokes one of them: thread winding onto a bobbin on the convent Singer, filling the spinning silver channel in even layers or with a bulge, depending on how her finger guides it.

She soaps her head and body, sluices off using a jug and thin cloth, washes her face and rinses again and is out of the tub almost at the same moment as the sister next door, who is Benedict, judging by the consoling 'There now' as she steps onto the floor. Each in her own stall, the women peel their arms and shoulders clear of the wet shifts and bunch them on the tops of their breasts. They get their heads and arms into clean shifts and arrange matters so that dry clothing follows wet down their unnaked bodies. They tip the tin tubs out onto the floor; grey water runs across it and drains through a slot in the wall.

The gloom of the place, the choking carbolic soap, the chill — these guarantee that the Mannamead Immaculates do not linger; six nuns are bathed and done in thirty minutes. The last in line hangs the tub on a hook on the wall then, her head hooded under a towel for the walk from the bathroom, returns to her cell for the ordeal of coif, wimple and veil.

Vergilius collects her weekly bundle of clothing from Perpetua and at the door to her cell pauses as she has learned to do when passing from the light of the day to the darkness of the room. Even so, her eyes take a moment to adjust. She closes the door and crosses the cell in a few steps, using more memory than senses, and deposits the black and white heap on the bed.

The narrow metal bedstead was donated to Mannamead Mission by a Christian Brothers school when the junior boys' dormitories were redecorated. On the underside of a tubular crosspiece at the head is scratched the word *poep*. Otherwise, the grey paint has held up well. There are two spots of red in the cell: on upside-down lids of Sunbeam floor polish that hold moats of liquid paraffin for each leg of the bed, put there to suffocate ants, and in the robes in a Sacred Heart print hanging on the wall. The flaming heart itself has faded to peach. Around the frame of the picture, pinned to the wall by its weight, are an iridescent scimitar feather left by one of the hadeda ibises that visit the mission grounds and a brittle palm blade folded into a cross, one of many made by Benedict and passed along the pews during Palm Sunday Mass the year before.

Vergilius ties herself into her weeds and carries the extra habit to an alcove set with shelves, packs it away and jerks closed the thin curtain that serves for a wardrobe door. Alongside the bed stands another donation, a melamine and sheet-metal bedside cupboard in decayed green, an unstable thing that makes a booming protest at the merest touch. She pulls the cupboard drawer out of its housing and sets this on the bed, then retrieves a folded veil from the back of the cavity and spreads it to reveal an old-fashioned cutthroat razor and a safety razor.

She sets these on the bed, side by side. She picks up the cutthroat and opens it; it resists. She tests the blade on the ball of her thumb; it is dull. She will have to steal the strop as well, or experiment with her belt. But not now; now, another bell is ringing. Vergilius pushes the blades to the back of the cavity and replaces the drawer. Her sins are: disobedience, despair. She pinches the skin of her left inner wrist and twists it as she whispers their names.

7

CALCOEN AND MADAM AND EVEN THE YOUNG MISTRESS
were like lines on a coloured wall showing scenes from the myths
or painted to resemble what it was not, marble and such, in the
rooms where the rest of us lived, we livelier characters of the day.
Surely by now Master had guessed from his wife's dark humours that
Le Voir was not at Vogelzang to bring suit for her hand or fortune –
for if he was, he was failing in it. Madam guarded the women's rooms
like a temple toad to bar men from there and kept an unfriendly
look for he that was the one admitted. Calcoen had the opportunity
to make contact with his step daughter only on her much accompanied excursions to the garden or veranda – he did not venture to
the kitchen, and she did not linger in the rest of the house – and with
this little to go on he seemed to deduce that she was ill, with an illness not specified, and that Le Voir was there because of that illness
and the peruking a ruse – in short, a sort of reverse of how it was.

But if he left the young mistress and her mother alone – as you
leave a heated iron when you have sealed your fingers thereon – he
was pulled towards Le Voir's company.

From time to time the bold naturalists who Le Voir so envied
would cross this plain and a few years later the more ambitious would
follow this with a published account of the journey. (The even more
ambitious, Le Voir said, would forego the travels, making their journey at a writing desk with another man's work open beside them.)
But it seemed to matter not whether the traveller was genuine and

remembered in these parts or just a one with his eye on what would sell: the result of all found an audience here – the naturalist's account thickened with Latin, the lemony diary of an astronomer priest, the mad guess work of a lively plagiariser. Calcoen's passion being the sub-cult of classification, he venerated the field's ranking scientist, the Swede who so confidently described people he had not met, he whose praises of me I had read in Calcoen's measuring book. A countryman and pupil of that man had passed through here, on the route Le Voir and I had taken, some years before. His account of his travels was much discussed, offering as it did a not all together sympathetic portrait of the masters.

Calcoen liked to show people that he sided with the naturalist in his amusement at such people, and hereby make it clear that he, Calcoen, was of a superior sort though of this place; Le Voir would not resist probing that vanity, darting and pecking at Calcoen, and the other fought back: if you have seen two cock sparrows in the dust begin their tournament with feather stirring and wing flurries, apply that to Le Voir and Calcoen seated with pipes on the veranda on a mild afternoon:

Le Voir: 'Your Swede now, he was not kind about the boor who "rushed between shelf and table", quoting the titles of all the books he owned right down to the printer's name and the bookseller's.'

'No, indeed – and the Josephus. Poor fellow! Josephus!' and Calcoen laughed a joyless laugh for Le Voir to understand that if he himself had ever given page traffic to Josephus, it had been as a green boy.

Le Voir: 'I regret the hint by him that you fellows are a dirty lot, and your daughters to be had for the price of a packet of needles.'

Calcoen made no answer but a show of sucking his pipe; it could not be answered – and what could not be resisted was Le Voir's next sortie, for here insult was met in the cladding Calcoen adored:

'And as for the cataloguing of the women of this place from best beddable to worst according to their origin' – &c. This last was a famous calumny much discussed in the town in that time, the worse and the funnier because in the list the pink and white homeland ladies were so little prized for tumbling, and the mere Malagasy girls so keenly sought for the sport.

Again the sucking, and a shifting of weight.

'Ah, this ancient world,' Le Voir began a new tack, and Calcoen, suspecting nothing, trimmed his sails to join him. He cleared his throat. Le Voir continued: 'And growing older all the time.'

Master hastened in: 'O, quite. The ancients would be astonished to hear that they were as much as five hundred years to the bad,' he said in the round tones of the academy. 'Fully half a millennium to the bad in reckoning the age of our planet–'

'Seventy-four thousand, eight hundred and thirty-two,' Le Voir interrupted, weary, dry.

Numbers, large numbers, are less easy to comprehend in another language than most other words, and the two men did not in the usual course all ways perfectly understand one another. But when Le Voir spoke this number his tone was clearer than his words and Calcoen flushed and left off the business with the pipe. Le Voir waited, made him ask, gave Calcoen his solicitude – had Calcoen not heard – surely sir at least a glimmering – the sensational experiments with iron balls heated to white hot and timed as they cooled? and the cunning extrapolation whereby so great an age could finally put to the earth? Aristotle's arithmetic, what was that in a time of experiment – '"Greece, the infant seat of arts and errors",' Le Voir said, with the insult of cool disinterest. 'It is universally acknowledged.'

I cannot say what brought Le Voir to the point of inviting his dislike. Perhaps it was the unease of Vogelzang that did it – Le Voir's means of looking out a strong wind to blow through him. But he ought not to have snorted. In the shadows of the veranda where I stood ready to hold their pipes and blow on the bowl when they sucked, I held myself still at his baiting.

'No one credits the ancients in such matters these days,' Le Voir resumed in a patient tone. 'Geognosts have given the lie to that child's play about Argonauts and the chronology and so forth. It is universally acknowledged.'

Calcoen was bewildered and must not let Le Voir know it, so he made to rise with a scattering of words about the business of the estate. Then he seemed to recollect himself as the master and the other as the visiting wigmaker, and settled back in his chair.

'This is quite amusing, Le Voir, but you will excuse me. I have matters to address,' and he underlined his dismissal by calling me forward to fill his cup, and in the end it was Le Voir who had to quit the field though he was not beaten.

The profit of that jealous exchange was that one had made himself an enemy – an enemy in whose house he lived and earned; and the other had been diminished in several ways, by being bested in the exchange (though who will ever admit that to his waking self) and worse, by learning in such a brutal manner of the new state of the world – for there, buried like a sleeping bee in a winding cloth of Latin in pages uncut 'til that evening, in a book on Calcoen's own shelves, was the proof of it: it had been discovered that this was a world not even so incomprehensibly old as six thousand or even ten thousand years, but seventy-four thousand and some, and even the 'and some' more than many spans of a man's life.

I could feel it with him: a man who had thought himself standing on a field, stripped of the cathedral buildings and reports of palaces that had sheltered him even as they limited his view, now seeing the field fold outwards until it is a plain, until it flows over the edge of the curving everywhere, stretching further away than could have been imagined. He has with him so few tools with which to begin to build his world over. It is too big for a mind to hold, a lonely task.

I am glad for this man that he may wake from this to a home kept ready by women and others of the living realm, where sugar has been shaved in a glittering heap and vapours curl from the cup and tobacco perfumes the air.

I took to the kitchen the cups and pot and set these on the side table beside the indoors water barrel. 'Geognost', indeed. It was all elbows as a word, although I could guess easily enough that it was trying to say 'knowledge of the earth'. I preferred 'geo-metry'. Through narrowed eyes I saw the angles of the window's small panes bisected by the line of a drying cloth hanging there and I squinted tighter to make out how the triangles found there sat, each with regard to the other.

And: 'Lord, Trijn, why you so cross?' said Jansie, hefting her body up the steps to find me narrowing my eyes at the wall. I tried to explain about the lines that were not there but yet tugged and hummed across the room and between the objects in it; Jansie watched my face, her mouth hanging. I stopped mid stream to look for a word and she took the conversation to be ended and rubbed her stomach and said something about movement there. The tom narrowed his eyes at her and when she sat tried to find a place on her lessening lap.

'He turns into a loving fellow when it gets cold,' she said, looping her arms to hold the cat on her knees. 'But you try to touch him when he does not want it and he will let you know about it, the ugly thing.'

I poured water into a butt and rinsed the cups. Derde Susann carried in the twitching body of a hen. She slammed it on the table edge to finish it off and hauled a pan of hot water to the front of the hearth and dropped the bird into it. Without she looked at Jansie she addressed her: 'If you carry on rubbing your stomach, girl, you will make a spoilt child grow there.'

Jansie smiled and pushed herself out of the chair to help Derde Susann pluck the scalded fowl. Derde Susann had news: music was come to Vogelzang. An estate down the road had bought a forte-piano and a musical tutor. The caravan fetching these from town had broken its journey here and the man would play tonight. But first there was a meal to cook and rooms to prepare, a wood pile to stock and lant to strain, beds to air, sheets to hem, floors to scrub, pots scour, candles make and sugar shave, spices crush and butter churn ... I could have understood geometry better had I not such busy hands and I yet with a measure of choice when seen against the kitchen women.

I thought of my mother, who never sat for a moment but seemed to never fully give her mind to the business of the passing day either. She all ways had an ear turned to the inner voices that discussed the pattern of our family story. And at that exact moment when I was lost in thought about my mother, Derde Susann asked me for her story – when my brother had been born, how many years between his and my births. She had the chicken's feet in her left hand, and with her right she ripped feathers from the carcass.

'The younger brothers and sisters – four of them in her skirts?'

Four born, four yet living. Evidence of my mother's fruitfulness impressed Jansie, who sidled towards me and for an instant rested her leg against mine as though to effect a transfer of that quality to herself. Derde Susann's glance flickered at this but all she said was: 'So she was a wet nurse, then. For them.'

I did not follow her reasoning but her conclusion was not wrong. There was all ways one there, as usual a thing as Ma and Papa, Old Mistress, the goats and the town, the mornings and the nights. I recollect a curious sensation around my mother as she nursed the infants, as though a field of repulsion and attraction enclosed her and the babe; by this I do not mean her disgust and the babe's need, but that these humours were present both in my mother. I was no doubt too young to have seen this but the sense of that tug and repulse is strong when I recall her nursing them.

Another memory: Tobie and I piling blossoms in the front yard to make streets and a town when a cart drew up and a most immense woman alighted in a sort of arrested tumble. The man with her reached into the hind part of the cart and fetched up a basket and followed her through our gate. She stopped next to Tobie and me, blocking the sun and frowning at our piles, then moved to the front stoep where our father waited. He took the basket and showed her into the house; her man leaned on the stoep wall, filled his pipe. After some time the woman emerged, carrying the basket, which the man took from her. We sat up from our game, stifling laughter as the man wedged a shoulder under her rump and heaved her onto the cart's seat and hurried around to take his seat before the whole tipped over. This time he placed the basket between them.

We went around the house to the back to discover what had been left, or what fetched away. Something of both, we found. This was repeated once, sometimes twice, each year. The infants were orphans cared for by the Chamber, which paid the Old Mistress for the use of our mother as their wet nurse, a grown orphan to care for infant orphans. For this she had been kept in milk since my birth.

I did not connect this in my thoughts with the pattern of her childbearing until that day in the kitchen when Derde Susann explained it to me and Jansie as she plunged the naked hen back into the pot, stripped out the guts and tossed them to the cat. It was why, said Derde Susann, their women had six, seven, ten children in as many years, passing them to us to be nursed and weaned, tricking their bodies, tricking ours.

'But this one is for us,' she said with a smile for Jansie, who beamed back at her. 'Bonded, but ours.'

The tom made a low growl and leapt to a ledge near the hearth and a moment later the knecht and the dogs filled the door way, he stamping his feet and grunting an order to Derde Susann about the musician's dinner. I set to work sorting vegetables from the store, with my hands in a box of onions, rubbing them between my palms to tell the firm from those we must use today.

The knecht left and the cat came down to be with us again. His fright at the dogs before they even arrived and Derde Susann speaking of my mother at the instant I was thinking of her: these phenomena were explained both by a theory I devised, my first. If you have seen dogs stand alert for their master long before you hear his approach, or had a girl alongside whom you are working of a sudden whistle the air you had in your mind, then you have seen it at work and perhaps thought it a marvellous proof of spirits among us, but it is not. I say it is simply the working of our senses and the dogs' senses, but the difference is this: the dog is not estranged from his. He is only his senses and pays them mind. He hears his master approaching and he rebounds to that. And he hears with all his hearing. With us, we hear the same squeak of a wheel as our fellow kitchen girl but we do not know that we hear it. Still, it acts on a deep part of our mind where the squeak summons up a certain tolderol, rolderol – in my mind, in my fellow's – and at the moment I think of it, she has, without effort or knowing why she so does, begun to whistle the same.

As for Derde Susann and my mother, perhaps I had on my face a look that was the twin of the look I had when I last spoke of Ma, and in Derde Susann's deep mind she recalled this and her mouth opened and she asked after her. What I am trying to say is that all signs of the spirit so called – these can be explained by our senses, in myself, in the tom, in the knecht's dogs. All can be explained if we only bring reason to the fore. There would be less mystery in the world if we were more aware. If we were more aware, there would be less mystery about us.

It did not rain that afternoon but the evening had the feeling of rain, so the men of Vogelzang heaved the wagon with the fortepiano through the double doors on the wainwright's end and into the workshop. There boys folded back the canvas and loosed some of the ropes holding the machine tight to the bed. They lit candles and lanterns, and chairs were brought for Master and Madam and their daughter and for Le Voir. Through the bustle I watched the knecht count the chairs; he left and returned with one for himself and set it down with the others, though slightly apart.

All of the estate was there, from Derde Susann to the meanest boy who lived Sunday to Sunday with the goats. The boys helped the music master onto the wagon bed and placed a chair for him. He started to see so many of us, seated in the rafters, leaning against tables and saddles, but made a bow and seated himself at the wider end of the machine. He raised his hands and placed them above the black keys, then moved his hands upon them with a motion somewhat like a dandy drawing attention to his fine waist coat by playing his spread fingers upon it. Then there was not a sound in the workshop but the dreadful noise from the instrument — a flat clanging, if I can describe it thus, the sound lemon juice on a tooth might make if it had a voice. We might have yet listened in amazement, for how were we to know this was not how this sort of music was meant to sound and the fault lay with us? had the dogs not set to howling every one, so perfectly giving voice to our own feeling that there came giggles and then hoots. The music master stopped, stood up on the wagon bed, turned stiffly this way and that way and made as if to step down, then rethought himself and held up his hands for silence: the instrument was yet suffering from the horrible – the horrible! – journey; we must grant him a moment to restore or partly restore its tone at least.

Someone kicked the dogs to hush them and cuffed the children and we watched as more ropes were undone and the music man delved into the belly of the machine to pull at the strings – for within it was strung like a guitar or many guitars and these struck with small wood hammers to bring out the sound – and producing a noise almost as bad to hear as the deliberate music but yet an entertainment to watch. Then he was satisfied and again we were quiet and he held his hands above the keys, then lowered them and it began, with the dropping of one pure sound, a whole sound in itself, then an insolent age before the next, holding us there until it came and making even the silence a new thing, thrilling us then with a run, the softer notes laying a path for the ones that chimed clearer. The patterns and repeats of the music put me in mind of a beautiful something held up for us to see from different sides, as though by family slaves at an estate sale.

I watched the shoulders of one of the little boys in front of me grow tight as the notes drifted higher. At my side, Derde Susann's eyes were closed. Her face was lifted towards the fortepiano wagon. Her mouth moved slightly – she was trying to catch the notes, to put her voice to them. On the wagon bed the music master frowned and thought hard, swaying his body to and from the machine as he gathered up all the lines of the song and brought them back down until they no longer crossed one another to make patterns on aether but returned to being part of one thing, and it ended.

We were unsure. For a moment there was thick silence then Le Voir cleared his throat and called 'Bravo!', and we followed with shouts and clapped hands. This time the music man's bow was deep enough that his wig must have slipped had he kept it longer. He held up his hand until our noise fell off, then signalled to those at the edge of the wagon and we were surprised when three of our Vogelzang men climbed up to join him there. Others handed them their instruments; these were the estate's band of minstrels who played at dances and kept time for stamping out the grapes. A few months before all you had heard was songs without end from the cellars, the music relying for its excellence on how sober were the players at that moment. But those songs were a handful of water next to the sea in relation to the music we had now heard.

The men were shy up on the wagon. The music master quietened the buzz of voices and spoke. The piece that this ensemble – he smiled at the word, but in a kind way – was to present had been scored for cello, viola and harpsichord but he and his fellow musicians – at which the man with the plucking bass and a lad, the one with the mandolin, cast a look at those hooting up at them – his fellow musicians had practised that afternoon and would present their interpretation on plucking bass, mandolin, guitar and fortepiano.

Well.

It was one thing to hear a new sort of music coming from a new sort of machine, but to see our scratch band around it, standing by their rough and patched boxes – to see, yes, and to hear! It began with the plucking bass. The master waved one hand in the air then cut downwards and at the same time nodded and the bass man played four slow notes, descending and staying low for another four steps like a man walking in quiet thought. I kept my eye on him – his hands held to that same pattern on the strings, over and over, well into the song. After the first eight he was joined by the guitar, plucking his four, then four, notes, almost the same, just different enough to excite the ear, like a round sung by children. Sure enough the mandolin joined for the third round and it with a degree more freedom than the other two. All the while the music master's hand kept time but now that fell to the strict motion of his head as he joined them, not with four notes following four but numberless notes running among them, submerging and appearing again, barefoot among the slave patterns.

Now Vogelzang's three played more softly although to the same rule and the fortepiano disappeared all together, as though it had moved far from us, then – my arms caught a chill – it returned, growing stronger with a forced velocity, and the Vogelzang line waked from thought and joined it. It moved higher, straining to make language with its sounds, to make a voice heard in our deeper minds, and the others supported it, then all seemed to recognise the reverend thing and the music moved to an end. The four musicians bowed together and rocked on their heels at the shout we raised.

I have thought often of that night and wondered how it might have looked from the outside had someone come to the doors: half a hundred people, variously perched, lit by tapers and lanterns, faces lit, turned upwards and along to the little stage, hands raised in the air as in faith.

The shouting died, people looked at their neighbours with grins and shining eyes and made ready to leave the place, but there came a terrible roar from beyond the room – YEEEAARGH! and a whip slapped the air and we could hear a wagon moving too fast, coming on the avenue with a frightening noise. YEEEAARGH! Crack! and a confusion of horns and bellowing and hoarse shouts as boys slowed and skidded and stopped the thing hard by the workshop.

It had begun to rain. We in the lit room crowded at the double doors to look as it came level. A lantern held by a boy showed within the wagon and we could see, across the small distance, a pallet and on it a sunken, fevered somebody and all we heard was the rain and the hard breathing of the oxen until a shriek with one voice, Madam and Jansie: 'Bastiaan!'

Beside me Derde Susann said under her breath, 'Beloved God.' And then she was ordering this and that man to carry the pallet and the young man to his lordlingshouse and the kitchen women to heat water and find her there. The man in the wagon was the son, the brother, come back to Vogelzang.

8

NOTHING EVER HAPPENS HERE, BUT SOMETHING IS HAPPENING now. Many things, in fact, but the biggest of them is the arrival of the Americans. Americans? Everyone knows they are not real outside the buttery colours of *Life* magazine, but here they come.

It is early morning but already a hot day when blue-black, yellow-eyed Chief Henry Kobe leans on the arm of his nephew Jacob and the two shuffle their way to a slatted Adirondack armchair on the hospital veranda, where the old man is supposed to spend the morning watching the hospital's doings and the passing traffic and dozing. His wife and minister come to see him and they discuss matters from home, and at 11 o'clock Vergilius brings the chief tea and medicine. She sets the tray on a table, slips the thermometer under his tongue and kneels at his side to take up his bony wrist, but feels him stiffen suddenly and exclaim around the glass tube. Vergilius is on her feet in a moment, her hand on his forehead as she looks around for help. Henry is staring ahead, astonished and rapt. Dismay surges through Vergilius. She makes soothing noises but her mind is scrambling; she thinks he is having a seizure, she thinks he is dying. He guesses this and snorts:

'Please, Sister, look! Look there!'

She follows his pointing finger over her shoulder to where a startling convoy is moving up the mission's driveway. Vergilius gapes to see it, then covers her embarrassment with brisk tucking and tugging at the chief's rug. Rose steps onto the veranda, and at her instruction Vergilius plucks the thermometer from the chief's lap and drops it into a kidney dish and sweeps down the steps, leaving her patient wheezing with soundless laughter.

The mission driveway and the Great North Road beyond are filled with a parade of many silver, loaf-shaped Airstream trailers, each with its truck, shimmering and undulating in the heat haze as they sway up the track towards the mission.

Vergilius strides down the driveway, a hand raised against them. About halfway between the mission and the Great North Road, standing tall as a saint before the slowing train, she flings an arm to the right. Henry Kobe watches as the convoy snakes off the driveway, down another short track and out of sight into the open veld between the mission and the hotel. In his buoyant thoughts the chief paints her as an angel turning aside temptation, or someone dictating to her great, shining fate its course.

'Ma'am.'

'Mornin' ma'am.'

'Good morning to you, Sister.'

'Thisaway, ma'am?'

In the dust of the convoy's passage Vergilius is greeted in American as each truck and trailer passes her until, with a bow and a gesture, she leaves them to follow one another into the field and walks back to the mission. She gives the chief a diluted smile as she mounts the stairs, and receives an amused look in return. From where they stand on the hospital veranda, the sisters' view of the caravan field is mostly blocked by thorn trees, but they can see the tops of some of the trailers as they manoeuvre to park in two huge, concentric circles.

When it seems the grinding of engines and the dust are done with, Rose gestures to Vergilius and they set out for the field. Women from the trucks are opening doors and windows on the trailers. Men fold out awnings and lawn chairs, picnic tables and American flags. Families stretch their bodies, plump cushions, call to one another.

Advancing among the aluminium-clad, boxy and many-studded trailers, Vergilius catches glimpses of her black and blurred reflection in the shiny sides, broken by slices of interiors – neat pastel homes wherein women are righting boxes of rice, setting out dishes, and, in one, smoothing a hand along an ironing board.

A man in a blue beret steps down from the lone golden trailer parked halfway along the inner ring to greet them in a loud voice, and the nuns turn towards him, dark robes flapping. Near the golden trailer two men bend over what looks like part of an axle. They are absorbed in a discussion, which the blue beret man interrupts to introduce the sisters. He makes a short speech, thanking Rose for the mission's hospitality, and suggests to the two men that they show the ah the ah ladies? the interior of an Airstream.

Before the sisters can step inside the nearest one, more visitors arrive across the veld – the village's two policemen, Louw smoothing his moustache, Teichert tugging at the tails of his brown suit while he skips to keep up. As they draw near, Vergilius hears the man at her elbow groan under his breath: 'Jesus H Christ!'

The man beside him warns: 'Frank.'

The man addressed as Frank leans behind Vergilius to root in a tool box. As his turn comes to greet the policemen he shrugs, holding out a greased jack as a reason not to shake their hands.

He is taller than Vergilius. He frowns as he listens to Teichert's remarks but the skin near his eyes is creased from smiling, or squinting in the sun. It is an outdoors face; his body is easy in its loose khaki trousers and open-necked, faded shirt. Vergilius notices his arms in their rolled-up shirt sleeves and his large hands twisting the jack as he stands, legs apart and easy, and hears out the smaller of the two policemen. The American is wearing a soft hat and there's a tidal mark of sweat where the crown meets the brim. His hair, cropped above the collar, has flecks of gold where it lies against his neck ... Vergilius feels eyes on her: her gaze, moving over the man, has been noticed by Mother Rose. She colours and takes a step back, out of the circle that widens as more villagers and more caravaners arrive.

Vergilius places a hand on the bright side of a trailer. It is, unnervingly, both cool and warm, or warm with the potential to cool quickly once out of the sun. She is puzzling it out, naming the sensation, when a pair of elderly twins take her arms, round women with pretty eyes who finish one another's sentences: Pie and Orie Badineaux out of Lake Charles, Louisiana and darlin', these heathen might be a bit strange around such as yourself, Sister, but we ourselves were educated by the Sisters of Notre Dame at the Infant Jesus Convent School and we have a fondness for the holy sisters and more than a bit of respect, Sister, healthy respect, my yes. They bustle Vergilius towards their trailer. They smell of baking and cut fruit.

Frank watches the tall nun as she bends to make sense of the sugary accent of whichever Badineaux is beating the hem of her habit with her hand before she will allow her to mount the single step to the silvery door, sending up gusts of dust and telling her, 'The Badineaux girls don't fuss about much, Sister honey, but we surely fuss about bringing the yard into the parlour.'

Frank puts down the greasy wrench, reaches for a cloth to wipe his hands.

On the hospital veranda, Henry Kobe stands with some effort, picks up his tea cup and takes a mouthful. He keeps his gaze on the dazzling laager amid the trees as he spits the ancestors' share on the driveway, then shuffles back to his chair where even the great caravan fades beside his preoccupation with his gut.

An acacia is a city of a million multifloreate leaves, of water moving up the capillaries day and night, the disputed territory of mantid and gecko, where ants milk aphids, aphids lay eggs, and tree frogs the size of a nun's thumbnail press themselves into the bark, praying,

O pass me by. For Mr and Mrs Ogden Buffmire of Beetle Lakes, Minnesota, however, all African acacias are blurs, even those in whose shade they tether their trailer. Back home, the Buffmires run the hardware store in Beetle Lakes, or have done for all the thirty-two years of their marriage; their second boy, Clark, is in charge now, and they are more often to be found on ambitious journeys with caravaners like themselves – United States of Americans of comfortable means, admirers of stick-to-it-iveness and can-do, who speak in new-minted word strings and believe in themselves and a more perfect Union, and trust in technology and the goodwill of men.

Mrs Buffmire and Ogden are part of this mighty caravan of Americans that will haul itself up the length of Africa. After it ends, months from now, they will park under a date palm in an Alexandrine campsite, upwind of a flaking pink latrine block, and Ogden will jam a card table into the sand outside the trailer and square upon it their travelling Remington. Mrs Buffmire will spend the cooler hours of the morning tapping out a history of the caravan, breaking off to tell Egyptian children to shoo but allowing no second thoughts to halt the flow of an account adapted from her diaries and Ogden's log. Completing her first book is a task she set herself before leaving Africa, and in five weeks a breathless draft will lie on the card table, weighted with a can of creamed corn.

Thirty-four Airstream trailers are making the journey from Cape Town to Cairo, one golden and thirty-three silvery fat cigar tubes fitted with many appliances, self-sufficient for weeks at a time when they carry their own gas bottles and generators to power their own refrigerators, and stoves, benches, beds and flush toilets, and hot showers, spare filters for the water purifiers, enzyme tablets for the septic tank, water hoses with large nozzles and spare dust filters for the ceiling vents, sheets of aluminium with which to patch the trailer's hide, jacks, pumps, axles and chocks, and more than enough toilet paper.

Mannamead's turn to host the caravan has come about a month into its journey when the caravan stops to regroup for the push north, and in the shadow of the palm, months from now, Mrs Buffmire will write of it:

In our last stopover before leaving the Union of South Africa (or, I should say, Republic!) for the *real* Africa, we made camp in the grounds of a Roman Catholic Mission Hospital south of the border with Southern Rhodesia. According to a rancher who was a familiar face at our camp, this was an 'outspan' in the Africaner language, when a wagon train in the olden days would stay to do repairs before embarking upon the subsequent stage of the 'trek'.

The sisters of Mannamead Mission were greatly interested in the trailers that appeared in their garden one morning, and their prayers went with us when the last of our party at last headed across the 'great grey green greasy Limpopo', on the far side of which lay ... Africa!

Mrs Buffmire has a lot to cover in her book – all those truck repairs on thronged roadsides and triumphant purchases of fruit or recognisable meat in flyblown marketplaces, and the aforegoing is all she will give to Mannamead; Slagterskop, when it comes a year or more later to read these few lines about a time that still gives them so much to talk about, will decide that for the duration of the outspan Mrs Buffmire must have been head down over a bucket of suds wiping down her upholstery.

Early in the morning on the third day of the outspan at Mannamead, the sound of the caravan youngsters warming up for a patriotic sing-along at the morning prayer service gets Frank out of his trailer and looking for escape. He unhitches and heads off in his truck, up the Great North Road. Not half a mile out he sees Vergilius and Jacob on the road ahead. She is mounted on a bicycle, he jogging beside her. Frank slows and coasts up to them, hearing through the truck's open window what sounds like an incantation until he recognises the rhythmic conjugation of Latin verbs. 'Rescindo, re-scindere, rescidi.' They notice him and the boy looks interested in his foreign truck, its different configuration. Frank gives them a good morning, smiles and gestures to the road ahead and drives on. In his rear-view mirror he sees them pick up their pace.

Vergilius neglects to call a halt until they have been on the road for far longer than usual. When they finally turn back to the mission she is overtired and she and Jacob are walking slowly along the road-side, wheeling the bike, hot and thirsty, with open veld beyond the barbed wire fencing on either side and no chance of water.

A couple of cars pass. In one of these is farmer Matthys de Kock. Vergilius's black habit makes him uneasy but if he sees her alone on the road he will always offer her a seat in his Studebaker; if, as now, she is walking with her munt, he tucks his chin and studies the odo-meter or taps the fuel gauge as he passes, and does not slow. For her part, Vergilius enjoys De Kock's stories about his forebears, but on his darker days she is happier to walk or ride her bicycle than share a car with him and his foul eugenics – that is, on days when she has not been so foolish as to drag her charge halfway to the border.

But Frank meets them, on his way back and about two hours after he passed them, his mood improved by the solitude and the sprightliness of the truck freed from the trailer. He pulls up along-side them and drawls, 'Need a ride, Ma'am?' and helps Jacob and Vergilius into the cab, stowing the bicycle and unhitching his water bottle from where it has been kept cool on the front grille. Vergilius is so relieved to be in the shade of the cab she almost pulls her veil from her head to let her damp hair dry, but she's still sticking to some of the rules and does not do so, not in front of the American man. He keeps the truck idling as she and Jacob take turns to suck water.

At Mannamead Frank opens Vergilius's door and hands her down from the cab in front of the mission hospital, but stops Jacob as he slides across the seat to the door and suggests that he might like to have a go at driving the truck. He is what, seventeen? Eighteen? Sixteen, right. And just graduated from high school? In the States, he would be borrowing his father's car, learning to drive. Jacob spins on his heel to ask permission of Vergilius, Frank grinning over his shoulder. Vergilius has hardly given her doubtful consent before man and boy have swapped sides and are lurching down the driveway in first gear, engine shrieking and Frank ostentatiously reclining away from the steering wheel. It is Driver's Ed on the Great North Road for the rest of the week, morning and afternoon, and in return Jacob helps Frank unpack, clean and repack his trailer and truck. While they work, they talk. Jacob has not had a real conversation with a man before, not until the chief arrived; visiting priests definitely do not count and Amos's dagga habit makes him dull company. Now he has his uncle and Frank in his daily life.

Jacob needs Vergilius, but he is nonetheless almost seventeen years old, and as he leaves her more and more for the company of the two men he is not gentle with her feelings. Soon he invites Frank to join the private morning ritual that he and Vergilius have shared, just the two of them, for the past few years.

At least the tall American does not speak more than is necessary, respecting the hush between the dawn chorus and the break of day as the three of them leave the mission grounds, walk up the road and turn onto the farm track. Jacob leaves them to jog down to the far end of the flat stretch of Bandolier's dirt road. Vergilius brings a stopwatch from the folds of her habit and hands it to the American. On the veranda of the farmhouse, Francis Shone, waiting there, picks up his binoculars and braces his elbows against his ribs to focus on her. She lifts her scapular to one side, takes in Frank's nod of readiness and sweeps down the cloth.

The American is impressed with Jacob's time and is, within moments, demonstrating other starting positions and talking of starting blocks, of smoothing the track, of finding him the right shoes. As they turn back towards the mission Vergilius sees that she and Jacob will not share the morning, just the two of them, while the American is at Mannamead.

That afternoon, watching Jacob and Frank working on the engine of the International together, Vergilius feels something relaxing in her, something that has stood sentry over her belief about the world and how it works. She is visited by the sudden thought, standing in the driveway at Mannamead, that she may have misinterpreted important parts of her life, but the prospect of going over it all again, re-remembering, defeats her. Perhaps she can start over instead. As she thinks this, her gaze falls on the tall American who in his easy way is leaning across the truck's exposed engine to accept a spanner from Jacob's hand. Now, when she has long since given up on finding whatever it was she needed, something unbidden is offering itself to her. It seems to her she has looked at the world blinkered by her wimple, seeing a narrow band of good feelings: the close corset of belief, the mighty project that is raising Jacob, the less complicated blessing of the natural world. Her emerging self is awakening to a new spectrum in all its subtlety and garishness. The feelings – of repulsion and attraction, of compulsion, most of all – are as agreeable and as mildly painful as working an underused muscle, as the sting of oxygen reddening her blood. It isn't Frank that makes her feel this way, or at least, not only him. It seems, these days, that life itself is moving through her, no longer washing past. Inside her veil Vergilius can hear the thump of her own pulse.

Some weeks after the caravan sets up camp in the mission grounds, Matthys de Kock eases his turquoise and cream Studebaker over the rutted road and finds Ogden Buffmire, who is on the lookout for a white face, any male. The two of them corner Frank and invite him for a drive.

A few miles along the road from Slagterskop and Mannamead lies Hoërskool Agricus, motto: Ad Astra Per Aspera, where the sons and daughters of the farmers and villagers board during the week. (Deep in the bush, on the Native Reserve, no child boards at a school whose pupils come from the sprawl of African villages lining the red road, but they are encouraged to sleep on the classroom floor and wash at the playground pump if the four-mile walk to school is too taxing to repeat twice a day.) It is of course to the farmers' children's school that De Kock carries his passengers in his American car.

As he drives, he tells the men about the recent history of the two nations that make up South Africa. Two nations? A question forms on Frank's lips, but Buffmire leans back from the front seat and pinches a fold of skin on Frank's hand, his head bobbing in De Kock's direction, mouthing the word 'white'. Two white nations, then, who fought two terrible wars here more than fifty years before, De Kock says, hostilities that in a manner of speaking are now to be concluded.

'You are fortunate, sirs, to see here a new country born.' He nods. 'Great times here for us, these days.'

The car turns onto a dirt track, and De Kock breaks off to give his attention to the road, sucking his teeth and hardening his belly as he eases the big car's underparts over the centre strip, holding his breath at each crackle under the tyres. With a gust of air released he turns off the track and rolls to a stop on a field in sight of the school buildings. Nearby, a few Native men in farm overalls are tapping at the armature for a grandstand. On the field itself, women haul a steel roller around the perimeter, their grunts carrying the barest cadence of a work song. De Kock ushers the Americans out of the car and stands with his hands on his hips, watching the women. He tells Frank and Buffmire: very soon now South Africa will turn its back on Britain, against whom it fought so bitterly and so well, and declare itself a sovereign republic, owing nothing to that queen whose head trembles under the weight of its diamonds. Along with nations up and down the continent, the southernmost is about to shrug off at least the trappings of colonialism, he says, and Slagterskop will play its part in marking the day. Hence the track and the bleachers and so forth.

The caravaners had wanted to be long gone when that day dawned but already they are behind schedule, and that after travelling on roads better than they are likely to find to the north. Catching their breath at Mannamead, the group has voted for a change of plan; they will leave in stages, with a small party staying back to wait for spares to arrive from America. The Mannamead group will comprise Ogden and Mrs Buffmire – no one outside their trailer is sure of her first name until she publishes her book – the two Miss Badineaux, one of whom has sprained her wrist and cannot manoeuvre the truck's steering wheel and change its gears with only one good arm, and Frank, who, as a single man, will act as escort to the sisters and has gladly accepted an assignment that will separate him from the main party for the better part of two months. The Buffmires, Badineaux and Frank know they are fated to be guests of honour at the republic festivities that De Kock describes as he walks the men around the field, sketching bandstand, podium, athletics track and grandstand where kikuyu grass now peters off into veld and workers watch them with unreadable eyes.

Suddenly the wooden framework of the grandstand groans and lists to one side. The men around it scatter, one jumping from the top of the creaking pile, and De Kock and Buffmire lunge to stop it collapsing. Frank jams a pole into place and it holds. He walks around the frame, taking in its design, pushing at some poles with the heel of his hand and kicking others, finds himself explaining to a red-faced De Kock how the main beams should be better placed and braced to create a stronger form. Buffmire and De Kock exchange a glance and then the American is congratulating Frank and volunteering to get up a work party to see the job done. Why, Frank here is an engineer – his job is building things, for gosh sakes. It is the least they can do. Frank looks over the veld. He thinks of the weeks ahead, of Jacob.

'We'll fix the bleachers, and put in a regular track,' he says as he thumps the side of his fist against the grandstand. 'A six-lane cinder track, an American track.'

By the time the northbound main body of caravaners leaves Mannamead and Slagterskop, Frank's grandstand framework is complete and workers are sandpapering pine planks for the seats. When, a few days later, the second splinter group heads east to Kruger, an athletics track has been marked around the perimeter of the rugby field and bricks hammered into the ground to form a channel for a mixture of red earth and claggier soil from near the river.

Frank and Jacob spend a day at the school with a plough lifted to the highest setting and hitched to a borrowed tractor, combing over the clods until the track lies as level as milk tart, ready for rolling. For the rolling, Frank has Jacob drive the truck slowly along the outer perimeter abreast of the tractor that he, Frank, pilots around the inner, with a pole slung between the two vehicles. The heavy roller is strapped to this. The workers and the women whose job it had been to pull the roller stand at the edge of the field to watch Jacob behind the wheel of the American's truck. As the afternoon wears on the ribbon of earth grows smoother and harder, and by the time De Kock loads the workers onto the back of his own truck and heads to his farm, Hoërskool Agricus has its American track and only the lane markings need to be set out.

The careful driving under the scrutiny of the workers and the farmer leaves Jacob and Frank with knotted shoulders. After parking the truck back at Mannamead's field behind the loose open square formed by the three remaining trailers, they set out camp chairs in front of Frank's Airstream, open a quart of beer and relax into the empty-minded ease of oxen unyoked.

Five nuns pass at a distance in the gloaming, towels slung over their shoulders. Vergilius brings up the rear, a head taller than the next tallest sister.

Jacob finishes his beer and leaves to be with the chief; Frank stays seated outside his trailer. His gramophone is set up in a cabinet inside the door and he rouses himself to choose a record and again to light a lamp. He hears the nuns returning. Murmurs carry across to him. Then he makes out a shape peeling off from the group and picking its way across the field towards him. Frank stands up as she steps into the field of his hurricane lamp. He sees with a small jolt that her head is uncovered; wet curls frame her forehead. Vergilius is clutching the ends of a towel around her neck and seeking his eyes with a mixture of wariness and defiance, her chin held stiffly out. Feeling off balance himself, Frank offers her the chair that Jacob left and reaches into the trailer to close the lid of the gramophone, damping the music. He sits and picks up his beer bottle, thrusts it towards her.

'May I offer you something? We have beer, cola … beer …'

Frank feels the knot in his shoulders pulse and burn as the woman stands mute and vulnerable, as though shedding a yard or so of black cloth from her head had taken so much courage, she had been left with only enough after that to carry her here.

'Thank you,' she says. It makes sense to them.

Vergilius prays to disappear, or for him to. Or for him to say something about her missing veil. An old moth confused by the lamp makes a tiny racket with her ragged wings against the glass.

This allows Vergilius a small noise of concern, which permits Frank to hurry to extinguish the light. In the darkness the music ends. The Misses Badineaux are with the chief and Jacob, and the Buffmires at supper in Slagterskop. The breeze brings a scent of dust. Some self-absorbed creature roots in the grass nearby.

Frank reaches up to cup his nape in the near darkness.

'Pardon me, but do they let you do that? Go bareheaded?'

'No, they do not … let me.'

The sound of a truck approaching the Airstreamers' field brings them both to their feet. In the seconds before the headlights find them their bodies brush against one another as Vergilius slips past him and away.

At the Airstream camp the daily roster of visitors and gawpers is down to Captain Teichert and a few snot-glazed children who stare at the trailers, unnerving Mrs Buffmire by creeping a little closer through the course of the day; at odd intervals one or the other yells Hello! and the lot of them, exhilarated by their daring, run away into the scrub. For most of Slagterskop the novelty of having Americans in their backyard has worn off.

Pie and Orie Badineaux cast about for something to do. On a Wednesday morning they jam their wide hats on their heads and cross the veld between the trailers and the mission. There they follow the shuffle of the women down the veranda to the clinic, patting the drum-tight blankets that bind the infants to their mothers' backs. The babies crane their heads out of their swaddling to look at the pale eyes and bright hair of the sisters. In a dim corridor where scents of breast milk, wood smoke and Lifebuoy soap combine, the sisters find a nun and ask to help. By the end of the morning Miss Pie and Miss Orie, lulled by words that run together and trail off in soft vowels, are batting away the thought that they could sell up, move to

Africa, see these infants every day, although not even the Immaculate sisters see these self-contained babies more than once a week.

The next day the Misses Badineaux look around more corners of the hospital and follow their curiosity into the adult wards; there they find the chief isolated aristocratically in a corner, asleep. On the bedside table next to him are a jug of water, a bottle of orange squash and a Jack London borrowed from Bandolier's library. Already he barely has the strength to hold the book. Sister Bernadette tells them that a doctor from Louis Trichardt came to Mannamead to hand over a supply of morphine for the chief and an estimate of the life in him, and that after he left Henry called Mother Rose to him and said he would pay for the care he would need. She would accept only one beast; he made it a cow in calf, and this he brought with him when he returned, says Bernadette with a lift of her hand in the direction of the mission's grounds.

The ladies sweep through in a whirl of blanket-smoothing and pillow-plumping, leaving a scent of face powder in their wake and jars of Amos's sweet peas on the window sills. They move their record player to the mission and in the afternoons play music for all to hide behind during the sponge baths. The Badineaux sisters are easy with men's bodies, and it shows when they rub eucalyptus salve into their patients' boyish backs, lift the leathery hands to take a pulse, or embrace an old man's waist for the journey down the length of the ward to the veranda. The chief turns towards the room, stays awake for longer between his drugged sleeps.

In Mannamead's dining room Rose has chosen the reading for the evening meal. It is from a letter written 1500 years before. Sister Patrick stands to read:

'Say not that you have chaste minds though you may have wanton eyes, for a wanton eye is the index of a wanton heart. And when wanton hearts exchange signals with each other in looks, though the tongue is silent, and are, by the force of sensual passion, pleased by the reciprocation of inflamed desire, their purity of character is gone, though their bodies are not defiled by any act of uncleanliness.'

Rose does not address her plate but keeps her rigid face turned to Vergilius for as long as it takes Patrick to get through it. Vergilius sets down her knife and fork, clasps her hands in her lap, locks her gaze there. Xavier, in fright, looks from Rose to Vergilius, chewing slackly, panic and avid enjoyment chasing each other across her face.

Patrick exhales heavily: 'Nor let her who fixes her eyes upon one of the other sex, and takes pleasure in his eye being fixed on her, imagine that the act is not observed by others; she is seen assuredly by those by whom she supposes herself not to be remarked ...'

God is an Immaculate sister, Vergilius thinks. Not a sparrow falls nor a heart creaks open but it is spied out.

Disobedience. Uncharitable thoughts.

Blasphemy, Rose would add.

'If you perceive in any one of your number this forwardness of eye warn her at once so that the evil which has begun may not go on but be checked immediately.'

Patrick rushes through to the end, inhales to the depths of her lungs and sits to bolt her potatoes and tinned fish. The other sisters keep their eyes fixed on their plates. After a cold age Rose snaps at Xavier to clear the table.

Next morning Rose telephones the bishop and the bishop sends his priest, a man of sixty years whose cement-coloured hair is shaved from the sides of his head and grows sparse and upright above that. Father Oliver Fisher closes himself in the parlour with Rose, then dismisses her and sends for Vergilius.

On her he first tries charm but he is not naturally charming. 'Young lady, young lady, what are we to do with you?'

He moves his head from side to side, purses his mouth. A spike of resentment flares in Vergilius but she keeps custody of her eyes as she sorts through the several assumptions in the priest's question. When she lifts her head she looks at him directly and for a moment too long without answering. He flushes, raises his voice, watches the colour drain from her face and thinks his sharp words might have won tears, at which he calls a halt and has her pour and hand him tea. Father Oliver drinks, sets down his cup, retrenches:

'All the visitors and the coming and going. You Mannamead sisters are not used to this sort of excitement. A certain level of discipline. The Rule of the order ... I have a copy of the Rule ...'

He leans on one buttock, reaches towards his jacket pocket. With a stiff, papal slide of her hand Vergilius gestures to a framed manuscript on the parlour wall:

'We have the Rule.'

The priest's irritation surges.

'The Rule which you vowed to keep. No one brought to bear any force when you entered and vowed, for the rest of your days.'

The mistress of novices who despaired of Vergilius a decade before would recognise the impenetrable tranquillity that descends on her now and not waste the ordnance. Oliver Fisher has to be told, and she tells him.

'I think this is no longer where I am meant to be.'

She says the words politely enough and without raising her eyes but they break against him like more defiance; he thrills and disgusts himself by wanting to draw back his arm and ...

'Your Mother Rose could not oppose a genuine ... But the timing ... Know your own mind, do you think you do know your own mind? Your bishop, your superior in Wexford, your Mother Rose ... none of them will support any appeal for a dispensation until you can show that you are able to reason clearly. You must prove your obedience to the Rule and to your community. You must ...'

It is wearying stuff, but, even though Vergilius is no longer receptive to sentences containing the injunctive, she knows the priest will prevail. Rose cannot write to Wexford, nor the mother house to Rome, without the bishop's permission, and on Father Oliver's advice – these are his parting words to Rose – the bishop will not give it. Give it time to blow over, he tells her. You all go through it, don't you?

She is still subject to the Rule; that night Rose locks her in her cell. She sends Xavier before dawn to unbolt the door.

9

I COULD HEAR A CURIOUS SOUND COMING FROM THE FRONT part of the house as I entered with coffee and hard biscuits for Madam. It was not regular but followed in the same order when it came: first the twitter of a song bird, then a jangle of thin metal, then silence. An interval, then it ran again. I stood in the hall that yet held the night chill at this early hour and there kept still. It came again – the questioning chirrup, the unmusical clang. My unease was such that I all but turned back to the kitchen to get Meerem to complete my walk, but a long silence calmed me and I started again – and gained the front room in time to hear the bird and see Madam slam her hand against the cage with a crazed look. The song bird stopped, its beak wide above a throat fluttering with fright. Madam stood over it, her hand raised, waiting for it or its fellow to make another sound.

I set down the tray and fled from her.

In the kitchen, Derde Susann dozed against a wall and Meerem was asleep at the table, her head in her arms. Our cook had been up until the wet dawn in the lordlingshouse at the side of the young man from the terrible wagon, spelling Le Voir and myself. Jansie had whimpered and darted about his bed and it was a relief when she dropped in a corner and slept there. He had not known her when she fell at his bed side clutching his hand and saying his name; he had looked at us and at her without interest.

The door opened and Le Voir came into the kitchen, greasy with fatigue. His hand shook as he took a cup from me, and he slouched at the table.

'Well, his blood is poisoned.'

He spoke to the air in front of his face, as though he had been asked why the young man had to die, answering with a shrug for the changeless 'because'. Because his blood …

We none of us moved for such a grey age that it was as though we had sunk together into a state deeper than sleep, in which the dying of Vogelzang's returned son was as unremarkable as the bread dough rising in the trough at the end of the table on this morning so cool as pewter.

After some while we heard the farm waking, though with other than the usual noises. There was shouting from many voices and to find the reason Le Voir and I moved to the door. Meerem joined us, and we three stood dull eyed before a dreadful scene. The second and third wagons of the young man's train had been out spanned on the avenue between the back of the main house and the lordlingshouse. The second yet wore its tilt of sailcloth and was yet neat, packed with trunks and boxes; only the guns and gunpowder had been brought in last night and locked in Calcoen's room. But the third had lost its cover, and its cargo, piled high on the bed and spilling over the sides, all but hid its bed from view.

We could make out that there had been some attempt at a system for the freight: heads at one end, then entire small bodies – I could make a porcupine, a couple of serval cats, a tyger wolf – and thought my tired eyes saw the dog creature menace the cats – then scores of stiff and bloody skins held down by the massive head of a rhinoceros, its top lip overlapping as though it would lisp a protest where it lay. Next was a heap of flesh and the skeleton of a many tiered drying frame that had listed and half collapsed. It was draped, piled, buried in grey and black and brown meat, and reaching for this two score of hands, and pushing back at them to defend it, sjambok and boot.

As we reeled at the sight and the smell Meerem pushed between me and Le Voir and ran down the stairs to claim her share.

'Was it his purpose to shoot every animal there is?' Le Voir muttered. 'Small wonder his body is as we saw it.'

Last night we had turned back layers of blankets and a kaross from the youth's body, then cut through his waist coat and shirt and peeled these off. I think I will never forget the sight of what we found. At first I thought it was caused by shadows or some other effect of the candle light upon his flesh but Derde Susann moved her lamp close to him and it was plain that what I had taken for a shadow was a black bruise covering his chest and right shoulder, which also was bloodshot and shiny with swelling. Le Voir moved the arm to find the wound that ought to account for this but found only raised glands in the pit. What we had seen last night and what we now watched with numb minds were the results of a hunting frenzy, a gluttony of killing that had battered the young man's body and filled his wagon with a tangle of hooves and blinded eyes.

The knecht and the wagon driver were winning against the ones clamouring for their share of the hunt; these last subsided to a more or less ordered group waiting their turn to be called. While the knecht's dogs ignored the crowding slaves and bent their heads to a wheel to lick the cold blood there, the hired hunter stood by the bed and hacked a slab of meat, green or less green as it came, and slapped it on the cupped hands of the next in line. With his hands full and held forward to protect his breeches, each one crossed the avenue to the end of the lordlingshouse and the slaves' kitchen to set his bounty direct on the coals or on irons braced across the fire, to his taste.

Derde Susann had awoken and was at the wagon, pointing out haunches and saddles to be brought to the kitchen and, as an after thought, the porcupine entire. With Vogelzang's people fetching off a double handful each there still was barely a change in the heap.

Le Voir left the scene for our patient, who had been placed in a small room opening directly onto the avenue about mid way down the lordlingshouse, and where the young mistress was there before him, holding her hurt brother's hand.

In the kitchen Derde Susann had already put Meerem to work skinning and dressing the legs; a boy was sent for extra milk and Jansie, called back to the kitchen, was making much of her task of scouring a wood bucket with lant and salt. When all was ready Derde Susann packed the meat into this and poured the boy's haul over it 'til the joints were white; as the milk soured it would keep them. She would roast the saddles today, one for a meal, one to be drowned in melted fat and like wise kept from putrefaction. The porcupine was for flaying, then into the chimney to cure above the fire to rough bacon.

Derde Susann was keeping Jansie busy, I saw, making up small tasks to succeed one another so that she was never still yet not tired out, and kept from panic in this way though every so often she looked about her with an open and bewildered glance; then Derde Susann moved to bring her back. Now she put a bowl of blood soup in Jansie's hands and told her to take it to the lordlinghouse. As Jansie left the kitchen, moving at a careful incline down the stairs, Derde Susann told me in a voice kept low, 'You go with her.'

She moved at her rolling gait – her belly was tight now, and full – but as though she were unsure of where to turn after three steps had carried her one way. I caught up to her and guided her 'til we reached the door way to the young master's room. His sister had wrung a cloth in water and placed it on his forehead. Le Voir leaned over him from the other side of the pallet; next to him a boy held out a jar. One at a time Le Voir fetched slim grey leeches from this and lowered them carefully to the awful shoulder and held still while the creatures swung about then found the skin and bit for blood. Now one doubled back and fastened on Le Voir's thumb; he clicked his tongue and tore it free, breaking it as he did so. He wiped the mess on his breeches.

Le Voir and the young mistress were silent as they worked. Neither paid us any mind where we stood at the end of the bed. As for the young master, he was breathing too fast – not panting, but taking no rest between breaths. A rash, hard at the edges, had taken hold in patches on his face and chest. He opened his eyes and turned them to the oily things swelling at his shoulder, then moved his head and watched his sister's face, his expression as still as a man reading. She moved off a way to wring the cloth and then he seemed to notice us at the end of his bed. Jansie made a sound, her free hand plucking at the skirts under her belly. At first he watched her with the same indifference, then his eyes moved to her breasts and belly and grew sharply alert for a time, though soon his overheated breathing and fever claimed him and his look settled back into those snake's eyes. Jansie thrust the bowl at me and sat on the floor, leaned against the pallet, a hand on the blankets over his feet, and so she stayed as the estate settled into the day and young mistress changed the water and swabbed her brother's burning body, and leeches unhooked from his flesh and rolled down the slope of his shoulder while he breathed without rest.

It was late morning when Madam came to her son's room. Derde Susann was taking a turn at nursing him; Le Voir and his other patient were about some business in the main house and Derde Susann and I had but removed a sheet from the young master's body and covered him in fresh when she stepped through the door. I shifted a low stool to the bed side for her. She leaned towards him and placed her hand on the blanket near his thigh and spoke to him in a voice of pleasant reason.

She said: 'Sebastiaan, do not again leave Vogelzang for such a long time. We have need of you here. I am not saying you should not have mounted your hunt, but now that is done you ought to prepare for your place here.'

Her manner was of a parent speaking to her child as an adult for the first time, offering and expecting new understanding between them.

'We will have your rhinoceros preserved for the wall. It will stand as proof of the expedition. At Bij-den-Rhee the brothers have brought back a savage from across the river; I am glad you brought us meat; animals are better, from a hunt. The boys say they will dress it as a civilised man. They have told the peruker to make a wig for it. So Vogelzang has this reputation, that it has fine things to offer. A peruker came while you were gone. You missed the harvest. Bastiaan ...' her voice trailed off, and there were only small sounds in the room, from the movement of Derde Susann's skirts, and the suck and hiss from him.

Madam looked over his face, down the length of his body, to Jansie's hand on his foot and she sang snatches of a country song under her breath as though she were alone in the room. Her eyes completed their circuit and came back to her own hand on the blanket.

'Well,' she said, 'you will rest and we will start over.'

She stood and turned away from him then stepped back to his bedside and bent to press a kiss on his forehead. He had not spoken while his mother was in the room – indeed had made barely one comprehensible sound since coming home the night before.

The doorway to the room filled again. Gottlieb Calcoen stayed on the threshold looking at each of us, looking again from the young master to Jansie. He was not Sebastiaan's father; he had been married to his mother for less than a decade and it was said there had been no ease on either part about the other – one master now, one who would own Vogelzang in due season. It was surely his right to visit his step son but all the same I was surprised to see him here. He took the stool Madam had sat in, flicking his skirts behind him.

The son was asleep or should I say his eyes were shut, for this could not be sleep that brought no change to his breathing. Calcoen waited, an air of busyness about him. For a moment I wondered whether he was about his weird science, some measurings to be done or an Observation on a Young Man Dying of Poison in the Blood.

Derde Susann and I busied ourselves with make work to stay in the room but we need not have fussed for, having but a moment before set himself down, Calcoen was stood again and looked about him with the same awake look and stiff smile as though acting a part, and I guessed that he had been told to visit the heir – told by some idea of rightness or by the mistress of Vogelzang – and he may as well have been at a reading of verse in Turkic for all he miscomprehended the meaning while he met the form.

The young man stirred and at that Calcoen turned in a hurry to leave, taking Derde Susann out with him. I could hear him on the avenue quizzing her about Jansie sitting on a cold floor – would it not harm her babe? – and at that I regretted thinking him not capable of human feeling.

Derde Susann came back into the room, sucking her teeth in disgust.

'There is only one person in this place that loves this boy apart from his sister, and it is not either of those two. Come, my girl,' this last to Jansie, whose shoulder she touched. 'Up you get.'

She took me aside and told me to fetch our shawls from the kitchen and return for Jansie – take her to the garden, up the mountain, any place but here.

Jansie almost nestled in my side as I spread her shawl on her shoulders, and allowed me to guide her out to the afternoon under the dripping trees of the avenue. Almost at once she began to speak of him.

'First I was his big sister – I am older than him by five years. Then he was my friend, only he was not all ways kind but I did not mind him.' She caught her breath. We walked down the avenue, towards the pondok. As we passed it Jansie covered her mouth with her hand and snorted.

'O goodness, we played in here!'

She spoke on about him, each second twisted oak or pathway holding a memory, lastly of that strange morning when Bastiaan and the young mistress returned so suddenly from their visit to the other farm, when the young mistress had fallen ill and been taken to the back room.

Bastiaan had been in such a passion when she, Jansie, took him his coffee in the lordlingshouse that morning, such a passion that she had dared to step close to him and put her hand on his arm, here, and she placed her hand on my arm and looked full in my face, and even swollen with carrying she was pretty as a kitten.

He had not hesitated, she said. She was his first and he hers, which was a wonder as she had been pursued for an age before by – by some other one, but she had all ways escaped that until then. Bastiaan and she cried after, the pair of them, in the sunny room in the lordlingshouse, on his bed, not in a field or behind the werf wall at night with the wild bush sounds nor forced in a front room with an old man's hand over your mouth and a piece of sugar afterwards to stop crying. Those at least were not her first, she said.

She was almost running; I took her by the waist and slowed her. We took the mountain path behind Vogelzang. I ought not to have stopped her flow for now she was thinking of Bastiaan again – Bastiaan dying in the room at our feet. At that moment the bell rang and we stopped on the path to watch people come from the buildings and vines and move to the kitchen end of the lordlingshouse. I kept an eye to our right, below, and sure enough a boy was on the path from the grove and Doof Hendrik coming up behind him and smacking him on the head.

I stopped for a moment before deciding to share my secret but it argued to be shared so I took her hand and said, 'Come, there is something to see here,' and led her along the path then down through the grove and into its clearing.

Work had begun on the roof of the structure. Beams ran from the outer walls to an upright pole off the centre and were lashed thereon with wet hide strips. The crossing laths were fastened on in parts; bundles of laths lay against the walls. From this angle it looked like nothing more than a pondok, better built than usual but not out of the usual type. I told Jansie about the inner wall spiralling towards the centre but I cannot say she comprehended that this was the same building whose foundations she had seen. She chafed to be back, and we took the path down to the avenue and to Bastiaan.

Vogelzang's son did not last the afternoon and soon was buried among the family graves near the grove. The men dug another hole, a pit beyond the werf, and there they buried the rotted meat and most of the horned heads and, after they had decided it among themselves, the head of the young master's rhinoceros.

The wigmaker had not put his hand to his craft since completing the goat's hair peruke for Calcoen in the first weeks of our time at the estate, but now wig making of a superior kind was upon us. First, the boys from Bij-den-Rhee called on Vogelzang. It was a month since Bastiaan's return and the house still dressed in black and grey. Madam would not receive them, and Calcoen had some how lost much of his position on the estate and was not expected to greet visitors as the master of a household that followed the mother's lead and used a diminishing tone and manner with him; there for it was the young mistress who came out of the front door to meet the brothers. She wore a dressed mutch and none would have guessed that beneath it she was bald as an egg nor must they, for the estate's troubles – the son's death after a profligate hunt, the mistress's crazed humours and brandy, the rightful master with no respect in his house, the trail of bad fortune at proud Vogelzang – was talked of on the plain, but in the person of the young mistress were tucked the estate's hopes and there dare not spread word of her condition how ever it may be guessed at in the household.

The Bij-den-Rhee boys were a pair, sturdy as buck, brisk and open. They tumbled from their cart, elbowing to be first to take the young mistress's hand where she waited on the veranda with Le Voir, and me in the back ground. One of the brothers made a nod to Le Voir; the other said, '*You* are the perew-ker?' – he minced the word – 'We had bet it would be some small fellow with airs.'

Le Voir accepted the compliment and I suppose the insult and beamed at their health and humour. The brothers seemed to prove that spring could arrive, even here.

'Idiot!' One brother pushed the other's shoulder. 'What about the princeling?'

And they stepped about and called and clapped their hands and on the cart a bundle of blankets stirred, to the surprise of the boy who had come to water the horses, and there emerged a young savage, he that the brothers had brought back from their hunt across the river. He stood on the bed of the cart with his hands on his hips, then swung to the ground and came to us yawning. In his appearance he was not many degrees unlike any civilised black one might see and he was handsome, with sharp cheeks and a shaped mouth. I was sorry to see that of bones through his nose and skins for his loins there were none; he wore breeches and a shirt, which breeches he now plucked from between his buttocks, though instead of shoes his wide feet rested on pieces of hide tied with cords.

Gaining the veranda, he stood before us, looking us over, with time taken over the bosoms and waist of the young mistress and my own, and so open and interested in his regard that none could resent it. It was Le Voir, though, who drew his most frank smile, for the Frenchman who topped us all fixed the savage with such a look of open interest himself it seemed we might watch friendship set there on the veranda.

Said one brother: 'His name is not possible for a civilised person to say; it has that kissing clucking sound.'

'A prince of some sort with his people. So we call him Majesty,' said the other. 'It is our sisters' idea to dress him as a man. The women at home are busy with a coat and so on and we thought it the thing to make a peruke to complete the picture.'

Le Voir had said it was the fashion at some courts to parade savages in powdered wigs and pale silk, for whose amusement I cannot say; here it seemed another plain farmer had caught a fancy to imitate. The wigmaker made the savage a bow, at which that same made it back and he took the hand of the Frenchman and did not let go of it but to switch hands so that they were side by side. Le Voir gave a mouth shrug and led his new friend into the house, by his hand. We set up in the long hall and laid our calliper, tape and paper upon the table. Jansie, red about her eyes and slow, brought coffee and brandy. She looked at the savage but showed no special interest and certainly if you did not know he came from people who hunted with spears and knew neither reading nor God you might say he was just a person like any other one.

Le Voir had him sit on a chair. 'Now, Majesty,' he said and showed him the tape, 'we will take the measure of you.'

He brought the tape towards the savage's head at which that pulled away, so Le Voir called me to him and commenced winding it about my head then unwinding it and reading the marks there on in dumb show. The Bij-den-Rhee boys exchanged looks at this but

Majesty took hold of Le Voir's hand with the tape and brought it to his own head. The calliper, that sinister pincer, presented a similar exception and that similarly resolved. Soon we had his numbers and now to style and colour.

The brothers would have no part of this but sipped brandy and milk and commented upon Majesty's own hair – dusty brown and soft as a cloud behind my hand as I held the end of the tape at his nape. Le Voir saw off relayed suggestions of a powdered wig for one in Majesty's own colour, or near to it, and we had by us a hank from Goa that would do.

The young mistress invited the brothers on a visit to the gardens and sent Jansie to bring a crock of preserve for them to take to their mother; I stayed to clear away our tools. Le Voir and the savage followed the gentry children; he told me later that among the budding trees what had drawn the visitor was Old Haarlem, at which tortoise he directed words in his savage lingua and with a fond manner.

Second among the spurs to Le Voir's industry there came a few days later a visit that we had anticipated and without which we could not complete the task that had brought us to the estate in the first instance: the arrival, with spring, of wild farmer Zacharias de Buys and his daughters with excellent hair.

They came at night, out spanning on the road that ran past the gates. At the next day's break Zacharias, Rachel and Hannah splashed their faces at the stream and walked up the drive where the dogs ran to find them. The oaks wore their tender small leaves and catkins; Zacharias stepped behind one and watered it as his daughters waited.

He was a man of ordinary height, his full beard trimmed to begin at the outskirts of his face and then not trimmed so that it came half way to his belt. He wore a wide hat, a waist coat and blue shirt, and trousers over hide shoes he likely had made himself. The girls like wise wore rough shoes, and simple dresses. Their heads and indeed their faces were hidden by bonnets that lay forward like a wagon tilt such that they could look nor left nor right but only down a narrow main of quilted cloth, and these with overlong skirts behind to hide their necks. They had, I suppose, fourteen and fifteen years, flanking their father as he came to the front door of Vogelzang to do his business with the peruker.

A boy had been left with the wagon and the span; the family's winter earnings were in that train: butter salted down and not new; slabs of soap, and ivory from the hunt. These would be turned to dollars in town and the rest of the year's survival depended on what was on that wagon, but luxury – small luxury, the only excess they would have – was under the deep bonnets of the daughters.

Le Voir had been waked from sleep in the lordlingshouse and was on the veranda to greet them.

'You have found us! You received my message? Of course, you received my message! Welcome, De Buys, young ladies.'

Le Voir and I had much enjoyed Zacharias's habit of saying the most patent thing in his slow voice in the manner of one imparting a prophecy, and he did not disappoint now.

'We were bound for the town where we might sell butter and such and the soap made by our mother and wife and also the other thing, to you. We thought to meet at your shop. We had agreed on this, you and I. At the pass keeper's house the man there told us that we would find you sooner than that. We drove them on, our team, and broke the journey here, last night. We are come.'

The De Buys kin stood in a row facing Le Voir for the span of the speech. When it ended, Zacharias stepped forward and took Le Voir's right hand in both of his and shook it; the daughters bobbed their bonnets.

In the kitchen Meerem had coffee heating and Derde Susann cut some porcupine; I carried this and bread to the hall. De Buys took a seat at the head of the table. Rachel poured his coffee, Hannah pulled a hunk from the round loaf and placed on this some of the rough bacon and put it before her father. The girls stood either side of his chair.

'I cannot approve of this place,' Zacharias told Le Voir. He took a deep drink of coffee. 'The trees alone must suck water like a greedy calf. The oxen are very fat.'

Le Voir, perhaps remembering the master and mistress in their beds close by, spoke low words about a fertile plain between mountains. This drew scorn from De Buys, and not over soft either: 'The farms on your plain are crowded upon one another, fence by fence. A man cannot breathe.'

He fell to his meal. When he was done he pushed his chair back from the table with an air that told us we could begin. The girls, from what I could see of their faces, were at the brink of crying though with no thought to disobey. De Buys noticed their distress and answered this as he adjusted his belt and broke wind: 'The daughter of my people is become cruel, like the ostriches in the wilderness. Leviticus four, verse three.'

He stood, took each by the shoulder and steered her after Le Voir to the eastern court yard. This was a sun trap sheltering a lemon tree, a tree bearing pomegranates and a trellis with a rose. The young mistress's window looked on it; had she chosen, she could have watched her new hair begin the passage to her head from theirs.

The elder girl sat at one end of a stone bench. I handed Le Voir a length of twine that had been run through soft tallow and he draped this on his shoulder at the ready. De Buys said, 'Rachel,' and she untied the ribbon on her bonnet and lifted it from her head, releasing an abundance of auburn hair. Le Voir dug his hands into the crown of it, spreading it in the slanting morning light. He separated a bunch about the thickness of a candle and tied it off, then had the big shears from my hand and cut above the cord. He handed the hank to me where I stood out of the girl's sight. It reached from my hand to below my elbow and was heavy as oiled silk.

The harvest from Rachel was three lengths, and three from Hannah. We had brought no mirror and for certain there was no such at their home, but each girl saw her own head in the other's and then the tears spilled. With a thickened voice De Buys told Le Voir: 'You have that which you wanted. You and I will conclude our business by and by. We will have a moment here.'

He positioned himself behind the girls where they sat on the bench. As I left the court yard with the hair laid in orderly fashion in a cloth, I turned to look at the family. He had a hand on the pale nape of each daughter. All three had closed their eyes and Zacharias was praying aloud for a blessing on their bowed, clipped heads.

Le Voir bade me take the hair to the back bed room before Calcoen or one of the household women should see it. As I passed through the hall one of the song birds made a peep; the other looked to be moulting but I did not stop to see. I held my breath as I crossed Madam's room but she was asleep or in a pretence of sleep and did not stir. The young mistress was awake and watched from her bed as I placed the bundle on the seat at the window. I had thought she might be interested in it but she turned away as though from some disgustful thing.

Back at the dining table the girls were restored to their bonnets. I arrived there as De Buys tucked the last of his coins into a pouch and deposited this in his hat, tipping it on his head and jamming it tight. It was the first I had seen him without it. He called the girls to his side and prepared to take his leave. It seemed the comfortable dining hall had no effect on him beyond that it produced some discomfort, what fine taste so ever it must be acknowledged to have. With a last shake of his head at the folly around him, De Buys formed his daughters into a line facing Le Voir and said:

'We have done our business with you that we came to this place to do by word of the pass keeper. I will shake your hand now and we will in span and join the road to the town.'

Zacharias's loud, slow speech had drawn Calcoen from his cot. He stood in the front room in his turban and silken robe and made as if to step forward to accept an introduction from the rough visitor and his plain daughters, but De Buys did not offer his hand nor directly look at Calcoen, and only startled him by suddenly declaiming as he left the house, a hand pointed upwards, past his hat:

'Woe to the bloody city! It is all lies and robbery; the prey departeth not; the noise of a whip, and the noise of the rattling of the wheels, and of the prancing horses, and of the jumping chariots!'

His voice grew fainter but I could make it out over the early morning sounds as he rounded out his cantation: 'Nations three, verses one and two.' He walked away from us, down the avenue, a daughter at each side, putting me in mind of pagan princesses walking with a tyger cat that was habituated to them but that was not tamed.

Le Voir rolled his eyes at me and breathed out. We turned into the house, where he made Calcoen some story about a travelling farmer breaking his fast at the estate, and I headed for the kitchen to do the same.

Now that we had the hair in hand and the fashioning of the wig was at last upon us, Le Voir lost his belief that it could be done, or rather, that he was equal to the work. For the rest of that day I caught sight of him in odd corners, scratching designs on paper, comparing this sketch with that, or he was in the garden peering into flowers, and once he called me over as I passed with an apron of herbs, to study my hair. He had me take off my cap and tip my head forward while he traced a pattern on my scalp and muttered about 'whorls and vortices'. You might think that a peruker who served his apprenticeship among ducal apartments would have nothing to fear from a hair piece for a farmer's daughter in a place that was not even a named country on a map, but the difference,

I surmise, was this: the fantastical powdered wigs for the ladies of his homeland had proclaimed themselves expensive and false — lavender- and rose-tinted towers of coarse stuff and flour, teased and shaped to the edge of parody's line. Now he had to learn about what he had been taught to cover up, and imitate it so that none should guess it was not entirely a natural thing.

We had already set up a wax head on the table in the back room, and Le Voir had pricked her dimensions on its surface; now he lifted my lace panels and smoothed them, one at a time, on the meridian and on the temporal. To add strength he laid a wide hatch work of galloon across the head but took care to keep the edges free of this, and fine. Lastly he lifted the lace at the nape and pinned the ends of two lengths of ribbon there. I set to stitching the lace into a whole, working directly on the wax head, employing the finest stitches and with an anxious master wigmaker breathing over me until he grew bored and was drawn to the hair.

He folded back the cloth and lifted one of the ropes from its companions, appraising it with a practical eye. The hair from the elder sister was a shade darker than from the other; this he would use for the line below the level of the ear, he said; the lighter hair would make the crown. He set out the hackle, laid a finger's width of hair across its many teeth and pulled it through until the hair lay in some sort of order. He could begin.

10

VERGILIUS IS LATE FOR LAUDS. SHE STANDS AT THE DOORWAY listening to the mutter of Latin, then enters the chapel and kneels in a pew at the back as Mother Rose raises her voice and bites out an emphatic bar of the prayer, teeth meeting like a badger's. Eyes lowered, Vergilius clenches her jaw at the reprimand. When she raises her head again she dislodges from her veil a tiny praying mantis. It lands on the back of the pew next to her hand and teeters there. Silent Contemplation finds Vergilius contemplating the insect, trying to fathom the working of its joints if it even has these, trying not to alarm it with her breath. At least this keeps her eyes downcast.

After lauds, when she is expected to break the fast with the sisters, Vergilius instead returns to her cell. She closes the door and crosses to the unsteady credenza next to the bed, pulls out the drawer and then the bundle of razors. She lays these and a pair of scissors from her sleeve in a menacing row on the blanket.

Since she entered the convent she has given herself orders for the smallest tasks and relied on the demands that inanimate objects will make when they are invoked, as if the tools, once assembled and waiting, oblige her to use them; twice a day it is the missal and rosary. Now, in obedience to the razors, she sits on the edge of the bed and reaches up under her veil to unpin it and the light wimple from the coif, then unties the chin straps of the cap itself and peels it away from her scalp and the edges of her face.

Her hair, once the dark gold of mountain water, is ash brown from lack of light and sticky with starch from the cap. She teases it away from her head with her fingers until joyless curls lie across her scalp. She can begin.

Twice since the night when she hid from her new sisters as they picked their way through the starlit dark from the hotel pool, twice in her ten years at Mannamead, Vergilius has fetched razors from the surgery and, in secret, cut her hair close to the scalp, then shaved her head and in so doing forced herself, at least until it has grown back, to stay in the order, where her baldness, the mark in a white woman of a convict or collaborator or denounced whore, would be hidden by the veil.

Now she has to tether her will again. From under her scapular she brings out a small mirror and props it against the crosspiece at the bed's head. She picks up the cutthroat, takes hold of a curl and turns towards the mirror. She slices into the hair, lays the lock on the veil and slices again.

At that moment her knee brushes the squat cupboard. It rocks wearily and booms, and she drops her hands to her lap and makes herself wait out the hollow din as a test of will surrendered and as a punishment, forbidding herself to put out a hand and still the thing. At last it trembles and stops. In the silence that follows Vergilius releases a sharp sound and chops it off by withholding her breath, then clenches her jaw to stop from crying out. Having been interrupted in her blind ritual she is no longer sure of how or whether to proceed: to force herself to stay or steel herself to leave.

After an age she allows her hands to tidy away the forbidden tools; she folds the razors and the locks she has cut into the veil and replaces them behind the drawer of the credenza.

She has surprised herself, as if, walking a familiar path through a familiar landscape, she has today come across a stream that yesterday was not there. Unprepared to plan and unwilling to pray,

Vergilius ignores the bathrooms she is meant to scrub, the patients waiting for her, her unfilled quota of contemplation, and curls instead on her side on the grey bed, wearing the robes and rosary of an Immaculate sister but breathing around the phlegmy word, 'ex-claustration', that fills her throat.

In the third hour of the crisis in her cell her spirits rise again and she who has struggled so successfully to subdue every new sensation with her intellect, who since late childhood has thought too much as a defence against feeling too much, is amazed to learn as she opens the door of her cell and steps into the late morning sun that sometimes the unthinkable thing turns into simply the next thing that you do. She takes a step, then another.

11

LE VOIR WORKED ON HIS MANY KNOTS IN THE BACK ROOM OF the house. In the vine yard they were digging about the vine stock and the small boys were put to picking snout beetles from the buds. In the kitchen Derde Susann found a new superstition or remembered an old one every day: knotting straw in strange shapes, slapping Jansie's hand away from her stomach, giving sharp warning if she stopped too long in a passage way or at the top of the stairs – this last invited a blocked passage for the babe, she said. Some times Jansie groaned when she walked, and rubbed her hips.

They fired the guns to tell us of ships in the bay and in haste new wine was loaded to be sent to the town on a pair of wagons. A third would follow with lesser barrels that had soured and been made over to vinegar; Caspar would take this to the port and sell it to ships to clean them from their effluent-splattered journey.

Calcoen rode with the first wagon, taking with him also Majesty's finished piece to leave at Bij-den-Rhee. Jansie stood beside me to watch them leave. She had folded in upon herself since Bastiaan's death as though to hold herself safe, and her babe. No more was she impatient to see her child; now she wanted to keep it within where, unborn, it could not so easily die. She had been proud of the special consideration her condition brought her, the particular attention from Calcoen. Now she said, as his wagon turned down the avenue and left our sight, 'I want it to come when he is away.'

She spoke as if just now realising this herself and though I asked what she meant by it she would not meet my eye nor answer, but only turned back to the house.

The master's folly in the grove was builded, roofed and white-washed and with a stout door. It was no longer guarded by Doof Hendrik nor any one but when I looked in at one of the high windows I could see only the blank white of the next wall of the spiral. It seemed, from what I could see from the aspect forced by the height and mean size of the window, that the floor was white as well, and there was draped a ceiling of pale cloth. I burned to know what was the object and intent of it. Le Voir was not interested to discuss it beyond to guess that it must have something to do with Master's limited views of science.

As I contemplated the building I heard Derde Susann call for me and took the path down to the avenue to meet her. She was seized with preparing a place for Jansie's lying in, today, she said. She had dreamed one of her dreams and it told her the birth was come soon.

On Vogelzang Sebastiaan and his sister had drawn first breath in the front room now occupied and occupied then by their mother. Other children of the estate had been born in the kitchen, a corner of the workshop, two or three caves in the mountain at the home-stead's back – the fashion in summer – and in the pondok where many had also been begun. Derde Susann had chosen a place for Jansie: a cave of middling size in the mountain face directly behind the homestead. We would begin today to make it ready, right away, while the knecht was in the vine yard and Master gone; she had an instinct to hide this from them, same as Jansie.

Derde Susann led me to the pantry and behind its door un-covered a pile, and we filled our arms and I followed her across the avenue and onto a mountain path.

Perhaps she had put out word that she wanted this cave for Jansie or perhaps it was that spring was not far enough come, for it wore signs of having been let alone since at least before the winter. Animals had been here and birds, though there was enough of a fire smell to keep the leopard away. It was in the main more of a flat place sheltered by a leaning rock but for on the right where a true cave split the wall. Derde Susann put down her bundle before this and we turned back for the rest.

The ground fell away in a number of rock slabs making a shallow stair of wide treads so that we walked three steps then stepped down, then two, then down. The bushes of the natural fields were in bloom with tiny flowers in purple and yellow and yellow-green across their tops, and the ground was busy with insects. I felt an up welling of gladness at the flowers, our female task, and as we headed down it seemed I heard Derde Susann hum a song.

In a corner of Melt's workshop was another hoard. A strung cot leaned against the wall. Derde Susann took hold of the webbing and toppled it towards her, then walked it until it lay on the floor. She loaded it with things from a stack by her side – a couple of wood buckets, a broom, a machete and sickle, sacks. We took an end apiece and bore the bed and cargo like wise past the lordlingshouse onto the path and up to the cave, walking with such purpose we stopped but once to catch breath.

We set our stretcher beside the other bundles. Derde Susann took up the broom and handed me the sickle, bidding me to cut heather for a mattress and to test that first for spring and for fragrance. I found upon the mountain side a type of bush that had the scent of cedar and cut arm loads of it and carried it up the flat steps. Derde Susann raised a cloud of dust to scatter feathers, droppings, the remains of some lovers' own fragrant bed that was now fallen to grey twigs and litter. She raised the broom over her head and swept the walls and ceiling of the cave, then sent me down to the house for a cup from the lant barrel and a bucket of water and she sprinkled the floor with these. Together we filled sacks with the sweet smelling brush, trampled these to pillows and tucked them on the cot. We carried this into the cave.

In a bundle Derde Susann found a handful of candle stubs she had saved. I set them in wall cracks and on ledges while she unfolded a heavy blanket and clean and patched sheets over our mattress and looped a length of rope under the top legs of the cot and laid the ends on the bed.

'For the pushing,' she said at my side look at this. 'Something to hold fast to when she has to push.' I was curious but also afraid.

We rested a while, then she sent me out with the machete for green boughs to block the entrance to animals and then again for dry wood, enough for a small fire. Each time I came to the cave she had brought more from the bundle – clean cloths, winding bandages, an infant's cap worked with red and green triangles, a jug of brandy stopped with cork. The afternoon sun reached into the cave and lit the bed, the buckets near by, the little cap.

Derde Susann placed her hands in the small of her back and leaned into them.

'The best day's work I done in years,' she said and we blocked the cave with the branches and splashed lant there to keep the place safe and headed down the mountain happy with what we had made. Tomorrow, if we could keep Jansie and Meerem back from pest duty among the vines, we would reward our work with showing it to them.

No one of us could have given a hard reason for hoping Jansie's babe would be born while Calcoen was away from here. It was not that he would by being there seize the child into bondage, a fate it would escape other wise; we knew as we knew that birds fly and men walk that enslavement depended on the mother's lot and a bond-maid's babe is born in bondage. Surely, marvellous stories had reached us of free born white women who had lain with bonded men, and their children ever after free and never a word said about it, not to their faces, and there was even told of a master who baptised the children got by his kitchen women but this we did not credit. Jansie, we knew, had hopes in that direction, believing Bastiaan had been the father of the child she carried and that his parent would know the babe and welcome it to the estate's sparse family, but she could not see past end of her nose, Jansie.

We began a time of waiting. Le Voir was yet knotting millennia of double strands of hair into my tatting; the young mistress watched and poured his brandy and coffee and stood at his side as he sat at the table, leaning into him as a cat will. Madam was in the front room, placed there each morning by Melt and left with her quiet birds and her counting books to work at these, or sit looking at the day, her cheeks wet, while the household fed and cleaned her and other wise walked a roundabout path to avoid that room. In the vine yard the scrimpy berries swelled; Allaman came to the kitchen steps with carrots; Caspar swapped a hare for a pot of lard.

In the kitchen we fell to the big cleaning. Meerem and Melt carried the kettle off the hearth and down the steps, setting it on a patch of ground between the steps and the avenue and the rest of us brought every piece of metal ware to join it. A station for the buckets and bread trough, the water barrels and chairs and table – every wood thing – we set up alongside this. We settled Jansie in the sun with salt and vinegar to scrub these in spells for as long as her gorge could stand the work. Up the stairs I was set to sweeping the hearth and carrying ashes to the midden. Meerem and Derde Susann emptied the larder onto the table in the hall of the house and closed the folding screen across the room against the dogs.

Melt had set a trivet over an open fire by the avenue and water was heating there on. Derde Susann ladled ash into this and dropped every piece of kitchen cloth but one apiece for Melt, Meerem, herself and me. These we tied across our mouths and noses and, thus, followed Melt indoors. He had a bucket in each hand taken from the lant barrel and, setting down one, took its brother in both hands and commenced to slop it over the floor and walls and we followed the while with coarse brushes, working it into the floor and greasy walls, holding our breath against the choking air. We completed this part of our deterge with much energy and fled the room to let the farm ammoniac do the work.

I joined Jansie at scrubbing each piece of wood ware 'til it was grey and furred; Melt settled near by to whittle a spoon for Derde Susann. He sent up a scatter of shavings as he flicked his knife against the outer side of the bowl, then flipped the piece and braced an end against his stomach to smooth the handle.

'Melt, thanks for this,' said Derde Susann. He nodded at her.

'You know,' she spoke on somewhat shyly, and this was rare enough that we sharpened our ears, 'You know, Melt, it would be a welcome something if you could make a cradle for Jansie's babe. It is long since there was a babe here, and the last cradle went off across the mountain.'

Melt stopped his carving and grinned at her, a frowning grin, and said: 'How many beds does one infant need?'

Puzzlement spread from this and only grew when we were made to understand two things: that he had made a cradle for Jansie's babe, of pear wood; and that no one of the kitchen women knew a thing about it. At last it came out that it was Calcoen had ordered Melt to build the little bed and he who fetched it away. Where it was none of those there could say. Jansie wanted to know about it, not to pick over the mystery, but to see what it looked like, how it moved. Did it have a hood? (it did), and a mattress? (Melt shrugged). What colour was pear?

He had scant details to offer and these she repeated to herself.

I listened to her, my hands pickling with the salt, and thought she spoke as one might about a fine thing that one did not absolutely believe to be real, but she was slow and dreamy in those swollen last days and I did not credit any new mood of hers.

'Well, one thing we can know: that baby is not to come today,' said Derde Susann and looked at Jansie, who had put down the bucket she had been scrubbing and was sitting, legs stretched in front of her and hands on the ground at her sides, her face loose as a dog's so that you thought any moment she might snatch a fly from the air with her mouth … she watched Jansie and laughed.

'If you have a big job of work in the house, washing the curtains or blooding the floor, choose a day when her time is all but come for nothing works like one about to birth. Like sparrows, back and forth, back and forth. But not today for this one.'

Derde Susann climbed to her feet and set off to get the boys started on a fresh supply of firewood to bring back to life her cleaned kitchen, and we packed it with the cleaned vessels, with no mistress to tell us and the work soon done.

On one of those days caught between Jansie not giving birth and there being little new to see with the fine work with the hair piece, Derde Susann asked me to fetch sugar from the master's room. Calcoen had trusted her with the key, being as she was neither crazy like the mistress nor lettered, because the sugar was locked in a box in a locked room that also contained his books and notes. I believe it was Le Voir he most wanted to keep from these and so the young mistress was locked out too. Derde Susann had sent me, in the midst of counting on her fingers to follow a particular receipt Le Voir had told her, because her usual girl was grieving over a shattered pot of conserve and would not be moved. 'Trijn, you go!' So there I was, the freakish reading thing, in the room and attracted by much besides the box which held the cones.

All was in high order. The main table was cleared but for these: a stack of leathern discs, strung on a thong, of shades from dull white to black by way of cream and brown and grading one to the other. I fanned them out and returned them to their stack: they were cool and smooth. Each was stamped with a numeral, I to XIII. The other thing on the desk was but a ledger marked on each page with ruled columns though none was headed.

I thought, as I unlocked the sugar box, that for all that Calcoen was a sour presence, there was a purpose about the room. I scratched and crumbled sugar into a cup, locked the chest and made to leave but did not yet. There was no place like it on Vogelzang; every other space crackled with unquietude – dipping and grinding and pinching in the kitchen, the slow pair in the back bed chamber, dull spite and badinage from the field men – even Melt's workshop had an air that looked sharply upon mere sitting in thought.

On the wall between the window and the door was pinned a chart. The greater part was taken up with a coast line and some parts inland. Set above this and slightly to one side was its context: the whole continent, indigestibly broad, its tip shaded like the grubby end of a stocking. On the detailed part I traced with my finger the river where we had crossed, and found our plain among the mountains. The few maps I had seen 'til then I had marked as witching things, holding impossible size in them. This plan was even more so for it showed where I was, though it was less familiar to me than maps of the place where books came from and which I would never see: the parent north, our closest neighbour though separated by the weight of this continent shown, like a cloud shape or a line in the sand, by outline only. On this map there were few stepping stones, barely a next named place to put your foot between here and there.

I opened the door and this drew Le Voir's notice as he stepped into the front room, and he crossed to me. I watched his face as he roved over the drawing, tilting his head to read the names of rivers, flicking back and forth between the town and our plain.

'I do not like to think too much on this Africa. It is too large and too empty,' he said. 'People like De Buys, they astonish me with their courage – or perhaps it is a lack in them; they cannot imagine. I think that is one way to be not afraid: in a covered wagon looking at the piece of the horizon your mind can hold, and do not suffer thoughts about endless lands and unknowable things.'

We locked Calcoen's room and Le Voir walked with me towards the kitchen.

'When I arrived in this place I felt I was drinking good wine. The days of fighting at home and the fear … then to find a place so warm, where you could walk in one direction until you could see only the sky and the land and make some bricks from the earth and build a house, like being a child – no money to pay, no guild to consult, no permission. It was not even a country, just land. Even though there were laws, notices about the number of gold buttons a clerk was allowed on his coat – that was the silliest of them, though many were silly – or who might sell his cabbages to another man, they were like the rules of the house at some country inn; even when they concerned matters of cattle and barter you might ignore them if you just left the place they were posted.'

We stopped in the hall.

'I used to think I could almost see the free land, the point at which you had moved far enough away from the castle men for their words to have no effect. The thought that there was a place beyond laws was marvellous to me. It was not like home, where the laws and the customs had been thrown over; this was where none had been, or none that could touch me. It was a chance to start again and do better. I felt younger in those first days.'

He looked about him. There were two paintings on the wall before us: a view of the roadstead at some port with ships set at intervals. The other was of Madam's mother, a lardy, scraped head. Le Voir made a small shiver, pulled his elbows tight to his coat. He had long suffered this peculiar fear of any picture that showed people or animals and, it seemed now, ships at anchor. A depiction of a house and lands and pictures of fruit in bowls or dead water fowl, only these were acceptable. The reason he gave was that a painting of a living thing showed it in such unnatural stillness as to make him think it had died but did not know it yet, or he had died with the image frozen on his eye. To learn such unguessable things as this about a person was delightful to me, as though one day to find the sky a rosy pink at noon.

He resumed: 'But when you think you have found a place without laws, you soon learn how far is that from freedom. You are hungry soon enough and you need shelter as well, and the next man needs shelter, he needs food, and so you make accommodations, and more accommodations with the man after the next man and these become convention and convention may as well be law for it binds you like law. Freedom, of course, comes in degrees. But when you had thought it a set thing those degrees are heavy things.

'What that did, seeing that laws were the outcome of being human with other humans, well, I think I began to be afraid of what I would become without people, out there, in the place beyond them.' He tapped his chest. 'Within a man, now that is a different matter.'

But he shook off his philosophies and took my elbow to walk me to the kitchen to see 'how our lady cook fares with the special brioche of Fallignac's filthy chef'.

The next morning they slaughtered an ox, the boys driving a three-faced blade into its tethered spine and flexing it there. With blood for the floor it was, curiously, immediately as Derde Susann had forespoke: Jansie changed from a blurred and aimless girl to an engine, spreading the stuff before it could congeal, rubbing it evenly across the packed earth. When it had dried she got on hands and knees and polished it in wide sweeps, her body rocking. Derde Susann caught my eye and smiled her turned down smile to have her speech so neatly come true. I felt a thrill at the baby coming at last and longed to be put to a task to help matters but Derde Susann shushed me, said it would be hours or even a day and a night.

From time to time as we worked Jansie stopped and pulled herself to her knees and held her belly or back for a spell, then bent again to her rocking. At last, with the floor gleaming underfoot, Derde Susann set Jansie down to gather her strength, and when the men had packed the kitchen hauled out a platter of kidneys and put Meerem and me to work to render their fat. By this I reckoned, because they slaughtered twice a year, that Le Voir and I had been here six months.

The afternoon passed. Meerem sliced fat, I stirred the kettle and kept the fire hot. Le Voir came to the kitchen for coffee and bread and went back to his knotting and we ate something at the cleared end of the table. Derde Susann pounded salt, the kettle filled to half and we strained the first yield into pots and picked and cleaned bay leaves to press on each as it set – a usual day but, of course, for Jansie. Seated or walking about the kitchen with her heavy sway, she was the focus of us all. The smallest grunt from her, and Meerem and I stiffened and waited out the murmurs between Derde Susann and Jansie – a question and a shake of the head, or a question and a noise of confirmation. Once Derde Susann knelt before Jansie and removed a petticoat and loosened strings about her clothing and felt under her skirts. She said, 'Not before night falls, my girl,' and movement began again among us.

The tom picked his way over the fresh floor to be near Jansie. She, I thought, was both aware of being watched and removed from us in a particular way, alone with her body's inner movement. It was almost dusk when she stood suddenly, bent forward, her hands on her knees, and made a groan, one with pain in it. At the same time and without a sound her feet and the floor were awash and though I had not seen Derde Susann move she was at Jansie's side, taking her weight, directing Meerem to bring the bucket of water filled in the day and me the pan which held knife, herbs, cloths. We waited until Jansie's body unclenched and she could stand straight again and then we moved at her pace and in procession down the steps, across the avenue and on the mountain path. By the last light we gained the cave and settled her on the cot. Jansie was quickly seized again and from now on each such brought her pain.

Meerem went down to lay out a meal for them in the house and I built a fire under the shelter, to one side of the cave entrance, and set a trivet and water on it. Meerem joined me there and after an hour or so of Jansie's sometime cries we dozed there. I woke once to hear Derde Susann singing under her breath as she stirred heated water in a pot of lavender heads. I looked into the cave; she had lit two candles. Jansie was lying on her side, one hand near her head, palm uppermost and the straining rope across it. Derde Susann whispered from close behind me, 'She's a strong little thing.' As we watched, Jansie woke and rolled to a tight hold, panting like a frightened cat. Derde Susann went to her. I watched a while and when Jansie eased I folded myself back into my cloak at the fire's edge, where Meerem snored, and slept again.

I was waked from deep sleep and that not gently by a bruising hand on my shoulder. It was Calcoen. Meerem was on her feet, blinking at the torch in Doof Hendrik's hand. A ghost stood at his shoulder. Calcoen was speaking to me, telling me to take myself back to the house, to go now. He said something about permission and about the mountain by night. He matched his order with wide motions of his arms, pointing down towards the homestead, saying 'Go! Go!' The arms were for Doof Hendrik to understand and indeed all the force in that place was with the deaf slave who shoved

Meerem and me across the space of the overhang, away from the cave. The stars lay at a wrong angle and by this my sleep soaked brain told me I had not in my life been awake at this hour. Doof Hendrik shoved a lit brand at me and I stepped down the rock ledges, torch in one hand and Meerem's hand in the other and we tumbled down the path with our light showing those on the mountain that we obeyed.

On the avenue Melt and Caspar worked to out span the team by lantern light. I rolled the torch on the ground and Meerem, still holding my hand, led the way up the stairs and into the kitchen. I could tell from the thick air that the household was asleep and at last, whimpering together like pups, we slept too.

When morning came Derde Susann was in her cot. I lay for a moment after waking, keeping still so as not to begin the day with its story of the night before. An unnameable fear was in me and I hugged myself against it. When the need to make water sent me to the corner pot my steps wakened Derde Susann, who sat up in her cot with her face in her hands. Her head was bare, a tangle of grey and black curls and a patch missing on one side to show bright white and red where the skin had come away. Her fingers moved from her face to the bright patch and she flinched at her own touch. She reached into a trunk at the end of the cot and pulled out a kerchief, and stood as though weights were tied on her shoulders and moved to the hearth, tucking her hair the while. Now Meerem waked and, seeing Derde Susann, asked in her balderdash tongue, with wide and hopeful eyes, if Jansie's baby had come and was it a girl?

Derde Susann dropped the grinder she was filling, moved as though to fly from the kitchen but she circled the table and returned to her bed and sat on its edge and held her face again and at last said that we were not to talk to her, she could not talk to us. Meerem and I scrambled for the coffee grinder and fitted the parts to one another and walked lightly to gather a meal for the household and ourselves. I did not feel we could ask whether Jansie was alive if a question about her babe produced such agitation and any way I was afraid to know. In the course of the early morning I went out to get from the others what they knew but the day was waking without ripple so I thought not to broach it with those without the kitchen, nor those within.

But after a time Derde Susann gathered herself and spoke to us: 'They made me leave her there. I tried to stay but Doof Hendrik made me come away' – a hand moved to her head – 'and there was a midwife come from town. A homeland one.' That was the pale ghost I saw and thought I dreamed.

'I brought out poor Bastiaan and his sister and every other baby on the estate and my own. Now he comes, this one, with a white woman from town!'

She looked at our faces, at the question there.

'She was strong when I left her and very near. It must be here by now. But we are not to help with it because he has brought a midwife from the Republic!'

Beneath her anger was sharp worry. Meerem and I stared at her but could not think up a question and only listened as timid girls to her bitter, heavy breathing, then we heard a new sound before we knew we heard it – some animal was on the kitchen stairs. Derde Susann closed her eyes and told Meerem to see what it was. Something in the sound of Meerem's returning step made me look over my shoulder, and I saw her move crab wise through the door, Jansie in her arms, across her body. Jansie, wrung with tiredness and no babe with her.

Now Derde Susann moved in jagged and swift fashion, directing Meerem to lay the girl on her bed, and me to make a tray of bread and meat and set it in the hall and hurry back. That done she closed the door that never was closed in the day and locked the outer door too against the sudden and undoubted danger we felt. She pulled a stool to the cot and leaned over to cradle Jansie, murmuring to her and kissing her head. We two drew close and did not speak, helpless while the fear grew in us.

Derde Susann left off holding Jansie to direct us to heat water, a great amount of water, and have one of the men fetch the half barrel they had used after my fever and prepare to bathe Jansie. While we did these things she quizzed Jansie closely, not about the babe for that must come later but about what had happened after the infant was delivered from her. Did she push again? Did she remember the midwife pressing on her belly, it would have been the worst pain of all, worse than the babe coming? Jansie did not recall such. No one had paid her any mind after the babe was come, she said, except that Calcoen had lifted her head and made her drink something and she had slept.

'Dear Jesus, she did not finish it,' Derde Susann said, and closed her eyes.

She lay Jansie back on the bed. She directed me to press her shoulders and Meerem to hold her knees apart and she reached into the girl with one hand and leaned all her weight on her forearm, this pressed across Jansie's belly. It was soon over. Jansie screamed and there was a scorched metal smell and a hot rush of blood, and then we led the trembling girl to the water. Derde Susann made a parcel of the bed covering and left the kitchen with this.

We did not cover over Jansie in the water but helped her to stand in the barrel and flushed water down her body. Derde Susann returned and washed her with a rag and we helped her to a cloth spread by the fire place where I knelt to dry her legs and feet. Meerem dressed her in one of Derde Susann's wide chemises, pulling her arms through the sleeves; I smoothed her hair. We brought her to the bed and she slept, waking at times but sinking back soon after. While she slept we opened the kitchen and went about our work, but I for one treated every person I met in that household and on the estate like my own enemy and looked at them with hot eyes, wanting them punished.

In fits and starts the next morning Jansie told us:

She had been afraid when Derde Susann was knocked down by Doof Hendrik and she could not see her by. Calcoen stayed at her bed only he would leave to look to the sky every so often as if expecting the dawn, with hard words for the strange woman and she short with him and with Jansie. She was not so gentle as Derde Susann and was drunk going by the smell of her, said Jansie. The pain was come more often and she was afraid, and thirsty, then the woman was winding the straining ropes about Jansie's arms and shouting at her to push and when she lifted her head she could see Calcoen at the end of the bed and at the cave door Doof Hendrik leering in, and she strained and pressed down and felt a new pain, a welcome cut feeling and release and she pushed again and Calcoen gave a shout, and the woman was at work with a knife and twine. Then Calcoen was at her head and lifting her shoulders and holding something to drink, and she so thirsty. The last thing was Calcoen telling her – and Jansie swallowed hard and would not say the words.

When she woke again, she said, the morning was come and she was alone in the cave and cold. The fire was out, bed rags stuck to her legs. She had got herself up and crawled and stepped down the mountain and Meerem found her on the kitchen steps and brought her within.

She told her tale as though expecting one of us to explain it to her – her manner asked, How came this to be? Here is what I heard and saw, what does it token?

Derde Susann patted Jansie on the knee and got to her feet, not ready to look beyond what was for she trafficked in practicals, at least in her awake hours where no dark ships followed. She took me aside and had me fetch a cabbage from Allaman and put it in the coolest part of the larder and mind that it was there, ready, and not cooked and eaten. Jansie's breasts would start to fill in the night and ache, and the cole leaves would ease that, she said, and it was so, though Derde Susann bound her bosom tight with winding strips. That was a night spent awake in the kitchen, and Jansie rocking with the heat of her hard packed bosom. She begged Derde Susann to loose the cloth and draw off milk but the cook set her jaw against Jansie's tears and threatened her with Madam's greed should she learn she was in milk and fit to earn dollars for them as a wet nurse away from Vogelzang.

A woman, a girl, seemed an animal-like creature to me if I took Jansie as the type, Jansie with a new agony each hour. I marvelled at her, at the condition, blown about by her body and so completely taken up by flesh and its humours with no place or calm moment for disengaged thought beside sensation and urge and the next sensation. What was Jansie but an upright beast bellowing to be milked, and for her lost calf?

And after all it was not greatly out of the usual course for a babe to die aborning.

And at least the mother was spared.

The household waited out our animus then approached with wanting to comfort her. Calcoen was about the place but the midwife he had brought from town had gone by the time Jansie was well enough to leave the kitchen; I would have forgotten to believe in her at all without Derde Susann's mutterings about drunken incompetents who left the mother in such a state and could not bring a babe safe to the world. She was nice about saying these things only when Jansie was not in ear shot to hear herself called mother; after another day even that dried up and the round of work claimed us, with only our gentle tendencies around Jansie as a new thing among us.

On the fourth day Jansie and I pulled a posy from Allaman's garden and walked to the graves beyond the werf. Estate-died freemen and family lay within a fenced ground and there was a larger plot for slaves to one side of this. In this side plot we walked among the hummocks of grass and bush between the odd wood board with a name and a date but found no fresh turned earth.

At length Jansie leaned over the fence at the family plot to look among the headstones that bore two or more names apiece above the dates but here, too, no earth was new. At last I read a marker as Bastiaan's and there she dropped her flowers. She said Calcoen must be waiting for her before burying her babe and I said I would ask Le Voir to say she was ready for that office.

But word came back that the babe had been laid in the ground the day it died, and we walked again to the plot beyond the werf. This time there was a mound. Meerem was with us and she and I moved to brace Jansie as we approached it but she stood still and collected. Her eyes travelled over the earth and the green wood marker where there was the year's date, 1794, and no name. On the way back she stumbled but when Meerem moved to take her arm she shook her off and walked behind us with no word.

Calcoen had brought a nanny and a billy from the fields and from town a she-ass, a white one. The men were building a pen for them at the edge of the grove, and a shelter; they were tethered under a tree and the goats had eaten a bare circle to the radius of their chain. I could see through the grove to the white hut; Doof Hendrik was back on duty there but I could only guess what Calcoen was about and I did not care overmuch. Part of me was doused in sadness and part was awake to the reactions and accommodations of everyone to the event, not least of all Jansie herself, who seemed to have become, along with sadder and quieter, somehow more intelligent, or perhaps I mean wiser. Where before she was like to drop or spill what so ever she took up, she now moved in a steady way that could be read as high competence. I caught her watching us with a new look, as though weighing our impulses, divining these beneath what we spoke them as.

There had long been suitors for her on the estate and beyond, men of her station held off by her being with the young master and then by her belly. These returned within the month to court her; if she did not make a move to meet them she at least heard them out, but there was something in her manner …

I watched her one of these afternoons with the man Adonis. Jansie was hemming a sheet at the foot of the kitchen stairs; Adonis leaned on the balustrade and told her a tale in which he shone, I forget the parts of it. I was picking over the dried peaches, sorting those we could keep from the brown and wasted ones, and keeping half an ear on their talk.

It was not what she said so much that sent him away as the air about her as she set her needle work in her lap and pressed Adonis: if he had her, what then?

Then love might grow.

And if love grows, what then? What then?

Flirtation on a sunny afternoon will not bear such weight. After a while the boys and men let her alone.

12

IN THESE LAST DAYS OF THE UNION, CAPTAIN TEICHERT IS gripped by the idea that something will happen to spoil or thwart the coming first day of the new republic, that it will happen here, and that he, Valentine Teichert, is the one to stop it. Slagterskop's Special Branch policeman locks away his files and thinks, then rises from his desk.

Pretoria is preoccupied with its own fears about the day; Teichert will not trouble Pretoria with his plan; he will use the materials he finds here. First, he visits the headmaster of the Hoërskool Agricus and has his proposition endorsed. Then he makes the rounds of the butchery and bottle store, arranges things with the hotel and travels to the next town to spend his own money at the OK Bazaars. On a Saturday afternoon after the rugby match he waits under the palm tree outside the Slagterskop Hotel; the headmaster delivers six tall boys; the policeman leads them through the hotel to a garden at the back where coals glow in a split steel drum and quart bottles of Lion Lager bob in melting ice in a metal washtub. On a table under a frangipani tree six new khaki bush hats jostle in a row. There is a board leaning against the trunk of the little tree; on it is a map showing the border region; a pearly pin lances the 'e' in 'Slagterskop'.

Warily at first – he is suddenly unsure about the hats – Teichert describes the lurking threat to the coming republic. The boys' grunts carry him along and he grows more confident as their eyes lock on his. From Westminster and Moscow it comes, he tells them, to attack this brave, this special nation, out of jealousy, out of blindness. He tells them, 'You ask yourselves, what can I do? But Captain Teichert says to you, sons: you must ask, what does my Fatherland want me to do?'

He nods, and nods again, then, realising from their waiting faces that he will have to treat the question as more than rhetorical, he tells them. After this he feeds them roasted meat and beer, has them repeat an oath of loyalty to the Afrikaner nation as each receives his hat. He listens as the boys mutter about this great thing they are part of, voices gruff or hoarse, bumping fists on one another's shoulders to outdo the other with their theories and plans. At nine o'clock the headmaster arrives to collect them, each boy clutching a hat and sleepy with beer and brotherhood, and the teacher and Teichert nod and shake hands like men of serious purpose who have done a serious and necessary thing.

The next night or the night after that the boys and the security policeman form what they call, among themselves, a commando. Teichert drives the truck, the boys are in the rear, encased by the vehicle's high sides as it sways and jolts along a dirt track for an hour, then turns onto the firebreak that marks the country's border. Teichert pulls up next to a thicket. They set off on foot, in single file, following one another into the dark veld.

Four hours later the truck retraces its route along the border cutting, down the farm track and onto the better road, two of the boys riding in the cab with Teichert and those behind sitting well forward on the truck bed, their blood toxic from the flow and ebb of adrenaline. Something trussed and hooded shares the bed of the truck, something that, although it makes less noise now, contributes an edge to the boys' jerky talk about anything but it, the bundle near the tailgate. It slides nearer as the truck pitches and yaws down an incline; a boy bares his teeth and extends his leg at an awkward angle to keep it away. The truck passes the sleeping village and its small laager of silver trailers and heads on towards the school. The boys have left off their shivering attempts at joking, at schoolboy gossip, and are silent. Some are asleep when Teichert stops in front of the hostel block. One of the boys climbs down to open the gate and Teichert cuts the engine and rolls through. The boys in the back wake and ease themselves onto the running board and step down. A schoolmaster in pyjamas and coat comes to meet them, flashlight sweeping along the path.

Teichert leans from the cab and tells the boys: 'Sons, men, good work tonight. I will tell your teacher, good work. The stuff' – he jerks his head in the direction of the truck bed – 'tonight it will be in a police cell. Now we will see if its Mr Hammarskjöld will come to save it.'

He gives a half laugh that sounds false to the boys already turning away from him towards the darkened building. They are beginning to dislike him too. Teichert is uncertain how to end things and nods once more.

'Really, sons, good work.'

He puts the truck into reverse and leaves the hostel grounds. The schoolboys head for their beds. Teichert drives past Slagters-kop; he is heading not for the police cells but back along the way they travelled; he turns onto the farm road and after about a mile he backs the vehicle carefully off the track to the edge of a donga a few yards into the veld; he sets the hand brake and climbs down from the cab. He jams rocks under the rear wheels for extra security, then walks around to the back, holding the sides of the truck to steady himself over the rocky ground, and opens the tailgate. He takes hold of one end of the heavy bundle and pulls it towards him. It slips with dense thuds off the truck and onto the lip of the gully. Teichert rocks the bundle under his boot and shoves it hard, sending it over the edge. He sighs at the noise coming from it as it drops down the donga, then he clips the tailgate closed and at that sound the bundle falls silent. Teichert stands a while, looking down at what he thinks is the shape, then he sucks his teeth and shakes himself back into action. He sings softly, a song from his days at Police College, a song about a brazen baboon: 'Bobbejaan klim die berg, so haastig en so lastig.'

He says to himself that he will be up the rest of the night, throwing rocks and branches down to cover it.

'O moenie huil nie,

O moenie treur nie.'

Don't cry, he sings, don't grieve ...

Within a day the news has spread through the district; a murmur even reaches Mannamead and brushes through the Airstream laager, and the waiters and cooks at the hotel where Teichert lives talk about what went on in the night. The old man who waits on the breakfast sitting makes a detour one morning to the chicken pen, there to fetch a pinch of dried scat, which he sprinkles over the bacon. He serves it to Teichert with a muttered 'Baas,' then stands in a corner of the dining room, a folded napkin over his forearm, and watches the policeman eat it. Others, younger and braver than he, scramble into the donga, remove the rocks and branches, take up the diminished bundle and bury it. Before they do so they find in one shoe a letter from a mother to her son, and bring it to their chief at Mannamead Mission Hospital.

'Infiltration'.

'Extraction of information'.

'Insurgent'.

The words are no more real to Teichert now than they were in Police College, and perhaps for that reason help to ease the prickling unease he feels about his first ... what? It cannot be murder, for what has he gained by it? His first kill? Does that imply there will be others, or that he will grow more adept at extracting information, learn to keep a cooler head when a political kaffir from New Brighton – that much the pass book revealed, the politics he guesses – should tremble before him, should give off such an intoxicating scent of fear?

He lines up the words and dials the number of Northern Transvaal Security Branch command. Holding the telephone receiver to his ear, reading from a piece of paper in front of him on the desk, he marshals the syllables in such strict order that he has trouble making his commandant understand. When he does make himself clear there is a pause and a sigh:

'What became of the body?'

'The body was disposed of on the farm Kruisfontein on the night of the incident.'

Following his commandant's lead into passive voice helps even more than the unfamiliar words, and Teichert realises with a wash of relief that he not only may relinquish the matter to the weary voice on the phone line, he is being encouraged to do so.

'Thoroughly disposed of? No chance that it will be found?'

'It is in a donga just off …'

'No! No … it is not necessary to go into detail.' Alarm flickers in the voice on the phone and therefore in Teichert, then is extinguished by more of the special words: 'Operational necessity', 'conditions in the field' and even 'initiative'. There will be a confidential report from Teichert, there will be an end to the matter.

As he replaces the black Bakelite receiver on the cradle, Valentine Teichert feels as if he has been jolted by a new awareness, as though he has taken a step down and found it shallower than his body allowed for. He feels, too, a pleasant hardening of resolve. He has established the parameters of his duty and his power; there can be nothing more extreme than what occurred with him and the boys, and Regional HQ has, if not dismissed it, then certainly not been moved to look into the matter. He has his orders, he has a district to keep secure and work to do.

After the work of the roller is done on the Agricus track, setting out the lanes and painting the lines are easy tasks and Frank and Jacob get through them in an afternoon, using modified pram wheels donated by Gupta and carried out to the sound of the workers nailing the last of the planks on Frank's redesigned bleachers. It being a Friday afternoon, the work parties have company: Agricus schoolboys practise scrumming and tossing the rugby ball to one another on the field in the centre of the new track; the thud of bodies and slap of leather carry on the thin air of winter. Schoolgirls sit cross-legged on the grass, watching the painting, glancing at the boys, marking their sidelong looks.

Frank has made a set of starting blocks, two wedges of old pine joined with sisal rope. He fetches these from his truck and slings them in a slow parabola to the boy, and jerks his head towards the track. Jacob trots over, limber from the afternoon's work, and allows Frank to set his feet against the blocks and show him how to splay his fingers. He presses himself into the surface, feeling his muscles coil and tense, then stands upright, flinging out his arms and legs as the American strolls further along the track to where it begins to curve around the field. Frank raises his arm and Jacob drops into a crouch.

It takes a few false starts until Jacob knows he is firing his limbs and sucking air into his lungs in the right sequence. The rugby players stand in groups, watching, and the bleacher builders straighten up to see him run. A few of the schoolgirls swivel to face Frank and Jacob. The rugby players snigger at the false starts but Frank ignores them and so does Jacob. Frank resets the stopwatch after each scrabbling beginning and captures the first proper run, when Jacob surges forward without stopping until he flies past the 100-yard mark; just as well, because the smooth track has robbed Jacob of a sense of his own speed. The short run is a burst of mindless energy, a revelation. The time is excellent, and Jacob knows he has only begun to wrest speed from the new track.

The rugby boys say nothing after Jacob's run, but a brief murmur swells from the girls and from the men on the bleachers. The Native boys and girls of the district are champion runners and Jacob's is a worthy run; the men catch Jacob's eye and lift their chins in salute.

Long shadows lie across the field and a cool wind springs up as the rugby players trail off, followed by the girls. The workers bundle their tools under the bleachers. Some strip to the waist to wash at a tap at the corner of a classroom. They make themselves cigarettes out of newspaper, BB tobacco and spit. Here and there they murmur a word about the boy's run, shake their heads in appreciation. Jacob and Frank pack up the truck and leave for Mannamead with Jacob driving.

Perhaps the rugby boys speak at supper that night about Jacob's run, or maybe one of the teachers saw the Native boy claim the maiden sprint down the track. However it is decided, on the following Monday there is new activity at the field. A team has dug holes in the hard ground at intervals around the perimeter and is setting creosoted blue-gum poles in these. A tractor and trailer are parked nearby and a pair of farmers watch the workers. Bales of fencing have been stacked at the edge of the field and alongside lie a pair of gates made from metal tubing and more chain-link. They may have needed help with making a running track, but fencing off land is something these children's parents know how to do.

Jacob comes to the track, the starting blocks over his shoulder, while the workers are wrestling with the gates, hammering at the bent bolts that protrude from the upright poles and serve as pin hinges. When they see Jacob the men stop and make way for him and he passes through the gap in the fence where the gates will hang. One of the Agricus boys calls to another, who comes to meet Jacob across the field, swinging a padlock at the end of a length of chain. Jacob locks eyes with the boy and backs out of the gate and stands there for a while, looking at the track as the men direct mutterings of disgust at the fence they are doing such a fine job of erecting.

Vergilius stands before Mother Rose's desk, shoulders back and eyes well and truly escaped from custody. She gives the impression of someone with a task to get out of the way. This, Rose's face says as she looks up at the woman who at thirty-six is still the youngest sister at Mannamead, is too irritating to be borne. What about humility? Obedience? What about the goad of that direct gaze?

Vergilius's own question hangs between them. Her letter to the Jesuit college in Rome? Has it passed inspection and been mailed? The letter is still in Rose's desk drawer and so she blocks the question with one of her own: what's the hurry? Jacob has been at Mannamead for ten years; there is no sudden need to send him to Rome. Let him sit his final exams here at Mannamead, then perhaps one of the … universities. Rose swallows the word 'Bantu'. As long as Jacob stays, Vergilius will stay, and – this Rose knows too, she was just the same – if she stays she will outlast the restlessness that comes over sisters as their bodies enter the urgent years. If a sister can keep herself in the order while her body flares and stirs, if she can see it through, she will come out the other side and know the ease when childbearing is no longer possible even in theory.

Rose knows she is forbidden to stand in the way of a sister's true wish to leave the order, but she wants to keep Vergilius here. She thinks she would not bear her escape. But Jacob? Jacob is nothing. They come and they go, these convent wards, petted and preferred like cats by this or that sister – or less than cats, because children are more trouble. They do not usually stay this long, particularly the boys, but this is the chief's nephew, and Vergilius is Vergilius.

Rose says: 'Leave them to me, the arrangements with Rome about Jacob. I expect they get a lot of this sort of thing. It might be months before we hear back from them.'

Vergilius smiles at her superior, nods her way out of the room, leaving Rose to slide her jaw at the trust in that smile; she reaches into the drawer, takes out the letter to the Jesus brothers and the letter to the scholarship fund, aligns the sheets of paper one on top of the other and rips them in two. Rose leans her elbows on the desk and clasps her hands before her mouth, then untangles her fingers and stipples them over her lips, her cheeks and eyelids, feeling her own skin.

13

LE VOIR FOUND ME IN THE KITCHEN AND CALLED ME TO THE
young mistress's room. I had a hand in the making of it, I should be
there when it was first worn, he said. I believe the truth of it was
that he and she were shy to go about it alone; they needed someone
without and within their conspiracy as lye to slow the reaction.

She had taken her place at the table before the glass. Le Voir
found his mark behind her. On a smaller table at Le Voir's side, a
wax head, and thereon the peruke. From the first I had been drawn
to wigs on their stands in Le Voir's shop in the town. The secretive
masks of the flat faces, topped with falls cut from a woman, the two
things, face and hair, taken apart and presented as on a dish, the
opposite of the head covering my mother and the other women
wore – a woman's hair for her husband's eyes only here existing by
artifice and without its power dispersed. No wonder at the queue of
townsmen at the shop to watch him harvest each time he cropped
the Buganese girls for a piece. The wig at Le Voir's elbow was quite
fine; he had almost invented our craft over to make it. A wig may be
a dead thing, repellent, but he had made the travelling farmer's
daughters' hair into a marvel of fullness and hollows, so like life it
had a special eerie aspect.

He unwrapped the turban from her head and was so familiar
now as to smooth a palm over her scalp after he bared it. Then he
placed his hands on her shoulders and looked her reflection in
the eye. The light from the window created delicate shadows on her
head, itself an uncommon strong sight. But no matter how fine her

skull and scalp, a woman is not permitted to be without hair: Le Voir lifted the peruke from below with spread fingers and slipped it onto her head and tugged it in place, and reached into her nape to tie the ribbons there. While he did this she did not look at herself but kept her gaze on his face in the mirror.

I could not account for how I felt at seeing her like this: I flushed, abashed, and could not account for it; fittings were in the usual course preening affairs or at worst matters for scorn at the vanity of clerks and whores – on these gaudy and drab people our hair pieces were by way of a degree this way or that – but on her it was too much and I blushed to see her, so discomfited I almost giggled at the stupid thought that on her the wig was too bald a thing.

She breathed in and on her exhalation lowered her eyes to look at herself, and pulled back quickly and slightly. Her eyes roamed over the tousled crown and fall of curls and back to their own reflection and away again; her nostrils whitened and she bit her lower lip; she looked about to weep. Le Voir was still close behind her. Now he touched her shoulders and indicated she should stand. She looked at her lap then sighed and rose and turned to him. He made an unsteady step backwards, away from her, then collected himself and took her hand to lead her into the day.

Her parents were in the front room when she entered in her proper clothes and without a turban or mutch for the first time in half a year. Calcoen looked up from a book in which he had been scratching and said, 'Good day,' and licked the lead and was back at his writing. Madam looked at her daughter from under her brows, slyly as at a shared secret. She lifted her arms and the girl went to her where she sat and into her embrace. As she held her, Madam lifted a hand and brought it shaking to the girl's head but did not quite touch it. When young mistress stood apart from her again her mother's gaze was fixed on the bird cage, and I wondered if she would come back to the world now that her plan to protect her daughter was done.

Le Voir walked the young mistress away from the front room, as far as the door to the kitchen. There she straightened her back to step in among the women. Derde Susann, Meerem and Jansie raised their heads, the cook with a sharp look for the girl, and she said quickly through a frightened smile, 'Give me something to do, Derde Susann, I am looking for work.'

While she stood there her hands moved often towards her shoulders where the new hair lay, until she took one tight in the other and held them at her waist. Derde Susann did not speak for a moment but looked hard at her and at me. Then she shrugged and said, 'We are baking,' and reached behind her to fetch an apron for the young mistress. She and I faced each other across the table, across hands sprinkling flour and slicing suet, and the look between us was made of doubt and shyness, some slight scorn for the others and a weariness, I thought, for being back in the world with fresh understanding of how matters conducted themselves here.

We exhausted the flour and Meerem fetched more, this fresh milled and yellow where we spilled it among the older stuff on the table. Derde Susann leaned from the door and called for Caspar to fetch us up some water for she could not spare Meerem. Melt answered with the bucket and stayed to look out for a split in the trough floor. He judged it no crisis, then leaned to see our work. I saw him look at her, the young mistress, with a judging eye and she flushed rosy at this and shifted something on the table – the shaker I think – with a quick, an angry, motion. That was all, but he knew from it that he must quit the kitchen, and did. I watched him out the door.

Like one sorting silks I looked at Melt's position among us: above the three kitchen women. Above me? Yes, because he was a man; no, because he was bonded; yes and no because of the feeling between us. Below the young mistress – but with his sex and status at such odds he was also apart from her how so ever he must yoke his movements to her humours. I irritated myself with this stacking of persons one above or below the other, felt as though I had half swallowed cotton thread that would not disgorge nor slip down. This way of sorting people that Calcoen held so high seemed to me did cover thought like mould on bread.

Having thought myself into an ill humour I asked leave of Derde Susann – as was fitting of my station – and left the kitchen for my own pursuits, as my station allowed. My impulse was to ask a shovel from Allaman and dig – dig a vegetable bed, or dig a hole, just so long as there was earth flying and the punch and slice of the spade into the ground. Flay us all and have done with skin, I thought.

'Were you a cat you would be growling.' Melt found me on the avenue and drew a softening from me with these words. I slowed my pace – I had begged no shovel – and turned at his touch on my elbow and followed him to the workshop. I had by then a place where I sat by habit, a stool near his bed at the side of the main work bench. I was familiar, also, with his work – the smoothing, when he rocked the plane with a sound like a pen hatching lines and brought cracked ribbons curling from the sliding box; I liked to watch him at the lathe, his pumping leg ignored as he held his mind on touching a glass-keen chisel to the wood, sliding close and away to form curves and bolder lines. Best of all was when the cutting was done and Melt took a piece of oily teak and pressed it against the turning wood so that a hard shine chased the raw wood ahead of it to the end of the piece, and he took his foot from the treadle and the spinning slowed and there was a table leg, by eye and hand made like the other three.

Today his work bench held a chair whose legs were in a clamp with raw plugs showing where the repair had been made. To one side were pieces of wood no bigger than his hand. They were finely finished, flat, square, smooth. He picked up two to show me.

'Spalted wood from a pear,' he said. 'It is not common, but you may find it on small pieces of stock. This mark is what killed the tree, though it shows up fine in the finished work.' A crooked line black as a quill's mark but deep in the wood ran across the pale grain.

'They are from the homeland, these curious bits; it seems these days every second piece I make is cut from wood brought on a ship. The forest is cut and gone from our bays; you've seen the giants from the mountains pass here on wagons? They that had stood since Creation are the last of their kind, all gone for floors and tables.'

Now he loosed the holding piece on one of the clamps, his head bent to listen to the joint. Satisfied at what it told him he loosed the other and lifted both clear of the chair; that he tested gently and then with a tug of the legs. They held and he quickly sliced the pegs level with the joint, then carried the chair across the workshop and set it on the bed of a cart there. With him some distance down the room and in a humour to talk, I was able to gather myself and ask him about the cradle for Jansie's babe – where did he think it to be now that the babe was—

He shook his head – perhaps the infant was buried in it, he said, for no casket had been ordered for it. Only a cradle.

He spoke of it as of a past season's concerns but I could not stop worrying at the cause and the manner of the babe's dying and who had attended it.

Jansie's grief had changed under the burden of these same suspicions; now she was not sunk in sorrow but rubbed raw by it, ready to start at any sound. One other change: she would not go near Calcoen. Meerem and I now saw to his pipe and the cleaning of his room, for though it was not within the gift of a bonded slave to refuse a task, Jansie did refuse if it should be for him or near to where he was. For the most part this could be got done beneath the notice of the household, but it was not in all ways possible that he and she should not meet, and this they did soon enough, one night:

Summer was upon Vogelzang like a close weaved blanket. In the usual way, the front part of the household had locked itself apart from us. Deep in that night Madam let herself through the main door out to the garden where Allaman found her riding Old Haarlem, the skirts of her night dress tangled and the tortoise tucked head and leg within his shell. Allaman pulled her off but she got away from him and hid and he feared for her and came to the kitchen to call us out. Derde Susann sent Meerem for Melt, lit lanterns for Jansie and me and sent us after her.

The leopard had lately been heard in the vine yard where he went after hares; Madam had gone that way, Allaman said, and I thought I saw a pale shape among the far rows. I handed my lantern to Jansie and clapped hands to warn any night hunter, and after a foolish chase in the lines we had her at last and between us drew her back to the house while she closed her eyes to hide from us and stumbled about.

Allaman left us at the front veranda. Madam called out when she saw he was not by; by then we were in the front room and her cries woke Calcoen, who blundered out of his store room study in his night shirt, his head bare and bristled above his thin neck. At this Jansie froze where she stood, holding the two lanterns. At first no one paid her any mind what with trying to get Madam to her room and young mistress come from her room and Melt from the hall and the dogs barking without. Then Calcoen called for more light, and now he noticed Jansie where she stood with the lanterns. He pushed his wife into Melt's arms and crossed the room to her. She was struck stiff, her shifting eyes giving her an aspect of a crazed animal. He pushed his face to hers and spoke the order again from a tight jaw, and at no response from her lifted his arm and struck her full and heavy. She fell against the wall and let go of a lantern that yet did not spill and he took this and turned back to Madam's room.

I think there is other work we do for them among the kneading and fetching and mopping: we are there when fright and fear and their own guilt want a box to hold them in.

Jansie cringed when I crossed the front room to take her to the kitchen; they were tying Madam to the heavens bed as we left. In the kitchen Derde Susann dabbed at Jansie's ear until the blood stopped welling.

The next morning Jansie walked unsteadily but although she would develop a shut-off, irritable air from that night, she was not wholly deaf, not like Doof Hendrik, and she yet lifted her head and listened for the sound she listened for – the wind, or something under the wind.

Vogelzang's people were at the outdoors slave kitchen at noon when Calcoen came there in a train, he in coat and new wig, then a boy with books and paraplendia, then a boy with a table and one with a chair. The knecht came behind. Some of the party set up the table and laid out ink and pens and so on; the knecht pressed those there into a line and called us from the kitchen to take our place, and sent a boy for Doof Hendrik. Calcoen sat at the table, pen at the ready over his ledger.

The knecht took charge of the line; he held in his hand the lanyard of polished leather pieces that I had handled in Calcoen's room. Each person that came forward was made to show his right arm with the sleeve loosed and pushed up as far as the shoulder. While the knecht was employed with so arranging the shirt he told each one's name to Calcoen and guessed his age and had from him his birth place if that were known. These the master of Vogelzang wrote in columns ready ruled on the page, I would see when it came to my turn. The knecht next took the wrist of the person and held it so that the arm was in Calcoen's view, and it must be kept thus while the knecht held discs against the skin to find a match, one for the outer side of the forearm and one for the inside arm higher up, that being hid from the sun in the usual course and paler. He would try several discs until Calcoen judged the correct one had been come upon and then, at a grunt from Calcoen, the knecht read off the numeral cut into the leather, only he gave the numbers as 'vee one' or 'one ex' as they came, for he was truly ignorant. These Calcoen noted under columns headed with little drawn pictures – a sun for the fore arm, a sickle moon for the upper.

We were some thirty in the line and the going slow. We preferred it to work we told each other, though uneasily, for there never was a new plan from a master that did not cost us in some way.

I was in the line behind Derde Susann, who balked at the knecht's pulling her chemise to expose the swinging purse of flesh on her arm but allowed herself only a hissed curse. Then it was my turn. I moved with haste to pull back my sleeve to give him no reason to lay a hand on me but he made to fuss with the cloth, rolling it back with care and with every turn pressing his plump knuckles to my breast. He groaned in his throat, looking into my eyes the while, until I lowered mine in shame. When they were done with me he made to roll the sleeve down my arm but I pulled away, and stumbled against Calcoen's table. I could hear the knecht snigger behind me as I ran to escape his sight, around the back of the workshop. There I turned my face to the wall, my arms held tight across my bosom, pressing into myself to remove the memory of his fist at my breast. I thought, I will find a stone and bite down on it and with my splintered teeth I will shred the skin from his face, and I rolled the curse in my mouth to get every taste of it, the more because that was the closest it would get to being.

I stiffened at the sound of a step and pressed myself into the wall, but it was Melt that found me there in the green undergrowth of the waste ground, dark as a shadow himself and gentle as he turned me from the wall and held me to him. I breathed in his scents of sweat and cut wood and also the milky smell a man will have when he thinks to lie with you. My arms had not erased the knecht's touch but it was wiped when I stood in Melt's arms.

The sounds of the farm picked up and our bodies parted; we did not make our way back to the press of people but bent at the waist and pushed through the undergrowth and upgrowth until we gained the open mountain beyond and hacked up this to come to the path. Melt pulled me to a flat rock in the shade of a sugar bush. He told me that, when the line was done, Calcoen had made the knecht hold out his arm and roll back the sleeve and read off his own number from a leathern disc. We made a hopeless, scornful laugh at the knecht being cast with us, though the man attracted as much contempt when the shifting ways of the estate put him for a moment with the masters. To be one of them but work as we did – both sides counted him a mean fellow.

'But Gottlieb Calcoen himself started here as a company knecht,' said Melt. 'He was hired by the first master to carry the whip.'

'Le Voir says Calcoen never sat on a horse before he was here. His father was a servant. He was a servant. Now he is served.'

Melt threw a stone. 'But what does it help to say he is not so high as he puts himself? Tyke or not, it is him I pay for licence to earn my peculium with the wood – but I save every coin, and they are starting to come from all over for my tables. I will set up a shop of furniture when I have bought my way out or they die.'

He sat, his knees drawn up and his forearms across these, looking out over the estate. He was quiet a spell, nor did I speak. We were so still that a sugar bird discounted us and slid across the face of the bush, moving between flowers fourfold its size on blurred wings. A skink claimed the rock at my feet. I breathed carefully and felt the blood move in my temples and thought I could hear the juices in the plant veins about us. As I write this now I cannot recall the work piece I have in my basket that I had out this morning or remember last night's meal, but the bright eye of the lizard and the click and whir of the bird on that afternoon – I can summon these and almost the scent of the bushes.

Where we sat we looked over the grove whose leafage in full summer all but hid the maze hut. Of a sudden I saw a flash of movement there, a silver flicker as though a pail of water were thrown. Then the sound of a door closing though I told myself that might have come from any place in the farm beyond. I kept an eye on the grove hut but there came no other movement, and Melt brought his mouth to mine and then I had no thought of someone being in that strange, unguessed at building.

The light of the moon on my eyelids woke me. It was the deep part of the night; Meerem and Derde Susann made identical snores as though finishing the other's sentences. The tom was awake and watching from his ledge, then he stretched and leapt to the sill and was gone. I eased the latch and followed him out of the house. On the avenue the light was bright enough for the trees to cast a weird dapple. Beyond, thick shadows twisted the look of the lordlings-house and workshop. I turned away from the buildings and walked up the avenue, the air cooler in parts against my face and my own footfall a haunting thing. The floating steps I took when I dreamed felt possible in the grey night.

The oaks ran out beyond the homestead before the path to the graves, and here no trees kept me from the moon. A tyger wolf called on the mountain and something barked. I held my hand before me, turned it over and back. I was unmarked and smooth, a creature of outcurved hips and long thighs, perfect under the moon and my mind in the state of a leaper at the last instant before the leap, my name a label pasted over a more secret name. From here I could see the kitchen ... the grove and at its back the dense mountain with its cave ... the path to the cemetery ... and the kitchen again: the compass of a small life that never caught, or did but sparked and died in the space of moments. I wanted to take Jansie's baby to my breast and rock it alive – and at that thought I wanted urgently to be back under my blankets among the female and food smells and I made for the homestead but now I felt daemons at my back and I clenched my teeth to stop from running into the tunnel of shade but strode on legs stiff with fright and up the steps and into the kitchen where I realised what I had seen before but not seen: Jansie was not in her blankets.

I had no courage to go back into the night to find her and though I tried to keep vigil for her it was soon morning and I was waking to the kitchen sounds and she like wise stirring in her bed clothes. She woke slowly, her skin papery with tiredness, her eyes sunk in green shadows. I guessed that last night was one of many she had spent awake but could not think where, unless some humour was drawing her to sit at the grave mound.

Jansie moved through her morning work like an ox after a long day's trek, with only weak habit keeping her from stopping where she stood. As was bound to happen she clutched too late at a crock and missed and it crashed to shards; Derde Susann sent her to fetch beets to get her away from the kitchen, and sent me after her a while later, when I found her curled asleep in the half-cellar under the kitchen stairs. She had, I was amazed to see, a smile at her mouth as though a glad secret came to her.

She began to draw the attention of even crazy Madam as she spilt the coffee and frightened the birds and dragged her feet on the floor of the front room, and Le Voir used a master's voice to her and ceased flirting. Do not think either that their lot made saints of those in shared bondage; we, her fellows in the kitchen and without, were quick to turn on her when her share of work fell to us and not careful to hide our grumbles as she fumbled this task or that. Now Jansie was a nuisance when just a day or so ago she had been Poor Jansie.

In part our looks were sour because now, after her stately grief and then her wildness, she had ceased all together to grieve in the proper way. I was not alone in seeing her smile, and not only in her sleep. She leaned on the werf wall, face turned to the sun, arms wrapped to herself and rocking, and moved dreamily in Allaman's garden and trailed a hand along the bushes, acting like one in love or some other mad creature. And every night that I was able to stay up long enough to see it, she left her bed and stole away out of the kitchen like a girl on her way to meet her lover.

14

ONE OF GERRIE SAAYMAN'S DAUGHTERS IS TROTTING AT THE side of the road where it passes her father's filling station, her hair swinging to her buoyant steps. Vergilius, on her bicycle, draws abreast of her and sees that she has a very young puppy in her arms, a relaxed puppy whose head jogs on the girl's shoulder. Clean hair and a puppy, the warm afternoon … the girl gives off contentment like a scent. She has no more prettiness than is lent to most creatures while they are young, and her dress hangs loosely and too long, but she has immersed herself in delight. God is Pinkie Saayman, Vergilius thinks, look upon her and be glad.

The girl reaches Gupta's after Vergilius but overtakes her on the steps. Vergilius stows the bike and enters the store where Mrs Gupta is setting jars of black and pink sweets on the counter at the level of the girl's eyes. She has another reason for gladness – a fistful of pennies.

'Six nigger balls and six Wilson's toffees and six Chappies and—' the girl looks at the coins in her palm. 'And that's all.'

She hefts the dog to free a hand, accepts the packet from Mrs Gupta and heads back into the street, chiding the puppy in baby talk as it tries to open the bag with its nose. Mrs Gupta stows the jars and turns to Vergilius. She shouts at her, 'Vikram! Lee Trikad!' and jabs a finger towards the door and in the direction of the town of Louis Trichardt. But Vergilius is not looking for Mr Gupta; she is about women's business. Tongue-tied by the old woman's refusal to speak to her, she smiles and says please and points to the shelves, and Mrs Gupta sighs and pulls down a bolt of cheap cloth, her eyebrows signalling that it cannot be this the nun is after. But Vergilius grins back and nods, so the old lady shrugs and brings down more – white bolts sprigged with blue flowers, brown with off-register yellow and red leaves, a peach expanse with a montage of lipsticks and French poodles.

Mrs Gupta claws about under the counter and brings up a shoebox of dress patterns and one of clouded packets of buttons. These she places on the counter with another shrug, but she has warmed to the task of advising Vergilius in dumb show, and is pleased by the subversion of it. She measures cloth, cuts and sorts and bundles the lot together, stares at Vergilius for a moment then taps herself on the chest and pantomimes turning the wheel of a sewing machine. Vergilius is so relieved at the offer, she barely glances at the sums Mrs Gupta pencils on the margin of a newspaper before agreeing, and accepts the old lady's tape measure and mimed directions to take, for the first time in her life, her own measurements; she does this over her habit, cinching the tape tighter in accordance with Mrs Gupta's gestures, there in the Slagterskop general store.

In the memory of Slagterskop Mrs Gupta has spoken no English but she does so now. In a haughty accent and measured syllables that suit her voice she names the next five days on her fingers. Vergilius understands, and bows and smiles her way out of the store and blows a breath of relief when she gains the veranda.

In one of those blurts of courage that she now makes every few days, she walked up the farm track that morning and asked Francis Shone for money for her new clothing in the unabashed way that one might request the loan of a book. He scrambled to empty his pockets for her before she should ask anyone else and was left reflecting on the difficulties of life outside the convent for such a one, the sort of person who might do things just because they felt right, accept too much, give away too much. Bound by precept her whole life, Vergilius seems to him to be ignorant of the rules as she breaks out in all directions, makes plans for her new life without any idea of her next step.

Insect life is a fund of metaphors, of course (we can use them for this because we can have only a sketchy idea of what goes on in an insect's life), and many suggest themselves to the farmer when he thinks about what Vergilius is going through. He pleases himself by deciding that this woman is not one to emerge trembling and vulnerable from her chrysalis, needing a safe place where she might harden her wings for flight. For her he chooses the mayfly's story: laid by a wary mother in an element not her own, a mayfly nymph must, when it grows up, leave the water so that it might fly. Some float up from a stream's rocky bottom, some crawl out on water plants to gain the air. Clear of the water, these crawling ones split their skin for the last time and flex their new wings.

But the emerging imago of one species does not come to the surface until the last moment, the moment that it completes its metamorphosis: when it is, by cell growth and chemicals and hormonal shifts, ready, the pre-adult clings to a stone a few inches below the surface of the water. A marathon swim past water weeds lies before it, through the water it needs now and the air its next self will need, and it works for hours to trap air until it holds a bubble roiling with energy, urgent to rise. When the moment comes, its last skin splits and the new creature effervesces up and through the meniscus carried by its air balloon, which bursts the surface and launches it into the atmosphere where it is born, reborn, able to fly the instant it is in the air.

These Ephemeroptera – wingéd creatures of but a day, as the Victorians translated their name – the farmer likes better even than purposeful Scarabidiae pressing against their own armour. He likes their story for her.

In the literal way of the district, Bandolier might have been named Motorkop or some such, because its distinguishing feature, to one seeing it from the road, is a substantial clump of boulders resembling an early motor car – one house-sized, square boulder set on a lower arrangement of rocks. But on Shone's first trek around his new farm many years before he had found a cracked leather bandolier on that same koppie, surely from the war; the belt had loops for shells and an arrangement of pouches, presumably for shot or bullets. He had crouched in the shade of a naboom and prised the flap of each pouch over its brass knob, finding in one a scrap of bandage dun and stiff with old blood, and decided on the strength of this to name the farm Bandolier. He liked the sound, the promise of arming oneself – but with blameless pouches that might, and sometimes might not, hold bullets. He liked the connection with history, though not such distant history as all that; he was absorbed in those days of change with a debate he thought of as 'what to take with one, what to leave behind', and the bandolier fit that too.

The belt itself, now crisp with dubbin, shiny as a beetle and hanging in the study at Bandolier, was not the only thing left by those who held the land before Shone. About eight years after naming Bandolier he had been led by the dogs into an overhang formed by a couple of the smaller boulders on another koppie where, on the sandy bottom of a little cave, he discovered a blue glass bead the thickness of a bee and half as long. More beads were half-concealed in the earth; he dug out the lot and some fragments of clay pot. Strung on a thong, they hung on the study wall too, lovely things with a layer of smoky indigo around a milky core, the whole with irregular facets. Some tribeswoman's trove, now his.

The koppie that might have named his farm, Motor Car Koppie, is crawling with Agricus boys when, two days before the first Republic Day, he passes it on his way to Slagterskop to collect the Monday post. Sergeant Louw has parked his truck at the foot of the koppie and he hails Shone from halfway up the main boulder. The farmer waves and drives on, leaving him and his schoolboy crew to the business of turning Bandolier's great boulder into a billboard for that nationalist week. Boys carry rocks the size of cabbages up the sloping face of the boulder, others slop these with whitewash and set them out to form '1961', the upside-down year. Shone sees no harm in it.

In the village a flag is flying for the first time in weeks from one of a pair of flagpoles in the sisal bed in front of the Slagterskop police station. It has three horizontal stripes: orange, white and sky blue. The white band has three smaller flags clustered in its centre, one of them a backwards Union Jack. Sergeant Louw hoped for a new standard to hoist this week, but it seems the scab flag of the twenties will still see service; this one Mrs Louw washed and ironed and he, at daybreak, ran up the pole.

Not long after that, among the acacias in the patch of veld between the mission and the village, Jacob was about.

He was carrying the starting blocks Frank made for him, and Vergilius's stopwatch, and at the stoep in front of the general store he found young Prakash Gupta, and the two of them set off towards the far side of the village. Jacob handed the stopwatch to Prakash and talked him through its workings, making young Gupta prove that he had the hang of it.

'But no one's even going to know.'

'No, we've got to get it right.'

The boys left the village and walked on, arriving within the hour at the Agricus sports grounds. No one was about. The drone of an anthem came from the school buildings. Prakash clawed himself up the chain link and over the gate, and braced it to stop its chiming as Jacob followed him up and over. Prakash headed for the mark on the track before the turn, 100 yards away. Jacob began his warm-up, shrugged off his jersey, put the blocks in place on the inside lane, nudged his feet against them and crouched, his head straining forward, his eyes on the empty mielie sack in Prakash's raised hand.

In the classrooms the Agricus boys and girls were settling down to study their separate history, wherein three ships come sailing by, wherein Jan and Maria plant cabbages in their rows and no Native comes to trouble them until those, perfidious, naked, who bow Piet into the kraal for the devil's dance, and even then there never is an inciting incident, for all is ordained, lacking any distribution of culpability, lacking reason …

Obedient to the flash of cloth, Jacob has launched himself down the track.

In Amos's room at Mannamead, behind the cloistered courtyard, a dusty plant with heart-shaped leaves climbs up to the high window and trails along the bare curtain rod. Its roots are in a pot on a saucer on the table next to the radiogram. Behind a panel in the back of the machine, warm from its workings, a handkerchief makes a parcel of a letter wrapped like a relic and tucked alongside half a dozen resinous seed heads drying in a row. This is the letter that went from a mother to her son, and from the chief to the convent handyman; it is the weightiest thing to have come Amos's way. He has read it twice and been pleased to see that it begins just as he was taught was the correct way to start a letter: 'Dear Son, How are you, I am fine.'

The sisters never come in here. No one but Jacob. Amos imagines leaving the room and taking the Great North Road. He will loosen the inner sole of his shoe, slide the letter in like the dead man did. He sees himself walking down the driveway and onto the road. His mind circles on itself … the shoe, the driveway, the road. Which way was New Brighton? How long would such a journey be? Two, three weeks? What papers does he need to travel so far? What reason can he give when they stop him? He slides one of his bent shoes out from under the bed and tests the inner sole. Where would he even go to seek permission to quit the small place where he is?

Amos leaves the letter in the handkerchief in the back of the radiogram. He crumbles one of the seed heads in his palm and reaches for the BB packet.

The letter is the last thing he thinks of as his mind slips into sleep, the letter and its writer, who does not know that her son is dead, nor where his body lies. It is a heavy thing, and Amos feels unquiet holding this knowledge, unable to warn the dead man's mother as she approaches its ambush.

15

IN THE USUAL COURSE OF THE DAY MEEREM COLLECTED WATER
from the stream in the morning, but today we were about butcher-
ing and salting down a veal calf that had died out of turn; Derde
Susann needed her for the heavy work, and so she sent Jansie and
me. We left the yoke – we could barely lift it – and took a bucket
apiece. The instant we were on the avenue Jansie lifted her chin and
tilted her head to listen, tensing in that way she had. I made a sound
of irritation and walked ahead of her.

To come to the stream you went to the end of the avenue and
followed a path along the outside of the werf wall. It was a neat
affair, flowing between banks with a rounded lip. The path tracked
it on the bank, ending at a beach where we could step into the water
and dip our buckets. I heard Jansie coming behind me, singing a
lullaby in slack snatches as she kept her mind on not tripping on the
path. She lifted a bunch of her skirt, took two steps into the stream
and tilted her bucket to collect water without water weed, and set it
on the bank, and this time tucked her skirts properly and was back
in the water with something taken from her pocket. It was a piece
of stuff that, as she held it in the current, unfolded itself into a small
jacket with sleeves and a ribbon at the neck. I said to myself, Jansie
has been making clothes for a babe. I thought it slowly to bring up
its utmost in the way of shock, for in actuality I was not shocked,
and when she straightened in the stream and told me with a simple
smile, 'My babe lives,' I just shook my head.

She laid the jacket on the grass, spreading the arms and smoothing the skirts and ribbons, and sat by it, her hands in her lap, an open smile on her mouth, and closed her eyes to feel the sun. I had gainsayings ready stocked against her madness and may as well use them; I said: 'We saw the grave. We put flowers there.'

She opened her eyes and looked at me.

'A grave is not my baby. May be not any babe; it may be a rock in the grave or no thing. But it is not my babe.'

I knelt beside her on the grass. The stream ran untroubled around the beach and made little sound. I asked her: 'Have you seen your babe?' and held my breath at cracking this door of madness for fear what was within would open its yellow eyes and see me there.

Jansie looked away downstream. 'I have not seen her. But I have heard her.'

This was the first time any of us had named the babe as a daughter. Hearing Jansie say, 'I have heard her' brought a lurch of hope in me as though it could be true. And with that in me I could not ask kind questions as might gently bring the mad girl back from madness. I turned away from her, took my bucket and left her on the grassy bank with the babe's jacket spread by her.

I was in sight of the kitchen when she caught me. She was out of breath and the bucket all but emptied and her skirt on that side wrapped to her leg, but when she stopped me and looked full into my face and said how I must not tell this thing to the others, held the chemise at her breast as if swearing on the milk that had gone wasted, she suddenly was almost sane. I regarded her a long instant, and it was a serious look we gave the other. Then I made her hold her bucket steady and tipped water from mine to hers so that both were scant but neither was empty, and what could you expect from girls sent for a woman's work? We walked on to the kitchen, something decided between us.

We could see the risks – I could – but the dangers could not be guessed by me nor Jansie, whose furthest terror to that day had been the night of birth and that not elected but only borne. This matter demanded that we discover courage in ourselves, for if there were a babe alive from that night in the cave she had been stole, and if she had been stole and was not stole away but at Vogelzang where her rightful mother could hear her – and if there were cries … well, that was so far as it would carry us.

Already I believed with half my mind what Jansie believed with all of hers, believed enough that I resolved to look around and see what was to be seen. I also had the thought, though unadmitted, how little I risked, not only because I was not bound to the estate but because, with the young mistress's disguise complete, there was less to keep us here every day: Le Voir had picked up some goat hair commissions from the farmers of the plain but his reason for being at Vogelzang was used and we could be for town any day that he chose or that Calcoen came into the real world long enough to suggest.

Le Voir was trapped in the front part of the estate, with adverse host and crazed hostess and him conceiving an attachment to their daughter. It was because of this last that I envied him least. Her confusion at the loss of her hair had hardened to self-love lost, and the splendid hair piece he had made for her was caught up in this so that she showed only dislike for it – stripped it from her head the instant she was in her room, pulled it on without care if she must enter shared rooms, affecting to be unmindful of how it looked, though waiting that small moment for him or me to tug it right, and her jaw held against joining in her own refigurement.

At dinner one night – most meals Le Voir took in the back room with the young mistress, and Calcoen took in his study, but from time to time Madam would break the surface and call for dinner in the proper room – at dinner one night at that time Calcoen's feeling for human contact was awakened. He made to parley first with his wife, who only regarded him as one might look at a dog giving chase to a flea about its body. He turned next to his step daughter and approved her looks and had the poor instinct to narrow this to her curls. She smiled the cooler the more he spoke about it – when he said how she had her good hair from her mother, how it was a woman's glory and so would be her dowry &c. At the end of this she took up the knife from the meat plate and sliced a lock of her hair piece and offered it to him as a keep sake. He, made timid by the violence in her movement and in the air about her, protested that she should not spoil her looks, at which she answered between her cold smile that he should not mind for surely it would grow back.

Le Voir was sickened when he told this scene to me, racked that his gift to her should be what she blamed him for, as though, by protecting her so well from any ill report the world might be allowed to make of her, he had passed judgment himself. He was the instrument of her mother's devisings and his a mother's dilemma: by disguising her child's flaw she made known that she saw there was a flaw to be hid, and this when a mother is bound to admit none. It was so neat a trap I could have made a theorem of it had I the heart.

He had sought me out after dinner and we shared a pipe at the werf wall, Old Haarlem cropping the grasses at our feet. I listened to Le Voir but also stopped listening as I worried over whether to tell him about Jansie and the babe. I thought he would take logic's part and dissuade me from it, this wild belief, and his argument would be strong; I could argue it myself.

But I wanted likelihood and old Ockham kept out of this, for it would only take Jansie and me back to the logical world of a baby dead at birth or murdered, and I wanted to believe Jansie when she said she lived. And so I told him nothing of it, but settled matters with myself, then gave an ear to Le Voir, who was saying something about the constellations.

Reason had no part in our taking this course but it was our sharpest tool as we advanced upon it. I put myself with Jansie the next morning packing the half-cellar, and set it out: we would break the problem into its parts, apply ourselves to each and work through the possibilities. I can see myself leaning back on my heels, a turnip in each hand, telling Jansie with a fine brave voice how we would proceed. I think she did not take in a word but was comforted by my way of setting it out. When I stopped my speech she laid a hand on my arm and said: 'I heard her last night.'

Whether that were true or no, whereas I had believed for these past weeks that Calcoen had murdered the babe or brought a woman from town to do it, now I must proceed as though he were behind its theft and keeping it alive. Why he should steal what was his own property I could not fathom, although the brigandage of slavery threw up laws where you might not expect them, and in a span lived beyond the rights of man there were yet rights (these were the customs accorded to property, yes, but when you are that property and the rule has to do with your not being destroyed or broken, you will take it). Even on that far plain we had law of a sort and the Fiscal would act if blood were drawn in a private whipping or a slave killed without sound cause, and perhaps even if a babe were stolen from its mother. I had a sense that what was afoot was outside the law – outside even its imagined misdeeds. So not killed, but not seen, so hid. Hid why? 'Why' almost brought it unstuck; I properly feared that the answer was like as not, Because I can. Because I do decree it so – as though you had asked, when asking why, not 'For what reason?' but instead 'By what right?'

But I had to start somewhere, and I would start with crediting Jansie's senses. I put away my turnips and told her I would keep watch with her tonight and listen for whether I could not also hear a babe cry.

We worked our day, ate our evening meal, cleared away the kitchen, sewed for a spell and then made our good night and pulled blankets over us. I lay on my back with my hands folded under my head, looking at the reeds lit with the glow from the fire and listening to Derde Susann settle with kindly words directed at her body – her hips, her thumbs, where ever the ache lodged tonight. Meerem was already snoring. It was an age before Derde Susann joined her but at last I heard my name whispered and I folded back the blanket and followed Jansie's blue shape to the door and into the night. We did not venture far: around the corner to the outside staircase that led to the attic above the front part of the house.

I had two reasons, or three, for choosing this place: my nervous instinct told me to seek high ground for safety and to give us the best hope of hearing a cry and of fixing its direction if we did; two, I had an idea that the space between the ceiling and the thatch – particularly where it swelled behind the front gable – was the only place to hide a living infant, and three, from here we would hear any commotion that should arise if our absence were found out. So we climbed the stairs and found the door at the top of these locked and barred, and settled against it. There was no moon but I could yet make out the tom coming up to investigate us. He greeted Jansie with his sound and found a place against her leg; she folded a hand around him and told him in a child's voice to keep still.

After a while, I own, some small resentment grew in me, as though Jansie ought to deliver the babe's cry now that I had paid with being there. As for Jansie, she seemed to feel me beside her as leave to rest at last and she slipped to sleep against me. I moved us around until her head lay in my lap, and laid my arms about her shoulders, eased my legs to a comfortable place. I felt, too, something of the fear and promise of my night walk. This was followed by melancholy that rose in me as if I were filling with cool water, until tears pricked behind my eyelids, but I opened them to the moon following its own mantle over the horizon. It rose so fast that I could fix a mark and look away and look back and see that mark passed. The tom stirred in the curve of Jansie's waist and she stirred under my arm and settled. I placed my hand on her cap, then back on her shoulder.

Derde Susann had told me Jansie's true story one afternoon during the grieving for her babe, while she slept in a corner of the kitchen:

When she was three years old she had sailed with her mother and their master for the homeland, coming from the empire's farthest outpost, and they broke their journey here. When they resumed it they left Jansie behind with her master's host; she never was sure why. The promise was to send for her within the year but within the year her mother was dead – freed by right as she stepped off the boat in the Low Countries and dead within six months of the small pox. Of the freedom Jansie learned in a letter her mother paid to have written and sent; of being orphaned she was told in a letter from their former master to Jansie's new owner, if that was in fact the office of the man with whom she had been left. He was an uncle of the Vogelzang family and on Madam's first marriage, to the man before Calcoen, Jansie formed part of her dowry, a gift from the uncle to the husband. And thus Jansie entered bondage without she ever was sold or bought; the child of a free mother, she was perhaps legally a free maid or had been at the moment when she was passed to a new home and an owner.

For years, as a kindness, Madam had read to Jansie her mother's letter to the little girl and the master's letter to the uncle. But when comprehension on Jansie's side or on Madam's dawned, the letters had been mislaid, remembered only as a sign that although she was now an orphan, her mother had meant to send for her. As for her bonded or not bonded status, Derde Susann said, Jansie shrank back from any essay at talking about this as though it threatened a second orphaning.

I had it in me to feel scorn at her going so easily along with her own enslavement – though why should the theft of her life be worse than a transaction in which money passed from the thief to the new owner? – but my surer instinct was to comprehend it. It is the fashion these days to share those wrenching tales of slavery escaped, but I find little in them to recognise. The high flown language sours on my tongue and the over strained telling of great struggle and great triumph have as their intent rather more of vengeance and ever-lasting reproach than of fact. From what I know of it, the state is a subtler thing once you are in it and so much the harder to escape for that.

Jansie could no more wake tomorrow and demand her liberty than a child can turn to her parent and simply walk away when next told to do this or not do that. For all the beatings and constraints or threats of it, more children could say no and meet with little real compulsion from their parents, but something locks their minds and keeps them obedient in action even in the face of their own muti-nous impulses, and so it was with Jansie, Derde Susann, Caspar, Melt and Meerem. Even when we ran away we did not escape it. La liberté, as Le Voir had said, tapping his chest, it is in here, and its obverse too. I would say that family is in there too, family in what-ever it comes dressed as, and sure as a hook through your skin so that the merest touch on the line will hold you there.

The moon was overhead, the tom had left us. Jansie slept on. At my back the house shed its heat. A plover's noise said the tom had reached the open ground between werf and road. The night closed in on our landing at the top of the stairs, then seemed to peel back and I heard the sound for some moments before I marked it: the cry of a very young infant, a thin bleat that tilted the world towards it and was answered in a whimper by Jansie where she lay across my lap, before she woke panting with fright.

Such a small noise, not so loud even as the plover, and we were not the only people to hear it. Jansie and I stood and had our feet on the step as we made to track it when a foot fall on the ground below had us shrink against the wall. Passing with a lantern swinging was a masculine shape I knew for Calcoen – the click of the front door, the sound of shoe leather on the veranda, these recalled sounds from our moments of fright told a story of him leaving his room. The lantern blinked out suddenly, and that told us he had turned a corner. We all but cracked bones so hard did we clutch one another; after a long while we stepped down the stairs and followed after him, for that way lay our kitchen where I now very greatly wanted to be if he was about in the night. We rounded the corner with cautious steps for what if we should see him stood there? But there was no living thing, nor any sense of one in the shadows, although the night was as quiet as it is after some passing thing has hushed the natural sounds. We two, our minds quite as startled, hobbled in an awkward clench to the kitchen stairs and up to safety.

Jansie was shivering. I brought her to my bed and laid her there and pressed myself along her. Her spasms quieted at last and I felt her sink to sleep. She must have been pulled there by great tiredness, for it was hours before I could close my eyes, not while thoughts of the baby would not leave my mind. In the safety of the kitchen I yet flinched at the sound of that thin cry, somewhere out there on Vogelzang.

16

THE DE KOCKS PROVIDED ONE VELDKORNET AND A HALF DOZEN
hard riders to their war against the English all those years ago,
seven brothers whose deaths in instalments by Lee-Metford and
Maxim gun hollowed their mother like a termite infestation; they
are, by the degree of their sacrifice, the district's most patriotic
family. Familie De Kock also sponsored a wagon in a re-enactment
in 1938 of the great migration that had brought their ancestors to
the Transvaal; Matthys de Kock, who is now a grown man with sons
and an American car, whipped a team of oxen into Pretoria as a
boy of nineteen, wearing a corduroy waistcoat and velskoene, embarrassed by the shouting men who met the procession of replica
wagons. He guided his team past tearooms and department stores
on the hard streets, then handed the reins to his brother and crawled
into the covered part of the wagon; there he lay on his back with his
head on a suitcase and looked at the tops of the buildings through
the jacaranda branches and thought that in the depths of the tall
buildings, behind their newspapers, there were Englishmen shaking
their heads at the enterprise, and this contributes to the irritation
that is his abiding memory of the entry into the capital. Aanstap,
rooies, die pad is lank en swaar … Get along, boys, it's a long, hard
road we're on.

These days it is the Afrikaners who are getting the big loans from
the Land Bank, ordering a new John Deere through the co-op,
donating an ox or a couple of sheep to the kerkbasaar and seeing
the sandstone steeple of the Nederduitse Gereformeerde Kerk rise

higher than the powder-blue bell tower of the Romans in Louis Trichardt. Gone are the farms named Doornfontein and Vlakteskop and Weenen. They have been replaced with sponsored signs that read like another new language until you realise they are compounds of the owner's first name and that of his wife – Plaas Marietjaart, and Henksantie Bonsmara Boerdery (Edms) Bpk.

The new prosperity, fuelled by an instinct for generosity and a tribal memory of the hungry years, guarantees a mountainous spread at every kerkbasaar or nagmaal, and today's Republiekdag feast will outdo these and set the board groaning with souskluitjies, sosaties, bredie, bobotie – heavy, soft food, smothered, fatty and sweet. Even the word for food, sounded well back in the mouth – 'kos' – makes a fat sound, thickening the throat.

A feast needs a centrepiece, and although she may be a De Kock by marriage only and really nothing more than a dowser's daughter from Soekmekaar, Aletta de Kock has claimed the right to provide it. Therefore: on the morning of the first Republic Day, the Studebaker eases over the road to a roped-off area at the side of the rugby field on the fringes of the school; as he always does, De Kock hisses and tenses his buttocks to encourage the car to suck in its belly as it moves over the tussocked road; today Mrs de Kock is too preoccupied to hiss back. On her lap is a tea tray covered in tinfoil, and on that a square cake in two tiers, with sugar flags crossed at each of the eight corners and on the topmost tier an arrangement of sugar proteas – not a flower whose size or colouring suggests it as a subject for re-production in sugar: its petals are brittle, its stamens packed solid, its stem as thick as a branch, and the least bulky variety is the size of a man's fist. Nonetheless, Mrs de Kock has had a go. It is a patriotic cake, this dense construction of fruit batter and marzipan, and weighs more than a baby.

Mrs de Kock does not breathe at all as De Kock eases the car off the track and heads over the veld to park beneath an acacia. He is concerned about finding shade for the car's upholstery and does not notice that, on Mrs de Kock's side of the car, he has parked too close to a springy young thorn tree. Nor is she expecting, as she clenches her thighs to hold the cake steady and flings open the door, to have it immediately flung shut again – or, misfortune on misfortune, not immediately; there is time for Mrs de Kock to swivel in her seat and point her knees towards the opening so that when it does rebound, the door catches her knee and delivers a jolt that climbs up her spine on one fork and on the other reaches to the topmost sugar petal of the protea cake. She lets fly a scream of fear for the cake that arrests field mice and jolts birds into flight. De Kock recognises his name across veld and sports fields and heads back to the car at a run. On the veranda of the school two De Kock children close their eyes. On the bleachers Francis Shone exchanges a weary smile with Frank.

The English farmer was almost a man before he learned that 'Afrikaner' was not an insult. If people everywhere establish their own outline by taking readings off those around them, and triangulate their group's position off others', the refinement here is that they seem to use, not the echo of unintrusive soundings, but the pitch and intensity of the outrage their sharp probes cause to others, and those in order to confirm something in themselves. They do it with bland smiles; Shone patronises De Kock, his neighbours do not bother to hide the co-op within the co-op that they operate when it comes to abattoir fees or maize prices or water rights, and when it suits them they join ranks to fear and loathe the Bantu in general, or bestow the shameful epithet 'good Bantu' on Zulus, setting them against the tetchy Venda, and the Venda affect to despise every other group, all of whom choose to dislike Boer or Settler more or less than Settler or Boer through the years.

Frank says: 'I understand your country, Shone: everyone here, every group, hates the other one.'

The papers – the English papers – are full of news of the 'clamp-down on civil liberties' planned under Verwoerd's republic; amid these high-minded warnings is a piping demand that the role of English-speakers in the 'building of this nation' be acknowledged. The end of hundred-and-fifty-five years of allegiance to the British crown is billed as a chance for reconciliation between the rockspiders and the rooinekke – an end to what they call 'the racial problem' – but at schools for English-speaking children, schools in the city, the masters encourage boys to use their Republic Day medals for target practice with catapults and air rifles.

In Slagterskop they accept where things stand. They are as men seated at rough tables, their grins turning to grimaces as they arm-wrestle.

And under their noses the hotel waiter smuggles men and women out of the country and in by night, and by day indulges in acts of breakfast sabotage with chicken shit; and the brows of the Afrikaans farmers bead with tension and their sons go to bed with scabbed knuckles, and Shone takes delivery of his books and catalogues and of their wives and sisters, and loses hours in the day putting a name to every arachnid, moth and mantid, finding for all creatures their double names of species and genus in the system where these outrank family, outrank kingdom.

The caravaners – Buffmires, Badineaux and Frank – are guests today, as are four of the Immaculate sisters, Xavier and Perpetua having stayed behind at Mannamead. Their party has been shown to chairs set out in concentric semicircles around a cairn and dais. They squint in the morning sun and, not sure how to behave, keep quiet and wave flies away from their solemn faces. First to be wheeled out is the real centrepiece of Slagterskop's commemoration of this first Republic Day, about the size of the cake and even heavier: a scale model of one of the cannons used at the Battle of Blood River. It will be mounted on the cairn in front of the school buildings, with a plaque. It came up by train and was fetched by De Kock yesterday from the railway siding on Bandolier; now it rests on a plank across a wheelbarrow in the shade of the new bleachers, manned by two of De Kock's farm boys in stiff new khaki overalls. Around the new South Africa a dozen miniature cannons will be honoured today.

The Agricus youngsters are in uniform – maroon-and-white striped blazers or the bush gear of the youth movement – and lined up behind the school buildings. The Afrikaners of Slagterskop began today with a church service; now comes the only slightly less sacred part of the day.

En hoor jy die magtige dreuning?
Oor die veld kom dit wyd gesweef:
Die lied van 'n volk se ontwaking
Wat harte laat sidder en beef.

The caravaners crane to Shone to understand the anthem the children sing as they file around the edge of the building and stand before the assembly. 'Do you hear, sweeping over the veld, the mighty roar of a nation's awakening, which makes hearts shudder and tremble' is about the sum of it, although it loses much in the translation.

'This is the song of young South Africa, this is the song … of young … South Africa.'

In the row of caravaners and nuns, Frank and Vergilius sit next to one another. His hands are on his knees, hers in her lap. There are speeches; there is a pause at the right time to hear a short speech by Verwoerd and a longer one from the new State President broadcast over the headmaster's wireless from a rain-washed Church Square in Pretoria. By the time the sun sets that evening, he says, we will be subjects no more, but citizens! Citizens of a republic.

The speeches end, the feast beckons, the athletics programme stretches before them like a salt pan that must be crossed. A headache slides between Shone's skull and brain as the clouds curdle in the white sky.

In nearby Slagterskop, Mr Gupta has overseen the whitewashing of a large rectangle on the side wall of his store. Old Mrs Gupta tipped a storeman to paint a pair of jaunty blue swags on either side of this. Several times Mr Gupta has almost managed to ask his mother about this but cannot frame the question, so there are swags, no comment. On the evening of the great events at the school, Mr Gupta has Prakash and Jacob and the storemen set out bales and empty mielie sacks in rows facing the wall. Operating outside himself in heady disobedience to the day, he has sent word into the back rooms of the village and it has spread to the Reserve.

As darkness falls he carries his projector out of the sitting room behind the shop, through the general store, and eases himself, tentative as a new mother carrying her baby, sideways down the steps into the street and around the corner to where the rows are packed with villagers. At their feet sit about twice as many Reserve Natives. Prakash pays out electrical extension cords in his father's wake; Gupta sets the machine on a table whose stability he has improved with flat stones and a wad of newspaper, and slowly releases his hold on it.

Rose and her more biddable sisters are back at Mannamead; at Gupta's, Pie and Orie Badineaux sit together, Vergilius shares a bale with Frank, the Buffmires fidget on another.

Mr Gupta flicks the switch and swashes of turquoise and amber ripple on the wall. He twists this and nudges that and the shapes resolve into three elongated horses, each with a stretched cowboy in the saddle; these thunder forward and skid to a halt; they stand frozen in their tracks as a giant cattle brand sears the words 'Riders of the High Sierra' across them and across the wall, and music warbles from a speaker in the projector's side.

In the warm, moth-strewn night Gupta mixes the reels and runs one twice, but his audience does not complain. The old men and old women, children, parents and even new teenagers join in loudly. A handful are seeing their first moving picture, if you do not count the old travelling movie vans with their Tea Market Expansion Bureau stories of Mr Tea, who wins a wife and a tennis trophy because he is an urban sophisticate who drinks the stuff, and Mr Skokiaan, drunk on pot liquor in his perilous shanty town, who does not. The flea pit in the town of Louis Trichardt is, of course, for the exclusive use of the white subjects, now citizens. But this is a real movie. There is incomprehensibly terse dialogue, and there are swinging fist fights. Each time a knuckle connects with a lawman's jaw the smack is drowned out by the audience – Slagterskop is making its own sound track. Factions choose their champions from among the bad and the good guys and with each blow the audience rises off its bales or to its knees on the ground and shouts 'Hau!' and 'Eh!' and other words of effort and manliness. They are on the edge of their seats so as not to miss a cue, and laughing to tears, complicit, for once, in the absurdity.

Gupta is embarrassed by this way of watching a film. He hopes the Americans can see that he knows better. Old Mrs Gupta, seated by his side, does not join in the noise, but, Gupta sees from the corner of his eye, she tenses and rises slightly with each punch and her fists, balled in her lap, threaten vaguely towards the screen. He shrugs and puffs out his cheeks. Tonight, anything goes. Tomorrow, who knows? Who knows what will happen in the new South Africa.

The farmer is seated behind the bale shared by Vergilius and Frank and he watches her more than the screen. He has in his thoughts called Vergilius beautiful, but thinks now that this may not be so. She is a tall, regular-featured woman of thirty-six years, one usually giving the impression that the warm blood of her body does not quite reach the surface of her skin … she is all of a colour, and that a flesh tone with some blue notes. The sense of remove about her is almost pornographic; the farmer can imagine a man spending himself upon her cool white body, not inside it. But, he thinks now, drunk on his banked anger at the day, and from sips at the hip-flask he shares with Frank, if he summons statuary to describe Vergilius, tonight he nominates alabaster, because in her high spirits she is lit with the illusion of warmth. She is flushed, alight at Frank's hand on her elbow, flaring her nostrils at the scent of sexual desire that rises from the throat of his shirt, and from her own body.

'Riders of the High Sierra' ends. The two of them heft their bale onto a pile against the wall of the general store, turn away from the crowd separating back into its parts and drift together into the veld beyond the village's circles of light. They stroll in the direction of the trailer outspan and the darkened mission, their steps slowing, their bodies swaying towards one another, and at easy intervals they speak about the day but mostly stay silent. In a moment they come abreast of the hotel. A tang of swimming pool chemicals cuts through the honeysuckle from the hedge that grows along a fence separating the hotel grounds from the veld. Vergilius pushes into a gap in the hedge and parts the branches. The pool area is in darkness. Metal lawn furniture makes a grey tracery where it is stacked against a wall and the water shifts as a breeze passes over it.

Frank moves past Vergilius and scales the fence. From the other side he leans over and reaches for her. She nudges a foot into a gap, steps up, and he half lifts, half guides her over, his hands holding her at the point where her waist swells to her hips. On the other side of the fence she draws away from him and moves to the pool, and kneels to fish out drowned and drowning insects from among the bougainvillea bracts that float there. When she looks up, Frank is naked, she thinks, where he steps into the water at the shallow end, although at this distance his body is a just denser shadow. He swims towards where she kneels, and treads water, looking up at her, then turns and swims underwater back to the far end of the pool. She hears a sigh as he breaks the surface.

She draws in her breath, then sits at the side of the pool and unbuckles her sandals, tugs off her stockings and slips her feet and lower legs into the water, her robe hoisted to her knees. From the sounds, he has submerged again; racing against him seeing her undress, she shucks her robe, tugs off her veils and cap and in her white shift slips into the pool. She ducks under the surface, pushing off the side towards the bottom where the water is cold and dense. Slow dolphin movements take her to him. They break the surface and their bodies do not touch but he circles her with coiling movements, moving closer, their faces almost meeting as she swivels to keep him in sight. The breeze has chilled the wet cloth on her shoulders; she dips them beneath the water. When she rises again, Frank is behind her. She braces her feet on the pool floor and her body against the water, trying to hold still, and his hands slide to her hips; he draws her to him. One of his arms circles her waist, one moves up to beneath her breasts. His cheek is against her shoulder; his head is turned away. Her breasts, unbound while the rest of her body is held so tightly against his, are nudged by the moving water. He moves her body with his, and deep in his throat he swallows sounds. Rocked in the water, she arches her spine and tilts her head back. Her eyes are open and she names the constellations in a whisper: the sisters, the great dog, the hunter.

17

'TO LIVE THE RITUALS WHICH ATTEND THE POSSIBLE existence of God eventually makes of one a believer.'

Le Voir was fond of quoting Pascal's wager for arguments beyond, I believe, the intention of its framer. He turned it to serve for proof of how any habit coupled to any humour – kindness, say, or love – would change any mind, and on slow days in our shop in town he had mused on experiments one ought to conduct in this vein – how a lady might be persuaded to make a pet of a rat and he become her friend, or a running boy be convinced of his worth by every day being bowed to by Le Voir and served a cake by me. Such were his plans, though the theory never needed to be put to the proof – that he thought it possible made it likely enough, and no rats nor boys had their minds changed by us. But we had need of changing some minds with ritual if we would discover the truth about the cry we had heard.

That morning, the morning after our few hours out in the night, I traced our passage from the bottom of the attic stairs to the corner of the house to discover where Calcoen had gone when he disappeared. From the corner I saw to my left the path to the graves; to my right the avenue where it ran between the kitchen on one side and the lordlingshouse and workshop on the other, and, directly ahead but set deeper towards the mountains than the other buildings, the grove with the pen for the goats and ass. For a moment I thought that it had been a goat we had heard, but in the next instant a wash of certainty told me my mind had made the leap ahead of my eyes and placed the babe in the curious hut. But if the maze hut then Doof Hendrik, the thrashing, violent slave hated by every creature on the estate.

The wager must convert him or lull him, and get him away from there long enough to see.

I longed for some one with whom to talk this over but there was none. Jansie had passed the duty of finding the babe square to me while she, waked from real sorrow and ready to be cunning, entered into a play act wherein she seemed to fit her sighs and looks to an idea of how a wronged woman ought to be. It amazed me to witness: she trailed about with an air that was a galloping parody of the real sadness that had soaked her through so lately. I ground my teeth to stop from snapping at her and was stopped every time by the need in her eyes as she some times looked at me. As well slap a bird who pretends with her dragging wing and fools no one but tells us by her pretending how keen is her need to save her chick.

Never the less, if Jansie could not be my conspirator she must be useful in other ways, this prettiest girl on Vogelzang.

Doof Hendrik no longer came down from the grove to the slave kitchen for his meal; the boy who had been used to go there to lead him down at the noon bell now made the journey every day with that one's bread and jug. Tomorrow we planned it would be Jansie who would fetch that to him and she did, with a swing in her walk and not a glance in his direction as she set the food down beside him where he gaped in the clearing to see her there. Again the next day she set the food by and he watched with wide eyes and wide mouth. On the third day he lunged for her and she stepped quick away and gave him over her shoulder a look to say she had not caught his exact meaning by this.

When I lost courage and tried to bring to consideration what could be the end of this sport, Jansie looked at the ground beyond me and said she would lie with him under the sun or in the front room with Madam by if it would get her babe to her. If it were a straight trade I believe she would have done this that day and not counted the cost of having her babe restored, but we could offer no bargain that would show we knew where for we traded. This was a slower game and already it told on Jansie's nerves, for it was a bad animal we baited.

And on the fifth day, without we had any thought that it was so close, we were brought to the danger point. We had a settled march by then, one that by now must be habit to the guard at the maze hut as well. At dawn that day we had shrugged out of our blankets, unrested from a night of 'what if' and reaching in our minds for the baby. I had dreamed again of a labyrinth; I was above it and plotted my way to its centre, whispering the choices at each turn; the dream labyrinth was not a spiral but a true maze such as Le Voir liked to test me with on a slate. But I could see my way through — if only for the next three turns, then I would stop and plot again, counting the decisions and dead ends on my fingers. When I entered it I did so at a run, though, and lost my way at once, pursued by a roar from within or chasing it until Jansie nudged me awake.

Then there had been the morning's work. From our hands there had not before come such even loaves or sticky preserves but nor so much caught afire nor dropped, nor so much grease on the floor. Work was the only thing that eased the burn in my shoulders, and though a house the like of Vogelzang will never run short of it, Jansie and I pushed ahead of ourselves, turning cheeses that need not be turned (but leaving half untouched), or freshening brine that could have gone another week (but forgetting to salt it).

The morning passed and the sun was overhead and the noon bell due in a short while; now urgent garden work must appear, to take us there. At the bottom of the kitchen stairs we parted, she going to catch the lad and get from him the half loaf, I across the avenue and up the slope to the grove, circling this until I came to the place we had marked with stones. Here I stopped to slow my heart's beat and my breath, for though the fearsome slave was deaf he had keen sight and I must be sure to move smooth as water through the place. I crept part way into the trees to a known grandfather tree whose broad trunk shielded me entire. This was about half way to my look out place where I could have clear sight of the maze hut and Doof Hendrik. Here I waited until I should hear Jansie's step and her message to me. This she sang, I think it was because the mind will not readily accept deafness so fully that it will test it with brazen speech, not when it knows what could happen should his eyes narrow and his voice be found of a sudden; you would have to be beyond instinct to speak plainly about a deaf man when he is near. So she sang in a high voice, 'You must come to watch, Trijn, the food is come' – but no words once she made it to the clearing for they said he could read meaning in the movement of a mouth and perhaps he could do this with sung words too; we did not know.

I left my tree and darted in plain sight (should he have turned his head) to a pair of sisters grown close together. Where they forked at about the height of my breast a feathery crop of growth gave a screen through which I could watch, my skirts tucked between my knees to narrow them. Jansie was crossing the clearing to where he crouched on a low stool, a knife and whittling branch in his hands. She had untied her chemise strings; the neck of it lay loose on one shoulder. Her feet, smeared with dust, yet picked in a delicate way across the ground and she turned her head and shrugged her chemise lower. But habit had made no friend of her; instead of settling into her play act she had daily grown more stiff with it. I studied him for signs that he suspected her, beyond the animal wariness he all ways showed, but saw only calculation as she moved to him and set the bread on the grass and offered sight of her bosom. The plan was to intoxicate him with her so he would follow her away from the hut, though thus far Doof Hendrik was planted on his stool with dense resolve to follow no one.

Now my airless fear was laid over with a prickle of fright as I watched her lose a battle within herself – so near to her babe (for so she thought), she could not keep a calculating head but was drawn bodily to the building. At first I took it, and implored that he took it, as a cruder sort of offering: she leaned her back against the hut wall, tilting her head and spreading her hands at her sides as though to draw warmth from the wall or warm it with her body. But she took her eyes off him and in an instant he uncoiled from his crouch and knocked her down with his fist to her head. She crumpled to the ground, against the wall. Doof Hendrik stood over her as if unsure how to go on. He leaned one hand on the wall and jerked his foot into her skirts, kicking them back to show her privities, his free hand burrowing in his breeches. She was gripped with fear, I could see, but yet stirred her legs to hold his gaze. Her right hand was flattened against the wall, her face turned to it, as if feeling and listening for and some how comforting the babe while her body held the jailor's eyes.

Jansie was concluding a bargain by which she would gain not a thing and lose much, not least her babe, for if she returned here after rape was done to her even Doof Hendrik in his brute mind would know it was not for him that she came. My mind stood numb as he bent over her – it was finished – an attack was as bad for our subterfuge as the visitation that would follow ...

Then my better mind acted and I threw back my head and let a wild scream use my throat and chest and voice, pressing the sound louder and higher even as Doof Hendrik, oblivious over his oblivious victim, unlaced his breeches flap. I drew breath and screamed again, even so hearing a commotion from the avenue and stopped of a sudden, my hand over my mouth, lest I spoil the semblance of who had made the cry.

The clearing darkened with men bent low to attack as they came. In my own flying tangle of branches and fleet steps I skirted the thronging space behind a screen of trees and was at the door to the white maze and through it. There I stopped short and in that pause the wall shook with a body thrown against it from the other side; in my breast the thump repeated in wild rhythms. I could see no more than a half dozen steps ahead to where the wall curved; soon the thrashing without was muffled, then faded to faint sounds of men crying out.

The passage way was cool underfoot and the air chill with the chalky smell of lime wash. Small windows set above head height at intervals wore muslin screens; these softened the light and seemed to round the edges where the wall met floor or ceiling. The light was weak, the colour of clean cow gut, but this changed as the curve tightened and by it I knew I had entered the second circle, one passage way away from the outer world. Now the windows were paler shapes in the fabric of the walls and the air had a blue tint. I heard my breathing and small sounds of fear that escaped my jaw. Courage guttered in me but turning around, turning my back on whatever lay ahead, was as horrible as broaching it; I crept on with limbs locked like a doll's, one foot, the other foot, and thereupon my breath stopped all together as a sudden curtain wrapped me round.

I blundered, ridiculous, in the cloth and fought it aside, making no cry but with panic loud in my throat. This was the heart of it. A rough circle, white above and below and on the walls, wide enough for a cot in the curve of the near wall and the rest taken up by a cradle in pale wood and in it a pale babe laying quite still and regarding me with dark unsurprise.

Then a stirring from the bed beside me and a bleary head where yellow strands parted and watery blue eyes swam in confusion, and the woman blew through her nose and made to pull herself out of the sheets but her attention was caught by a tumbling jar, and she snatched at it. I stepped backward and fled with a lurching, skipping step down the tight-curving passage until I slammed out of the door and never mind who should see, but they were all gone and I, too, through the grove and skirting the other way to come to the kitchen as one from the workshops, to find it deserted but for the tom. He yawned and closed his eyes to see me. I was seated at the table stitching a cap when they came to the kitchen. I had not used the time to think of an excuse for my absence from a scene that must have drawn all the estate; my mind was a locked room and I looked up calmly as they tumbled into the room a-jitter with voices and bright eyes. Jansie was not with them.

I should have been there: Doof Hendrik had forced Jansie, had almost taken her, had tried to force her with a knife at her throat; Melt and Caspar and two field men had held him down, fought him off, thrown him against a wall; he was cut down and dead from a knife, he lay senseless in the grove, he was in the lorldingshouse snarling under lock and key.

Melt favoured his right leg; it needed dressing for a cut above the knee and I took him aside to do this. I seated him and drew off water from the kettle and he rolled his breeches while I fetched honey and dry lavender from the larder. When I returned, Calcoen was in the room – the unthinkable thing – but I did not remark on this even to myself. If the sun should judder and switch course one could not mark something so small as Calcoen in the room. I ignored him and settled to wash Melt's wound. On the other side of the table Calcoen found his master's voice, rebuking us for the morning's doings and demanding an accounting of Caspar.

I bent over Melt's leg. He brought his head close to mine and said, 'I thought it was you when I heard the scream. I was sure it was you.'

I did not answer him. The cut was clear of dried blood and welling with fresh. It was deep and must be sewn. I stood to fetch a needle and the movement drew Calcoen's eye. He spoke on about low and animal passions but circled the table as he did, and his interest shifted to Melt. I watched him as he took in the cloth pink with water and blood. Still holding forth to the silent men and women, making less sense with each word, he carried a kerchief to his mouth and regarded Melt, then stooped and with his free hand touched a finger to the centre of the cut where it gaped in a leaf shape and moved the kerchief aside to sniff at this. Next his tongue darted out and touched lightly to the dot of blood. He held up his finger and turned it to the light. Melt did not move; he caught my eye with a look that shared something with how you would be if you were of a sudden the chief interest of a beast. His held-wide eyes said, Keep still. As for Calcoen, he looked again at the wound and made a thin sound – perhaps with the fellow feeling we may feel cut us at a wound, though I would have said then that it was a species of disgust that moved him.

In any event he had lost interest in the men and after a half aware look around him he returned to the body of the house. Melt let out his breath. I passed a needle and thread through the honey pot and set to closing the cut while he held fast to my shoulders against the extra pain I brought him. As I worked on it I saw over again that finger touching it, quickly, in its very centre.

In the small hours I had come to believe that it had been a goat I had heard that night on the attic steps with Jansie. No babe's cry could get out of that chalky shell. That the bleat of a nanny had led to the babe was a gift of chance and Jansie's keener hearing though she were half deaf. I would put no greater weight to it than that, though my thoughts returned to it, seeking a better reason.

Doof Hendrik was in shackles in the lordlingshouse (the least satisfying story was the actual one) and Jansie in a locked room by him to wait for the Fiscal. Calcoen had set his knecht to guard the outbuilding, and I knew that with our soft and pitted young knecht on duty at the maze hut entry was mine if I waited; in a few days he would be lax enough.

Of the woman I had encountered there I was less certain. Probability said she was the midwife – that and the smell of brandy in the inner room when I recalled Jansie had said this about the woman who took her baby from her – but what was her work now? To guard the babe? Why? That she had to do with Calcoen's studies I had no doubt, but what part of them? White walls, white floors, white animals, white nurse ... only a simple man would equate the colour found in birdlime with a person's state of being white – that is if you reckoned without the crazed magic where words took meanings beyond sense. They had described and defined the natural world, these men of science, and even (we heard a story from their homeland) conquered the air. Was the vogue now to experiment on ourselves – let me say rather, on those of us still lacking perfection, so children, so women, so any of us who were not male, adult, Homo Europeanus, being as we were most in need of the crucible work?

I shook off these thoughts and set myself after trapping to win time to think and some noisy plover birds to turn into calm pie when I had got them, with mace and wine. I found my frogs and set two traps and trailed the cords back to the werf wall where I settled in the grass to wait and there laid out my recollections in a row, thus:

The babe in the cradle had moved less than is the wont of an infant; its arms were not bound, yet did not wave in the breeze-tossed way a babe's arms will.

It was sweet smelling, there for clean, there for cared for.

The woman on the bed: her chemise was stained with milk: she was feeding the babe herself and probably drinking from the she ass and nanny. The small room in the maze hut was sweet, there for clean too – breast milk, babe, the woman's brandy, a good mixture to the nose at least; no tobacco nor hint of corruption. There. I had exhausted every sensation gathered in the less than quarter minute I was in the room. Now to deduce, thus:

Calcoen was spending effort to keep the babe alive and he had planned for this, but not for it to be raised as his own or as his grand child, whichever of he and Bastiaan was decided had fathered it. He was spending effort to keep the babe a secret from Madam, from its own mother, from all on Vogelzang but a thuggee slave and fuddled wet nurse. Was the shape of the hut an over elaborate design to keep the babe's cries from the estate? This seemed possible, but something about it yet troubled my mind. Alive, hidden, fed, raised in secret. Some whiff of science.

Not one but two frogs were being pecked to pulp by plovers, and I jerked the lines and one, two the baskets fell. None was there to see but two birds lolled in my apron as I came to the kitchen, their necks twisted and moreover an egg light in my hand. I had time ahead of me to plan, and a pie to prepare. When the household slept tonight I would take a dish of it to Jansie's window and reason with her about her babe.

We may think, when we consider the business of being a slave or owner of slaves, that it is a thing cut in stone – he is master, and thus; she is slave, and thus. But it is people that take the parts, not words on stone. As an example: on Vogelzang, Calcoen, master to the mistress, was owner with her of thirty souls. But when he had chided us in the kitchen that day his hands shook and he met no man nor woman's eye. He was Master; he was afraid. Not fifty slaves, not two hundred, will insure such a man of his right to his titles. An inward-turned loathing, a twisted conception of how it is to be among people, will tilt his outward actions and make him unable to effect a natural command over those below him in the room. Sensing he has no man's respect and no slave's, he insists the louder upon the respect built into his office and demands it the more strictly for being unable to command it. It is a sort of hysteria and Calcoen full in its sway, and not a human soul on the estate but knew it and even the hounds showed it with the shamed look of disappointment that a big dog will give an unsatisfactory man.

For another example: the knecht. When last he and I had any business he had touched my person and bought with his sly way my sure hatred. But now he had found manners from a new quarter; I learned this when Derde Susann bid me take a pitcher of ale to him at the hut in the grove where he now kept watch. I feared what he might do and kept a distance between us as I came to the clearing but he made no move by word or touch or even sneer, only watched me from sidelong eyes with his own wariness. I set down the ale and left, and no harm had come.

On the avenue, Melt was waiting and asked for my report on the knecht; he nodded when I gave it and said one word, 'Good,' and by this I knew that slave had mastered freeman and warned him off.

I took a pair of hens from the fattening hok next to the kitchen stairs and tossed them into the grove and a handful of corn after them, more than they saw in a week, and thereafter spent my afternoon in a pretence of trying to capture them while I kept watch on the maze hut and they made nests undisturbed by me. At first there was little to see. The knecht sat on Doof Hendrik's stool against the wall, looking about him, stretching his mouth and pulling back his shoulders to stay alert, but it must have been dull work with only the distant estate sounds for company and not a soul to shout an order to. I made no secret of being in the grove, made a loud 'Here, chick chick' and a regular sigh at the cunning fowl, and he made to oil his whip or scrape his tobacco pipe rather than look at me.

Calcoen came to the grove with a sack on his shoulder and ordered the knecht to the workshop until he should be called back. I shrank behind a tree but kept watch and saw him enter the hut. I waited until the afternoon was all but over, but he did not emerge and I left to visit Jansie and keep a pretence of work in the kitchen. It was late in the day when I chanced to be on the stairs and saw him return with an empty sack and putting something in the pocket of his coat. He barked the knecht's name as he passed the workshop and, when that one came from the slave kitchen, jerked his head towards the grove and watched his man hurry to his new post.

Another day when I was by, the knecht was roused by having the door over his shoulder open of a sudden and out came a pale pair of arms and a bucket at the end of them and flung the contents in an arc. Next, an untidy head looked around the corner of the door. Who was the more surprised? Who knows what Calcoen had told the knecht when he set him to guard the hut but it must not have included the intelligence that this woman lived within. In their startled way the two even nodded good day to one another before she tucked back away. I could sense her on the other side of the wall; he looked about himself as if wanting some one to tell of this.

For the rest of that afternoon the knecht fussed with the maze hut, pressing his ear to the wall, walking its perimeter, slowing at the forbidden door as if this would cause it to fly open again.

18

A 16-WHEELER BARRELLING DOWN THE GREAT NORTH ROAD
with a cargo of retreaded tyres roars across the plain, the hard, re-
flective sides of the horse a moving light in the dark landscape of
round boulders and candelabra trees pointing starwards. The driver
flinches as he feels his wheels fling into the night some very young
or very old animal, something without the wit to get out of the
way. As the pantechnicon passes the butchery whose stoep light behind the flyscreens is the first human sign for miles, the truck slows
slightly and the driver shifts down. The brakes hiss and the engine
whines as the gears engage and in the long grass of the verge a slim
jackrabbit freezes in her tracks. The creature stays perfectly still, un-
blinking, for some moments, until the thudding of her own heart
is louder than the fading rumble of the truck.

The noise wakes Chief Henry Kobe in his bed in the men's ward
of Mannamead Mission Hospital. Orie Badineaux tucked him into
bed hours ago with pills she watched him drink. They were designed
to put him to sleep and keep him there until morning; she had not
reckoned on her patient being woken at such a difficult time, when
the pain in his gut forbids further sleep and there are hours of night
to come.

He pretends to be willing himself, chief-like, to lie still and ignore
his body until either dawn or sleep arrives, but soon finds this not
worth the effort and instead pushes back the sheet covering his
wasting legs and eases himself out of bed. His movements are ex-
quisitely slow but still he stands too fast. He holds on to the bed

frame until the singing darkness clears and he can make out the ward floor well enough to shuffle into his slippers and out of the room.

This early in the morning, before the birds wake, the air holds pockets of warm and cooler air, and a dusty scent of wild sage. He savours these as he moves towards the two steps dropping from the veranda to the driveway, hearing his own short exhalations as though they come from someone else. The pain in his gut is still there, but, as with the pockets of air, he seems to move in and out of awareness of it. The chief shakes off his slippers and steps, careful as a spider, down the steps and gains the soft dust of the driveway. Without thinking at all about where he is headed, enjoying the mechanics of each step in his hip sockets, in the tendons behind his knees, he sets off down the driveway, in the direction of the Great North Road that disturbed his sleep. A peristalsis of pain and ease, pain and ease, carries him gradually to the road and there he decides, takes a full breath and sets course for Bandolier, where he was born.

The room shudders. Vergilius hears the smack of flesh hitting metal but, half asleep, cannot name it. Frank is on his feet in the trailer's main room, grabbing his trousers, slapping on a flashlight, illuminating Xavier at the door, her righteous spite.

'You you you YOU YOU YOU!' Shocking without her headdress, short hair bristling with curl papers screwed tight, white scalp showing between them, spittle snapping like an electrical short circuit, she shoulders Frank aside and plucks Vergilius from the bedchamber of the Airstream, lunges for her and slaps at her thighs and breasts and stomach. Frank pins Xavier's arms from behind long enough for Vergilius to fight her way into the robe of her habit.

Clothed, bareheaded, Vergilius stands before Frank and tries to make herself heard above Xavier's triumphant you YOU! She has to weave her head to meet his eyes as Xavier bobs and cranes to beat upon Vergilius with her accusation. They find one another but there is, at last, nothing sayable between Xavier's greedy panting. Then Xavier breaks free and seizes Vergilius's wrist, wrenching her through the trailer, into the night – or morning, thinks Vergilius, for isn't it pale enough to see two Badineaux behind the blinds of their trailer, and Ogden Buffmire in his robe, pyjamas just so, slippers even, watching at the door of his trailer, his hand covering his mouth? Beyond the trailers, Mannamead's veranda is lit with a scattering of lanterns, and dark shapes are moving there.

On the other side of the Great North Road, the waning stars light the homestead at Bandolier. The farmer had given garden space to a wisteria some years before; it is in its full-bodied prime, holding up a corner of the veranda and, each spring, filling it with flowers. Now, at the start of the dry season, the mother plant is mounting its attempt on the rest of the farm. A warm wind is blowing about this plain at the foot of the mountains and has set the plant's seed pods cracking open with small reports, much like paper crumpled against one's ear. Shone likes the optimistic sound of the wisteria ejecting its flat brown seeds the size and shape of a trouser button. In the morning, he thinks, I'll have one of Daniel's daughters gather them for propagation and I'll offer the seedlings to the sisters at Mannamead.

Having been startled awake by the plant's urges and then embarrassed to find the mastiffs that sleep in the bedroom regarding him with blank expectation as he sits upright in bed, Shone is slow to react to a new sound from beyond the garden, but not so the dogs. They set up a sustained low growl and the younger is a split second from letting fly with his roaring bark when Shone tells him to shut up. He eases out of bed and limps to the window in his bare feet. By his side the dogs set up a thin whine, their wet eyes asking permission to investigate.

Something is out there, beyond the fence that runs higher than a man's height around the homestead. The garden itself is all shadow and patches of pale lawn that seem to shift as he stares. He holds himself still, waiting for whatever it might be, but nothing shows itself. A jackal calls from the far end of the home camp that lies between the house and the railway line, and he pulls back from the window. At last he feels foolish about standing in the middle of the darkened bedroom and makes his way back to bed. The mastiffs will not settle; they continue their tjank and whine but he dozes again as the night air cools before dawn and the crackling of the seed pods falters and stops.

Before morning comes, Mariah Kobe walks stiffly from her room at the back of the milking shed, her long apron picking up the early light. She carries an enamel bowl of mieliepap pot scrapings for the dogs and a jug of fresh milk for the farmer's tea. In her apron pocket is a key to the padlock on the homestead gate.

From a dozen steps away she sees a foreign shape against the fence. In a few more steps she sees it is a man, his hands curled at his chest, his legs folded against his body. On the other side of the fence, inside the garden, the dogs sniff and nudge him but they are more interested in her and the food than in the stranger and that is how, in the same moment that Mrs Kobe recognises the man as her brother, she knows that he is not alive.

She drops the jug and the basin, runs to him. Her howl hurtles Shone into the garden where he sees her cradling the body of the chief. Then another pietà: Frank's truck pulls up alongside Mrs Kobe. On the seat: Vergilius, with Jacob's body across her lap.

The women open farmhouse bedrooms, rooms that have not been used for years, one to receive the body of the chief, one for Jacob. Frank and Shone hover as Mrs Kobe and Vergilius tend to the boy's body, then fetch water and cloths and prepare to wash the chief's.

They send Frank to Mannamead Mission to fetch the great wife and he returns with her and the induna, followed by the Badineaux in their truck. The chief's man squats in the backyard, smoking and looking into the distance; the women set about their work. In the afternoon, undertakers from the location near the town bring a casket with golden plaques and handles and forty minutes later they half-wheel, half-carry it out of the house. The Tribal Authority car arrives to take the great wife and induna to their kraal with the news that, in the idiom of a royal death, the pool has dried up and the crocodile has departed. The chief's ancestors lie in a grave on holy land near where he died, on Bandolier, but it is the law now that this chief will be buried in anonymous new ground behind a fence in the Native Reserve, and he is taken away.

Mrs Kobe stays behind and is standing at Jacob's bedside, adjusting a blanket, when Vergilius brings the farmer into the room. The boy is awake but turns his head to the wall as they enter. Shone takes inventory of what is broken on Jacob's body, what is whole: one eye swollen shut, one untouched. Both hands and one arm show sickening signs that, within the swollen skin, bones have broken or shifted. Missing teeth, revealed by the teeth still in his mouth; lips cut. Ribs or a rib cracked, judging by the way he flinches at his own movements. Fuck you! Fuck you for doing this to our boy! The farmer feels the shout inside his head; it is directed at Jacob, or his attackers.

Frank knocks, holds out a bundle of clothes, a shirt, shoes. Vergilius must have sent him to Gupta's. He sets another parcel on a chair by the door; later, without ceremony, Vergilius will move it to a room made ready for her. She still wears the habit of the Immaculates for the rest of that day.

The first to arrive are the Buffmires, Mr and Mrs, dressed formally, he in a jacket, she in a pastel frock. They have come, it is apparent, on a mission to pull their fellow American away from the Communist-Catholic-Native scandal.

'Inappropriate' is a serviceable word, and given weight by the way Mrs Buffmire signals with a tilt of the head and Mr Buffmire invites Shone out of his own front room and on to the veranda to use it.

At last they leave.

Mrs Kobe finds him on the veranda and brings a tray bearing a tea pot, a cup, a milk jug under its beaded net. She sets it on the table and Shone looks up, almost meeting her eyes. Their shared knowledge of the boy in the back room is between them, a small inventory of memories, but it is not in them to speak of this.

Somehow that night supper is eaten, Jacob is drugged to sleep. Vergilius leaves his side and finds a bed, and Shone paces on the veranda, the dogs' claws clicking beside him as he navigates the outline of his house, suddenly so full of other people, and finally takes the handle of the door and goes inside.

19

LE VOIR CALLED ME TO THE BACK ROOM. BOOKS AND belongings leaned upon an open trunk on the floor. Young mistress stood at her bed and did not turn her head at my entrance. On her table the wig stand reflected back in the looking glass, hair framing a blank face.

Poor Le Voir. He wanted to speak of her but even had she been gone from the room he was so bothered as to know not where to enter the subject. After our months at Vogelzang he had to show for his labours a journal setting down Old Haarlem's habits and a fine hair piece for a client who despised it. Other than that he had an awareness that the spectrum of passions he would feel was wider than he had imagined – awareness he may have foregone to have back the easy sceptic's tools that had carried him through his days before we came here.

Their acquaintance had been formed and was growing outside of convention. Some times that is the let but here it was a hindrance; every advance of regard from him or her was blocked by the business of her needing help to hide her disfigurement and him being the one to supply it. Le Voir had never credited Madam's guess that it was a sluttish contagion that caused her daughter to lose her hair, but the theory itself was another corruption between them and she conscious of this too.

But it was not about that aspect of the young mistress that he had called me to speak – nothing so natural as that. I am older, as I write this, than Le Voir was that day, and now that he is the younger I may pardon him. But not then.

First he invited me to sit. His hands turned from chin to waist coat until he seemed to recollect what he had seen men do and held them one in the other behind his back. He clamped his lips and cleared his throat. His eyes moved to her and back to me but would not meet mine. He addressed, comical to relate, my knees.

'There is a matter I am bound to discuss. By duty and, ah, convention. No, that's not right. By conviction.'

I thought he was trying to make me laugh and I smiled up into his face to encourage him. My smile gave him the resolve he had sought and, flushing in the face, he found the words.

'Do not laugh! Serious trouble has found you, Katrijn. You are accused of theft, of the theft of' – and his voice stuck in his throat, then he resumed – 'of an item from this room.'

He put all this effort into his address, but she for whom it was performed had moved to the window and was directing her attention to the court yard out side. It flashed to my mind that this was a test she had set him, whether he knew it or not. In accusing me he had met it; the rest was of less interest to her.

A blush of shame heated my face as though I had taken whatever it was but my protest died on my lips before the greater hurt that he could suspect me. He made some more sounds about 'trust' and 'envy' and my mouth curled in an ugly gape and I began to weep, despairing at myself for so doing, and at that he made to approach, his kerchief ready in his hand but she turned from the window at this, tense as a cobra snake to see him weaken.

'I did not do this. And I do not …' but I could not finish, I could not say, I do not love you any more, for such words were not spoken between us.

'You were admitted to a position of trust in this room and you have, ah, abused it. There is some matter also of ribbons and such

215

gone missing,' and he gestured towards the table. 'But that is perhaps not what we need to discuss now. The young mistress will be generous with you – she offers you the chance to simply return what you have taken if you wish to keep our affection.'

By this offer she sentenced me to a limbo of no before and no after, no punishment but a purgatory of suspicion, for we two alone knew there was nothing to return, and she alone was believed when she said there was. I was suddenly so weary as to fall to sleep where I sat and would protest no more for the denial made me sound, even to myself, guilty. I was dismissed to the kitchen and noticed as I was perhaps not intended to that upon my entry there Derde Susann picked up her keys where they lay on the table and slipped them in her apron. Meerem stared at me from under her brows.

I thought that for how ever many days they still had together he would have to prove his regard by choosing her again and again over all things he loved, to atone for how they had met. But philosophy was not topmost in my mind that day. Indeed, these thoughts of recollection are not yet all together calm these several years since I knew the pain of losing Le Voir's regard – or rather his loyalty, for he could not truly have believed I stole, surely?

I was dulled so by it that I could not run to the grove and play the heedless game with the hens. I tried once but the knecht sensed my clumsiness and in it something he did not trust and chased me from the place. I bought Jansie her food at her locked room but could not keep my mind on comforting her. The babe, I confess it, lay only at the edge of my mind, barely real to me, and I counted it a help that she were kept in such a manner that I need not trouble to address the problem of her until I must. All day I smelled tears, cold, salty, cavelike. I tried to harden my mind against all people, told myself I had a goal of being alone, of shedding people to come to this perfect and dry state of solitariness.

Then the New Year was come and Derde Susann put us to pounding cinnamon and crushing nuts for the special baking. She liked to make a pie and what was New Year's but an excess of these; it seemed the table was never without a paste manufactory at one end and at the other chopping and beating and crushing of meat and fruit and spices. At least in the kitchen I had the bustle of Derde Susann and Meerem to resist.

Young mistress joined us one morning for the fine cakes. Unlike most of what we produced in the kitchen, if you discount Le Voir's fanciful receipts, the fine cakes' measures and means were precise and it was the practice on the estate for the young mistress to stand at the head of the table and call the amounts; as a child new to her letters she had spelled out the half fourth barrel of flour and set a woman to pounding it fine while at her instruction another drew off a set measure of yeast and added that to a mingel of cream and so on. Even Meerem was lively on fine cakes day.

Today young mistress took her place at the head of the table where were laid out pounded sugar, rose water and a knob of seasoned ambergris among the common stuff. She took the receipt from her sleeve but though she cleared her throat and tried, she went no further than 'take twelve eggs ... eight without the white ...' She stopped and looked us over as we stood at our stations about the table, at Derde Susann's watching eyes, Meerem's urging childish look, and asked: 'What of Jansie?'

Derde Susann exchanged a glance with me and opened her mouth to answer but young mistress put her finger and thumb to her brow and said, 'Of course. That day with Doof Hendrik,' and looked about her again. We shuffled where we stood and Derde Susann said, as though to encourage a child who has forgotten its recitation, 'A half loot mace? Tempered with sugar, three-quarter pound?'

But young mistress only sighed and handed the paper to her,

saying in a weary way: 'You know it by heart. And one of you reads, in any event. You have less need of me now.'

She untied her apron ribbons and left the kitchen. Derde Susann handed the paper to me and with a throat aching for being held so stiff I began to read and the women to follow, though Meerem regarded me throughout as if I were telling lies at the kitchen table.

Amid endless thoughts of the babe I resumed my long walks, now amid the haze of high summer. I traced the course of the stream and visited the far fields of cattle. In the vine yard the plants grew thick to carry their packed berries and all was neat and fine and at one remove from life. When I had exhausted the low-lying farm land I took myself up the mountain, along the familiar track with its view of the white handful of buildings and avenue. I had in mind to visit Jansie's cave. I wanted things to be made real again before the confusion and pain of that night were so dispersed by regularity and the small politics of the farm until they were nothing but an inconvenient thought. Jansie and her babe were out of sight – the babe dead, for all the estate knew, and the sometime mother locked in a room in the lordlingshouse – as though the place itself had shrugged them off. The babe's confinement and Jansie's lay so heavily that I could not contemplate stepping out of the worn path of my days to try to effect change to either state.

I turned up the face of the mountain. It was hard going in the heat of the day and I stopped by one of the hundreds of streams that made their way down the slope, although most dried up in this season. This one was a smear of wetness on a rock where I bent my head to suck at it. When I was done I sat dully there in the sun. The natural sounds began again around me now that I was stopped, then came another sound – a shriek that might have been a bird but was not, not quite. It was from among a stand of sugar bushes to the side and somewhat lower down. For a long moment I was too weary to do anything about it – tired in my mind, which shut down to any new alarum – but the stronger drive all ways is to know, and at last that picked me up and sent me to it.

The shriek may have been almost like that of a bird but the thrashing of the bushes promised a large beast was there and I held my breath for fear it was our leopard. I circled at a small distance and lowered myself behind a rock, a stone ready in my hand. At this elevation my view improved and so at once I made out it was a pair of humans in the bushes – it was the knecht and the wet nurse from the maze hut. 'They have found each other,' was the thought that came to me.

There was idiot delight on his face as he hefted her this way and that to spare their bodies the rocky ground. She clutched hands full of his flesh. Soon their faces took on a particular concentration and hers a look near to fury as she strained with him; I left my hiding place and circled back to the path and downwards to the homestead, feeling in my mind the sting of some small hope: the knecht had done for us what we could not achieve with Doof Hendrik, for now the babe must be unguarded within and without the hut! This sudden opening scattered my thoughts – do I go to the babe and take her now? To Jansie?

For the first time I faced the problem of what we would do if we had the babe. What Jansie would do. We could try to join the maroon at Hang Klip, though it sat more like a fable with me than real life. We had whispered about it but we were neither of us bonded slaves, her case being less clear than mine it is true, but none the less should we declare ourselves maroon, we would declare ourselves slaves on the run, and it was a slippery thing, the chute from here to there.

I decided on the avenue that I would leave the timing of the matter to the Fiscal who surely must be on his rounds now that New

Year was over, and I would in the mean while prepare us. Where ever it would end, there would be a journey before. That much I could hold in my head as an object. If a journey, then food to carry and I became a forager about the house and farm, a thief as I had been labelled. Food was easy – the cellar bulged with dried fruit and a pot of larded meat would not be missed; the workshop boys sometimes helped themselves to this and Derde Susann conspired in that (though let a cup of flour be begged from the kitchen proper and she would chase them down the stairs).

Food was got with ease but I had in mind that we would need a knife also and a hatchet – to defend us, to make shelter, my planning was not nice to that degree, but we needed a hatchet, on that I was decided. On the estate there was one place for these both. The key to Calcoen's room opened a door upon valuables such as tea and sugar; it also opened to another key, kept some place in the room, to another room, the twin of the young mistress's on the other side of the hall. In the back room on this side was kept all weaponry – the guns, gunpowder, shot and moulds and ingots and flints and any dangerous farm tools – mattocks, on the more nervous estates, could take up half such a room but on Vogelzang these bided in the lordlingshouse, though yet under lock there too; here fear of us drew the line at axes and hatchets. These sat in the back room of the master's study until handed to a sober slave and then under the eye of the knecht, when it was time to cut sugar bush for firewood or hack at the remains of a tree to get what we could for the kitchen range and Madam's eternal foot stove. Knives were another matter; each male slave had one about him although this was supposed to be forbid them. I knew that there were a few knives in the back room where none bothered to go so far as to requisition them to keep the play act alive that we had them not.

Calcoen alone had the key to the inner room, and kept it in his study. Even were he to go abroad again I knew the household would not now send me to fetch sugar. I would have to get his key myself and though I feared to do this the greater part of me relished being brought to the point. Like a savage dashing to smack his reed on the flank of a bull to prove his courage, I was fired to do it. That none should know of my daring bothered me not; I lived in a cold place within myself where none could visit and I needed no other body near by to prove my frigid will. To have so loved that isolation was an evil, I own it, but I will not deny that it bore my weight when I needed.

I became a spy in the homestead where I might have been happier to ignore all those within. I volunteered to take the tray where ever coffee was to be fetched and the next morning I stopped Meerem and said I would carry the night pots from the three rooms. I had set my chin against who so ever I should find in the back bed room but it was empty of them. Madam was yet abed in hers and started to see me there and made as if to deny me her stinking pot but I pretended I did not see her and took it up. I emptied those of mother and daughter and left the pots in the sun while I returned for the father's. He was not there! My eyes darted across the table top for a hiding place for the key, when a step in the hall beyond sent me to the cot from beneath which I fetched the pot, and I was swift gone from there.

He hardly moved for the rest of the day and locked the room when he did but the next morning I was on the kitchen stairs when I saw Apollo make for the front of the house; I flew around the opposite side and from behind one of the great flower pots kept watch through the window as he entered the front. Calcoen came out to speak with him and then re-entered his study alone, fumbled beneath his bed – I must have been right by it – and stood and crossed to unlock the inner door.

Then it was a matter of waiting and watching and within three days I had my hatchet and knife and fresh sight of his papers too.

These were notations on only one person, an Eva, measured on successive dates as though she were expected to somehow change (and this she did not, being awarded many similar numbers in her rows and a 11 under the little moon sign for entry upon entry). It looked a foolish business and I forgot it until I was half way back to the kitchen, the knife and hatchet in my chemise, when I went sick with the thought: he was measuring the babe! It was a filthy thing that he should include a babe in his science but I was sure of it: she was kept in the hut in order that he could chart her, and it was for this the babe must lie still as a loaf in a white room!

And then I knew for certain: if it hurt her not, just as much as if it hurt her, these measurings as of a calf or corn stalk must be stopped. The human babe must be removed from this, whatever it was. There was hurt in it, I knew. If not pain now, then pain in store.

20

VERGILIUS WAKES AFTER DAYBREAK TO THE CLIPPED SHH-SHH, shh-shh of a twig broom on bare earth outside the bedroom window. The even strokes are overlaid by a song, a list of sorrows between sounds of exertion. She holds her breath to hear, then exhales and a prayer flows into her mind by rote or by grace. She sits up and puts a hand on the parcel of clothes by her bed, taps the brown paper with her fingers, then rises and shrugs her Immaculate robe over the shift she slept in. Where the veil is she cannot say.

Jacob is dozing amid signs that his grandmother has already tended to him this morning. The farmhouse is quiet. Vergilius returns to her bedroom and collects the parcel, goes in search of a bathroom. She finds it, but the deep bath is in use, lined with packets taped in rows on the inner sides of the tub. Mrs Kobe comes upon her there:

'Tcha, the bath is this way. That one is for the master's funny things.'

She leads the way into the garden, following a path that disappears around the side of the house and into a thicket of bougainvillea the size of a hut. It is hollow inside and open to the sky. The outer walls formed by the plant, or colony of plants, are dark green, flecked with hot-pink papery bracts; the inner are a bare tangle of branches. At this time of day the light reaches the room they form via layers of leaves. Clay garden pots attached to the branches with wire hold brown orchids, a clutch of giant moths suspended on their stalks. A floor of turquoise painted cement, a broad ledge of the same, and suspended above them a shower head the size of a dinner plate. Mrs Kobe sets down the towels she has carried in and gestures towards a dented bowl, roughly perforated; it holds a loofah and a shampoo bottle.

Vergilius takes her time. She inhales sandalwood soap, the farmer's scent. She squeezes the loofah and enjoys the way it retakes its shape. She takes off her sandals, then her robe, and sits on the ledge beneath a corona of flowers and listens to bees draining them. She hears a bucket set down on a hard floor, some way off, and a calf moaning in the cattle shed; insect sounds and the silvery drip from the showerhead and her own breathing. She stands and turns the taps, then steps away from the spray and, in one movement, lifts the shift over her head and casts it away. Naked for the first time in years, at least a dozen. Naked under the sky for the first time ever. Cool air on her skin, then steam breaking against her stomach and nipples. She holds her arms away from her sides and steps into the water, into a feast of lather and scrubbing, heat and open sky, steam curling like Sanskrit around her shoulders, until the sun reaches over the wall of branches and lights the spray.

She closes the taps and folds herself in one of Mrs Kobe's towels and wraps another around her head, the feel of it taking her back to her mother's bath-time embrace. Vergilius sits on the ledge and sets to work on the string of the package from Gupta's, from which there emerge a dress of blue and white stripes; one of green flowers on a white ground; a tangle of stiffened cloth and hooks that she knows is a brassiere; cotton underpants. Each dress is finished with buttons, a zip, a hook and eye, and hemmed with even stitches. She shakes them out and something falls from the folds – a sprig of lemon verbena. Vergilius sits in stillness, crushing the leaves, before climbing into the strengthless bits of cloth. She tries to ignore the new clothes as she made herself disregard the habit when she first wore it years ago; this stuff is so light she feels she might tear it just by breathing too deeply and lifting her ribs.

21

SOON THE FISCAL WAS COME. THEY HAD SENT WORD AHEAD and for a day we roasted this and baked that. Allaman drew off wine and brought brandy and in the kitchen we delved for a crock of brandied grapes put to soaking after a fat summer and picked and polished a dish of fruit to set on the table. Madam was tied into her dark silks. The younger wore the hair.

Le Voir and Calcoen met the Fiscal at the front steps and flanked him into the house. They had no choice but to put me to wait on them and thereby I saw him. I was ready for an ordinary some body, perhaps fat, but the Fiscal that year was a well set man with a curled head of grey hair and sharp eyes that forced a distance between him and you. They brought him first to the front room and the young mistress kept a hand on her mother's shoulder where she sat by her cage of birds. I brought coffee and a dish of the brandied fruits, and the talk among them moved along. I stood back and looked them over, the family, and wondered at how moderate – how prosperous and sane – they could appear and in how fine a balance this illusion stood, teetering here between solid land owner and crazed cataloguer of the world, there between a girl easy of nature until she was cruel and on her way to following her mother, and her mother, her face puffed with wine, half way to madness but nodding now and casting her eyes to her lap in modesty. Only Le Voir among them could have withstood a closer eye for he was as he seemed to be, and for this moment released from his thrall and sharing fresh conversation with a proper man. I smiled to see him and drew a narrowed look from young mistress for it.

The actual work of the Fiscal was done in an hour of him seated on our finest chair under an oak, hearing Melt, Caspar and others describe the fight. There followed dull-eyed Jansie, who said she had gone to the hut to take Doof Hendrik a meal and denied any plan to lie with him. Doof Hendrik was called, but what was the use? Even though he glared at the Fiscal to find his meaning from the movement of that one's lips, he could not answer but with a sound like a sea lion barking and a lurch against his chained hands as he tried to tell his side, and by each served only to underline his bad name.

He would be flogged four pipes for his attack on her and for having a knife and cutting Melt there with, the Fiscal ruled. They took him direct to the tree whose branches formed a natural frame for it and at that he understood their meaning, and there they stripped him and the knecht filled the first pipe and lit it and made a play of a casual drawing as though he were smoking after his dinner. The house party stayed for less than four strokes before moving to the front room and waiting upon their dinner.

Jansie was released and in the kitchen, held to Derde Susann's bosom, both shaking; Meerem and I could not stay there but carried out the dishes and set them amid the table. They were seated with Master and Mistress at either end and Melt in clean clothes was stood there behind Madam to attend her.

Their minds were split between the food before them and the sounds without, for though he did not speak, Doof Hendrik yet screamed.

At last Calcoen set down his knife and said, 'Why did the good Lord make them thus?'

It was not intended for an answer but Le Voir answered any way:

'Rather more of man's governance and enslavement have made them thus, perhaps.'

The 'perhaps' was for the Fiscal's sake, the thinnest gilding. And they were in the cock pit. Cataloguer battled geognost over lamb cutlet pie. Lettuce was passed steaming in its bowl while Calcoen led with horse and degenerate ass, man and degenerate dark man. They were fierce with having an audience for they could say worse and not be clouted on the ear for it; they contained themselves in hot politeness, and they could count points, having in the room, actually, a judge.

Calcoen affected a casual laugh: 'Ah, you are so busy reinventing La Société you have not even half a mind for science. Now I, I am a farmer and a scientist and about inventing all of the day. I do not need the rights of man to set my course; I can see it before me: a potato without corruption is an incontestable thing; you need only look at it. It is the same with a human – fair of skin, straight of limb – a glossy coat, eh, my child?' – this to the young mistress – 'these are proof of pure bred health. That is the human perfection we will reach.' (Did Le Voir think to reach across the fruit bowl and snatch the proof of human perfection from her head? I did, where I stood behind his chair.)

Calcoen was in flight, riding a warm wind of his own production and straining his voice to be heard above the punishment sounds.

'I will give your man this: he said an interesting thing about the dark skinned, how many generations would have to pass for some dark men to turn white were they moved as a tribe to his country and kept to themselves there.'

'A more northerly country than his was proposed,' said Le Voir, and the Fiscal's lips formed the word 'northerly' with him.

'North, north,' said Calcoen and passed a hand across his face to brush the irritation there. 'But the pointed end of the matter is this: he trusts a climate to change a species' characteristics—'

'Because he seeks to prove that the reason some have darker skin is to do with the sun, not the distance they were born from the Caucus mountains, or the wickedness of Noah's son—'

'You will allow me to complete my thought, I think? The point is this: there may be no need to wait those generations for their skin to grow fair and in the mean time forget why we started in the first place.'

He held up a hand to command their full regard, and waited out a long cry from without.

'Gentlemen, in *one generation* it can be done. This can be proved. Do not ask me now, but mark these words.'

Melt had shadowed Madam's movements as she reached for a cup of wine or grabbed at the food on her plate, but now she pushed his hand away and spoke, fixing her husband with a dead eye:

'She is not your child.' For a cold moment I thought she spoke of the babe, but then saw it was his talk moments ago of her own daughter's healthy head that Madam addressed.

The Fiscal was equal to the silence that followed this. He sipped wine, wiped his mouth on his sleeve and leaned back with the easy use of time that is the privilege of a man who knows he will be listened to when at last he speaks, as he now did.

'I find myself in sympathy with another countryman of yours' – this to Le Voir – 'who said that if a stranger to Earth should study us as we study animals or insects, he would find the human world identical to the physical and organic spheres in principle but' – and now he addressed himself to his host – 'when one of us undertakes such a study of his own human species, I believe the exact words were, "the observer is part of the society he observes, and truth can only be judged, imprisoned or bribed".'

If I had been allowed to speak I would have thanked him; as matters stood, I gave him the best of the preserves and tamped his pipe with especial care for my own satisfaction.

Madam spoke, and again with a terrible eye on Calcoen:

'Is it you that would cheat God, Gottlieb? God will not be cheated, not by you.'

At which she nodded to the Fiscal and signed to Melt to help her stand and they left the dining place for her stove in the front room. But what is a wife's scorn when a man serves science?

The Fiscal must have had a light heart to be leaving the estate when, the next morning, his carriage drove down the avenue and he quit Vogelzang.

I visited the babe the next afternoon, timed after Calcoen had been and gone from the hut and when the knecht had taken his one up the mountain. As before, sounds from without weakened the deeper I went into the hut. I was full of fear that I should be discovered but that is an all together different species from the dread I had felt the previous time I walked this strange corridor; now I knew that it had an end and I was pulled forward by the thought of seeing the babe where before I had felt myself repulsed by imaginings. My breathing, though I yet heard it loud in the echoing shell, was easier.

Soon I gained the inner room and crossed at once to the cradle there. The babe was not asleep but lay so very still; only her eyes moved; her head did not lean or shift with them. I moved smoothly to spare her a fright and made high sweet sounds, these softer than I would address to a healthy babe; I had already pinned her in my thoughts as not quite that. Now to fold back the blankets from her body. As I removed the last of these one of her hands made to explore the cool air, but she could not lift it; her arm only flopped one way to the side of the cradle and then the other to her rounded belly. She was not under fed, but weak withal; her nether limbs lay as the blanket had pressed them, bowed between her hips and the inward turned soles of her feet.

I had lifted several new siblings by then; the business of supporting loose necks and heavy heads was a natural thing with me and I slid a cupped hand to hold her head and get the other arm under her. She was warm as a babe is warm and smelled sweet and made no cry, but still I came close to dropping her that first time. As a sleeping kitten is to a lively one, as, I almost fear to say, a dead plover is, she was so loose about her limbs as to all but fall out of my arms. The thing of it was, though, that she was lively, to go by her eyes and expression. She made those low watery sounds babies make; she was a bright infant in a damaged body was my verdict. I had been prepared for tender feelings; now here was pity too.

We moved to the bed and I sat and folded the blankets to hold her limbs close to her body and rocked my own body. She was a pretty babe, with her mother's eyes and little chin, her lashes just so, just so her nose and mouth. I looked about more thoroughly at the room I had glimpsed before, though the yield was still thin: round and white and dim. One cradle rocking to a stand-still. One cot, on which we sat, a slattern's nest with, yes, a jug I pulled from under me and a cask by my foot. A pot for her doings, which put me in mind of the babe's and I looked for evidence of washing but saw only a store of small linens in piles leaning this way and that. Did Calcoen remove the soiled cloths when he came? Likely yes. Did he wash them himself? I could not paint it in my imagination.

A basket held cheese rinds and a heel of bread and another jug, of milk leavings thickened but not yet sour. An easy inventory. I turned my thoughts again to the babe. She was regarding me with a grave auditing look, half of recognition and half discovery. I took a hand in mine but felt no answering clutch so presented a finger to her fist and she tried to take hold of it but her fingers only lay on mine. I could not make it out, for she was so bright of eye and other wise sound.

I began to think of bringing her to her cradle when the matter was settled for me with the curtain parting. Having startled himself with startling me, the tom proceeded to sniff the room and I to realise that I had left an open door to announce to all what was amiss at the hut, and I wrapped her and placed her in the cradle, bent to kiss her forehead and, snatching the cat, was down the corridor into Calcoen's wrath for all I knew – but it was only a door swinging in the wind that met us and that swiftly made aright and we two innocent in the sun. The suddenness of my taking leave left no time to feel its wrench; that visited as I climbed the stairs to the kitchen and I held a hand to my stomach against it.

Jansie was within and Meerem and the cook, and as I joined them at the table she was telling her tale of attack and imprisonment for not the first time going by the scant attention Derde Susann gave her, though Meerem was again alarmed at the knife and the prison room and so forth.

I had spent time at the window to her room impressing upon her that she must bury deep any thought of her babe being alive for by that means she would keep it so until we could get ourselves to a better place, and I thought as I listened to her that she had heeded me for she was mystified as to why she should be attacked of a sudden (why out of the ordinary why when there were ten men to every woman and the kitchen locked from within each night against them). I thought, too, that she, its mother, would not be able to leave alone the weak babe I had seen that day; should she go into the spiral house with me, her proper love for her babe would cost us our chance of saving it.

I waited until she and Meerem left the room with arms full of linens then quizzed Derde Susann on what could cause a babe to be weak in its grip and limbs, all of this wrapped in pretend gossip from another estate about a babe there. It was a wasted invention; she knew of no such affliction on a babe, had not heard of such; knew rather of its opposite with limbs thrashing in fever; it sounded serious to her and the babe not long to live; I should reach down the rusk crock and fetch a bowl of curds from the larder. Dinner.

Le Voir had more help to give with his surgeon's work informing it: he had seen such among the poor of his home town, among children born in autumn or early winter, he thought it had to do with the sun on limbs as they formed, like the heat of a hen's brooding body, like sunlight to any growing thing.

Our conversation about this was a cool matter. He essayed a formal manner, an air of sorrow as the nobler side of reproof. I would unbend no more, having approached and sought his counsel on the matter of weak infants, which he surely took for a ruse but having given it did not terminate the encounter and we stood in a golden and blue morning over the giant shell whose owner was asleep or bored with us. Le Voir had cut a runner from a rose bush and he beat the grass with it. His coat buckled at his shoulders and his cheek flesh was looser on his face. I studied Old Haarlem's shell, the colours of honey where the dew had touched it, dull higher up after months of summer.

At the exact moment Le Voir and I sighed, but even that brought no more than a shallow smile to his face and no remark on it. There was much I wanted to say to him, of matters recent and undated – how I had never taken the young mistress's things and that he surely knew this; how I needed him, wanted him to set my resolve amid the changes I faced, to back me when I refused to occupy the narrow band of ways open to me – tell me I need not be the creature described in my natal chart by the old man my mother paid for the diagram; that nor need I be this Asiaticus creature Calcoen set me down as. I would not be those things, or not those things alone. I needed Le Voir to help me hone my resolve and my argument – to support me, yes, but provide new channels also. My throat hurt with the things I did not say to him about matters recent and not. Chief of these was the babe.

But if he was my teacher he was also only a man of two and thirty and adrift in a strange land. How my need must have pressed on him! Perhaps there were more reasons than one for his having conspired with her attempt to cut me down.

There was something Le Voir wanted to say to me that morning; not an apology – I wait for it yet. No, it was, when it came at last, the news that the young mistress had in the convention of the women of the estate made him an offer of marriage.

M'sieur Le Voir ... He used to speak of three principal constraints on freedom and how man had created them all to keep himself tame and unfree. Of them, he had escaped God, and Nation had ejected him as a wigmaker to doomed royalty, but Family will all ways find you, like shot in a roasted guinea fowl waits to crack your tooth: here it was in the person of jealous she with her vine yards and house who yet wanted more. He never saw her straight or at least did not at that moment, for he softened after giving his news and began to speak of a place for me in the household upon his marriage.

I heard him without sounding the rude snort that was in me at this, and at last left him there and turned back to the house with a hollow sensation, a dull, hollow sensation that I would rather cut my own arm's flesh than feel over again.

Home sharpened in my inner eye as my only object now. Home and the babe; I could not see how I would hide Jansie but I knew I had to get her and her babe away from this place and myself too. That I must do this without Le Voir's protection meant I was hobbled, but resolve won out over desolation if only by the thickness of a hair.

If I had stopped for an instant to question whether this was in my power or was my obligation to carry out I might not have tried –

but I did not entertain the thought. Jansie impelled me there with her trust that I would and could take care of this; when I told her the barest intent of my plan – that we must quit the place – she smiled and nodded as if at a known fact.

There was one other I had to tell, and not merely because I would need his aid; I found him in the workshop, running a curious small plane along the edge of a table top. He stopped his work to show the shaped blade that left its positive half in an incurved and out-stepped pattern the length of the wood. He was working on the table's narrow end and tense with the tool's wanting to nick and jud-der on the cross grain.

I broached the subject, with no mention of the babe but as a general query on the matter of escape. The maroon life that was some times the means of fine boasts among us on the estate – 'I should say that I will not be here much longer; I am away to join them at Hang Klip at the next moon' and the like – was not a subject on which any in bondage had timid views, but Melt yet surprised me with his and their direction.

'You will not ever find me taking that path,' was his opening.

'But freedom—'

'Freedom? To sleep in a cave and cook snakes on a fire! And choose thieving as a trade?'

I trimmed for another tack: 'If I were to need to go to the town without sanction from the estate—'

'Why should you travel illegally?' He looked me full in the face and I could only mumble about it being a matter of cargo I would take with – 'Not stolen!' I blurted, for he must have heard the ill reports about me.

But 'I would not guess stolen, Trijn,' was the calm rejoinder.

He turned back to his work and for a while the sound of steel against wood was our conversation. Then he straightened his back and ran his thumb along the table edge.

'This will be complete today. It and its companion' – he indicated a half made matching piece – 'will travel to town before the month is out. Should we meet a traveller on the road she might ride with us. And her cargo also.'

I must suppose he knew that I would not return when I had left the estate, but he did not ask why again and only bent to his work.

Calcoen said: 'When you came here I had in mind that you were after milking the old Bessie. But it was the heifer you had your eye on.'

Silence, then a sigh and Le Voir's voice: 'I had no thought of any pursuit of that kind. It was a job of work to come to, to hire our craft. And to see the country.'

A snort. I thought, he has taught himself to lie well.

The sucking of pipes. Another sigh, from a narrower chest.

'Well.' More sucking sounds. 'Well, I am master of the estate yet, I suppose. While she lives and does not divorce me, and of a portion of it when she is gone insane or dead of the drink. I need a few months more, a year, then I shall have a claim to rather more than this groom's share of some outpost farm. Science is happening here under your nose. I am breaking ground, the first to tread this path.'

'A better potato digger?' Le Voir's voice was cool; it choked Calcoen, to go by the splutters and coughing.

They were on the side of the homestead on a bench beyond the court yard, near to the entrance to the root cellar. From there I could hear them where they sat in the last light of the day. Le Voir had come to tell Calcoen that he was to be his son in law, which had not held that one's interest for more than a moment before he was back at his one passion.

'You cannot see it. Not all can see it. But this place is a laboratory where in we will settle the principles of humanity.'

Calcoen then echoed a thing I had heard from Le Voir, who in our days in town would sit on the steps of the shop, pipe and wine to hand, and say that here 'Musselman and red coat and black fellow and yellow man and sailor and clerk's wife and whore will all pass by if you but sit a while'. Calcoen's version was thus: 'Black savage and white man and all manner between are here for us to study, as fine a set of specimens as could be ordered from an expedition's duplicates. You have to be blind not to see that there will come no better chance to settle the differences, to mark out the specifications of each type and work on perfecting the lesser.'

'I wonder,' Le Voir began in that dangerous voice that plucked the flaw in an argument and laid it out as on silk, 'whether one would be so eager to advance this science if it were blue eyes and pink in the cheek that were the mark of that lesser type? If they should send a raiding party to your capital to carry off the unwanted ones, the ones pushed to the front of the crowd … we might stop to consider where we might be in a crowd like that, among our fellows, if it were fair people who stood in bondage.

'Your science seems to me to lack the first requirement: it is not disinterested. There is something behind these studies. A lack.'

'O let us hear the philosopher on the iniquities of our system! You will have the running of the estate soon enough; let us see you grow any thing here by your labour or hired labour. There is none to hire! Here is land for the taking and sun shining all the year and water but who will work it if not them? What draws you here is what drew me, Le Voir, the chance to expand your knowledge, to study and experiment. I know it. And this you will not do if there is not another to clean the vines and tend the beeves.

'Come to me in a year and we will see how many of these wretches are yet here and how they are even increased, and how many manumitted by your hand.'

A pipe knocked on the end of a bench. A man spat but whether in answer to Calcoen's argument or to underline it I could not tell.

Calcoen again, sounding like a one who had aged between that outburst and these words: 'And you will tell yourself that you have taken them into your home as a part of your family; you will count their bread and new breeches a sign of your patronage and feel irritation for the play acting of their thanks. You will know yourself to be a benign force in their lives, a rescuer who has brought to civilisation these wretched of the earth, and you will bestow your smiles on them. I look after them, they look after me, you will say to any who ask. That is what you will do.'

He was walking away from Le Voir as he spoke his last words.

'You will fear them and need them in equal measure. And they you.'

I could not credit it that Le Voir should turn from his freedom to join himself to this life but I had not estimated the spell under which he had fallen. He was a man caught in a passion, for the girl, yes, but it was most of all this place that held him and gave him that ease you will see in a person who is where he believes he ought to be.

He barely spoke of this to me – I expect he spoke of it to no one but his journals – yet it could be seen in him when, for an instance, he returned to the homestead at dusk, striding down the mountain side, craning his head around arms full of enormous blooms.

'Look,' he says in my memory, tipping them onto the table in the kitchen. 'Manly flowers! Tree flowers made from vellum and velvet!'

Derde Susann at once seizes the flowers and upends them over a bowl to get the nectar that gives the name to the sugar bush. Some hold enough to pour out in a dribble, others but drops for he has carried them careless of this. What so ever she can get she boils to make a piney linctus, the best I will ever taste. As for Le Voir, he spends hours cutting the blooms apart and taking pains with drawing the results with so fine a hand you would think a lady held the pen. Some of them are the size and shape of a dainty cup, others almost the dimensions of a child's head, and all growing on the slope behind the estate. He dries some in the lordlingshouse and they crackle apart in his hands and give up their seeds.

'Roses are soft things, no substance there. That is part of their appeal, that they will not last the week; they tell us the world is so dear but we cannot stay. We die, the rose dies. There are flowers that last a day only and those not even cut for a bouquet but on their mother plants. They bud and bloom and start on their fruit in the space of a day as if a hand had moved across a carpet and changed the colour, then smoothed the other way and the change is gone. Bloomed and gone between two sunsets. But here are these masculine heads with petals like the scales of armour and a dome furred like an animal, even with a trim of fur – who ever saw such on a flower?'

There is no understanding the passion that grips some one when the frenzy of collecting meets a hunger waked by discovery – when they meet in one, his passion carries him to a place I do not follow. That was Le Voir and the flowers he found upon coming to the estate, and beside his passion the likes of its master and mistress were mere irritations, ephemeral creatures that would soon pass.

And yet, before he stood to follow Calcoen into the house, he sighed like a man with a long journey ahead of him.

22

'YOU'RE BLEEDING AGAIN,' SAYS JACOB.

This time it is from cracked lips but could as likely be from torn cuticles, or a patch of inflamed skin on her elbow where she scratched for a minute with ragged fingernails. Jacob can see out of both eyes. His arm is in plaster from near his elbow to beyond his wrist, his ribs are bound with bandages, his knuckles less bruised and wearing a dusting of scabs. Vergilius probes her lip with her tongue, then sucks her bottom lip into her mouth to hide it as she bends to fondle the ears of one of the dogs.

'Don't change the subject.'

The two of them are seated on the grass at the edge of the garden, where the ground drops away to open veld. To their right, in the distance, the farm track runs between its rows of grey-green sisals. Ahead is a field of grasses where rust-coloured cattle gather at a salt lick and in the shade of thorn trees. A railway line at the edge of this pasture marks the boundary of the farm, the tracks raised on a berm of gravel and fool's gold. The northbound train from Johannesburg is due to pass within minutes; they have taken to waiting together to watch it go by, or stop if there is something for or from Bandolier. The subject Jacob stands accused of changing is related to the train – will he go? What will he do? He needs to be told, if only to have something to argue against.

Vergilius is trying to persuade him that staying is not an option. Not after the beating that left him lying broken at the door of Mannamead Mission on Republic Day night.

He blamed her for that, through hot tears: 'There isn't any law! A person can't trust any of you!' The first words Jacob spoke, through his broken mouth, were to his pillow but directed, the adults in the room knew, at Vergilius. His neck strained with anger but his strength failed and he closed his eyes (his eye), holding back tears. Shone, Mrs Kobe, Vergilius, said nothing. Then Vergilius moved closer to the bed and spoke his name. He opened his eyes, and this time his face contorted, and the tears came.

'You told me! You said they worked by the law but there's no law! They didn't even fight properly. They didn't warn me, they just jumped me, all of them, and he was with them, that new policeman, he was making them hit me.'

He spoke as though she could explain this to him. That was over a week ago. Now she says to him: 'If you stay, you could end up at the bottom of a donga. You must go to the city, or you must leave the country altogether.'

'How is there "must"? And how come *I* must go?'

'It won't be for long. This can't go on for much longer. Whatever they say. But, for now, you are living in a place where you can't even run a better time than a white boy without getting beaten half to death for it. So don't expect the law to help you, Jacob. I was wrong about that. I'm sorry. I was wrong.'

He is sixteen years old. Perhaps he can feel over again the pain of being cast out of Bandolier as a small boy, as though it has stayed keen all this time. But if he leaves again, this time he will not be taken by the hand and walked down the track like a boy setting off on an outing with his grandmother.

'And you? What will you do? I don't think you can stay here … not on the farm. You can't believe the stuff they are saying, about—'

'About me and him?' She bends her head towards the farmhouse. 'They should be grateful about the way this is all going,' she says. 'I'm not laying charges against the people who did this to you; I'm not causing a big stink at Mannamead about leaving; I'm not push-ing off with some American in his caravan – don't look so surprised, boyo, I know that's what they're saying about that too.' She plucks a stem of grass. 'I think I am being very polite, on the whole.'

Had Vergilius ever come across someone like herself she may have changed, or tried to. But she has never run into the sort of forthrightness that is her manner, has not been on the receiving end of so blunt an instrument. Any girlishness she carried with her from girlhood was scoured off during Formation at the mother house; if that was when she acquired the direct gaze and assump-tion of her own rightness, well, she has kept both since she shucked off the habit and started to wear the cotton dresses.

At odd moments in the day she withdraws from the others on Bandolier. Sitting at Jacob's bedside, on the veranda with a cup of tea, walking in the garden, taking up the history of the wigmaker's apprentice that Shone has pressed on her, she has the air of someone, engaged in a long argument, who has listened to the other side and is now – as the silences descend – ready with her rebuttal, or to advance a new line.

She falls silent now, but breaks off her thoughts to watch the train as it steams around the bend and whistles in greeting to them or as a warning to something on the tracks.

'A virgin birth on Bandolier!'

The awkward shout is Shone's, coming from his study window as Vergilius passes the side of the house. She frowns, waiting for a punchline, but in his careless and lifted mood he just laughs.

'Come into my parlour and all will be revealed.'

On a table in the corner of the study a glass battery case the size of a child's torso holds a layer of sand with a scattering of seeds and a branch of fresh acacia leaning against a drier one. Vergilius joins him as he brings his face close to the case, and obeys his hand, which warns her to keep still. He says, hardly moving his mouth: 'This case has been kept closed for months now, except when I give her a fresh branch – she doesn't need anything else; she's a vegetarian. She was. So, no other Phasmatodea out or in ... no male visitors, yes? Just me, but even so ...'

With his shoulder he nudges Vergilius until she can see past an outcrop of leaves to the green branch, where, as they watch, a slight thickening separates itself from the main bark and moves with a diffident, preoccupied motion towards the leaves that will complete its illusion. It has green-blonde legs the thickness of a hair on either side of a thread-thick abdomen.

'Hatched this morning. I didn't see it happen but there's the egg case – that split seed pod next to the dry leaf? Made straight for the branch, had a meal. A virgin birth ... but the virgin herself died in the effort of laying all those eggs.'

Shone risks a gesture and points to the dried branch where there is another acacia-branch stick insect, ten times the size of the young one and apparently not so much frozen in the face of a predator as dead. He proves this by beating gently on the glass with the side of his fist; the mother's lifeless body trembles with each blow; the infant, being alive, is struck quite still.

'It's gone into shock. A kind of a fit. Not playing dead or anything. Nothing cunning about it, Skaife says.'

He nudges her away from the case. A movement in a corner of the ceiling catches her eye; it is a mantid as big as her thumb. She keeps it in the periphery of her vision as the farmer tells her how a scarcity of males among this type of stick insect means the females have evolved to do without them, to be capable of parthenogenesis; she listens to him and nods, and raises her eyes to the ceiling in time to see the mantid tilt its head and quiz a moth before snatching it to its death. As she watches the insects the farmer looks at her face and his features move to echo the expression on hers.

'There's something else I'd like to show you,' he says. 'But it's not ready yet. Soon.'

He is laying out his treasure for her, piece by piece. Late that afternoon he unhooks the string of blue glass beads from the nail they share with the bandolier, whistles up the dogs and piles them, Vergilius and Jacob into the jeep. Jacob braces himself in the passenger seat; Vergilius and the mastiffs share the rear well. She stands, holding on to the cross bar, her legs set wide to roll with the jeep. Letting the torque carry them and the wheels find the easiest path in deference to Jacob's healing bones, Shone heads for a particular koppie, down a track clogged with drifts of sand. Young thorn trees have claimed the centre strip and they screech on the undercarriage as the jeep rattles and whines over them.

In the shadow of a boulder at the foot of the koppie Shone draws the jeep off the track and into a circle. The dogs leap to the ground, the scent of a leopard in their heads, and snuffle and swallow around the base of the boulder. Shone leads the way between it and the next, even larger, mound of biscuit-coloured rock, up a narrow path forced by the roots of a strangler fig. The trunk of the tree, which winds like a broad balustrade along the path, is worn smooth with the passage of other animals that use the track. In one place a roughened spot is smeared with blood and a tuft of hair as coarse as a beard.

They reach a clearing, raised about a man's height from the level where the jeep stands. It is shaded by the fig; to the side a cave is formed by a flat roof of rock resting at a slant on several boulders. It is broad and shallow and lit by a shaft of light towards the back where the slab ends. Caught in the sunlight on the sandy floor, a miniature stand of new growth – bush spinach, perhaps – glows like a monstrance. Vergilius and Jacob are drawn into the cave, walking, then crouching, then on hands and knees.

'That's what happened with me.' Shone stands outside the cave, smiling at them. 'The same light – I couldn't resist. And that's when

I saw the first one, lying on the sand, like it was put there for some-one to find.' He tosses the string of beads to Jacob, who catches it and lets it trickle through his hands to the sand. No one says a word; even the dogs slow their panting and, with a wet 'clop' apiece, grow quiet. A burial site? A trysting place? A safe nursery? Each of them imagines a context for the little woman — they assume a woman, a physically small woman — whose beads the farmer dug up. Vergilius rests the fingers of one hand on the beads, half-buried again in the sand.

Shone takes a seat on a rock, his walking stick beside him. They keep so still that wasps fly straight towards their heads, veering only when they feel the heat of their skin. A babbler troupe arrives in the branches of the fig to chide and bicker. The shadows are long when the dogs at last sigh and nudge the farmer and it is evening by the time they return to the house, where Mrs Kobe has fired up the generator and switched on the lights.

Days pass, so crammed with change and colour that Shone almost loses his rhythm of time, but here it is nonetheless: the standing appointment at the Slagterskop police station where Captain Val-entine Teichert is waiting to hear his confession.

It is just as well there is something that compels him to leave the farm; they are becoming too much a world of their own, as though the vacuum of his isolation is pulling Jacob and Vergilius towards him, however unsure he is that this is what he wants. He wants to have them always at Bandolier with him; he insists upon the return of his formless days when he padded from study to workshop to cattle kraal and never spoke a word of English and heard only the murmurs of Mrs Kobe to tell him a meal was on the table, or Daniel's careful sentences about seed, or diesel for the tractor. He wants to inhale, to taste, this woman who fills his ears and eyes; he itches to peel her away from his skin. He cannot be certain she has rejoined the world, although every day she walks more freely, less like a nun held close in upon herself. Shone watches this, unable to say whether he wants it or not. If she ceases being a nun she might remove even that thread that links her to him; a real woman would not look past his failings. So goes his conversation with himself as he circles around this chance of having a family.

He returns from Slagterskop with news: more Americans have arrived, and the lot of them will leave in a matter of days. He watches Vergilius's face as he tells her this; she looks at Jacob. She is asking the boy, Will you be in that caravan?

Shone does not tell his household about the meeting with Teichert, what was said and unsaid. When supper is done with and Vergilius and Jacob asleep or reading in their rooms and Mrs Kobe has left the homestead for the compound, he moves to the veranda and recalls the afternoon.

Teichert and he both carried something to use against the other in the office off the charge room at the police station. Shone's turned out to be the weaker; all he held was fresh knowledge of Jacob's beating and a murder on a twisting farm road near a donga late one night, when boys were blooded and Teichert tested the limits of his power and found, with a lurch of imbalance, that there barely was a limit at all. Shone laid these things out and in the office that afternoon he learned what the Native people in the district did not question: the servants of the law are above the law. With the statutes at his disposal Teichert could make a formal case that would condone or even endorse the killing of the New Brighton man, or he could dispense with the paperwork and go altogether unchallenged. The assault on Jacob was beneath mention.

This Teichert told the English-speaking farmer across the desk from him. Told him with a sneer, of course, but he also used the steady tones of a magistrate explaining a point of legislation – instructive, immitigable.

Then Teichert showed his hand, leading, as Shone had, with the law. He said he had applied to Pretoria to have the far Northern Transvaal's only listed Communist banned. Did Shone realise the implications of this? Teichert did not wait for an answer. The implications – he enjoyed the word, implic-haitians – are that the banned person, that will be you, Francis James Shone, shall be confined to this magisterial district; that he shall report every week to this police station; that he shall meet with no more than one other person at any time and then only those on a list of approved persons and approved persons, you must know, may include house servants but shall not include jumped-up kaffir boys with ideas about being white and shall not include Americans stupid about how things work in the Republic of South Africa and shall not, as he said, include more than one person at a time, so if you go into a shop and there is someone there already you have to wait outside until there is only the shopkeeper left and then you can enter, and the same in any other place …

Because this is not likely, he said, you most probably must make other arrangements. You will not speak in public. The usual restrictions on what you write will apply, and he waved a hand to denote the obviousness of this.

But we are not uncivilised people, Mr Shone: it says here that if persons attending a gathering are drawn from the *family* group, this will not fall within the prohibition. He looked the farmer in the eye and smiled a smile so corrosive it should have dissolved his teeth.

Teichert expected to hear from Pretoria within the week. He expected his recommendation would be approved.

The farmer has mentioned none of this to his new household; it seems impossible that he should be imprisoned in his home because decades ago he signed on with a league of clever, bickering men and women and since then has, what, remained seditiously English? Has made unguarded remarks about something so casual and yet so crucial as the race words his neighbours used? He is sure they could know nothing about the letters and money exchanged at Bandolier, the odd night's shelter given in the compound to the young men who pass this way. He hardly knows of these things himself, his subversive activity amounting to little more than leaving cash in the usual place and turning a blind eye at the usual time, and the vague feeling that, although he may not have engineered it, somewhere on Bandolier the right thing is being done.

It has been like this for years, at little cost to himself, as keenly amateur a revolutionary as he is an entomologist. Now, at no cost to the state, he is to be imprisoned. His crimen laesae majestatis amounts to disagreeing. The banning is as unjust as death. He will not look for how or whether he brought it on himself. The wages of dissent are not this. Not among civilised men. But the wages of dissent are not this only until it is decided that they are. It seems impossible, but it is only too possible in the new South Africa.

He thinks, as he touches the head of one of his dogs, as the moths beat against the light, that he will not tell his household about this. He feels, when the anger washes back, ashamed, as if he has done something wrong and been found out, and this is his punishment.

23

BELOVED, YOU ASKED TO KNOW THIS STORY; PERHAPS AFTER reading so far you know enough. I could end this in a word or two and spare you a closer look at what came next, after the flogging, after the Fiscal left; I do not want to tell it. But I watch my ink mark this page and I do not see my way to leaving you without the proof …

Enough of vague snatches and lost history. This at least, this contained and unknown life, shall be set down as it came.

So:

Doof Hendrik's flogging took him to the edge of life and there he clung. He lay on a straw mattress in a corner of the workshop, his back weeping and bubbling 'til he was recollected and Meerem sent to wash him and lay on bandages. She let us know when she came in low spirits to the kitchen that he had lain still the whole while she tended his back, his head turned towards her, his eyes blinking through the spokes of a wagon wheel by his body. When she looked back from the door his eyes were closed and she guessed that he slept. Derde Susann sent her back with a bowl of something and a loaf. The Lord knows how he had survived until then; perhaps some boy had been sent by the men with water.

In a week's time he was seen about the place and fetched his own food and there was much talk in the kitchen of what would – what ought to – become of him and many warnings to Jansie to keep away from where she might find him. There was no question of settling the matter by selling him; the harvest would come again and he a worthy strong worker who you could lead to the end of a vine row and he would not lift his head until he had reached the other end, though none wanted to partner him for his knife darted to cut the bunches with no regard for hands on the other side. No, even if a price could be got for a wild deaf slave, Vogelzang had use for him, and Jansie was bound to encounter him and hurry to the kitchen at least once a day breathing hard with the news that she had done so, though only at a distance as far as I could tell.

But he did not go after her in person. It was known that she doted on the tom, and this stood proxy when Doof Hendrik took his revenge. At first he flung what so ever was to hand when he crossed paths with the animal but after it dodged each stone and clod, the slave entered a chase that we ridiculed though it yet had a twitch of danger in it: clapping his hands in the tom's face, snatching at it, hurting it if he could. The effect was to make our easy kitchen cat a dark-browed lurker that started at the merest new thing and snatched at food where before he had taken it as his due.

Doof Hendrik duly was thus revenged on Jansie, who had poured into the pet her passions about her babe and now was half crazed at seeing the tom turn wild, or worse than wild, for it yet part trusted her, crying from dark corners but not daring to come to her lap. Within days it was full feral – but still trapped with us. As though it were tied there, it did not leave the homestead, however it bared its teeth against the scent of people, and with at any corner the threat of Doof Hendrik to kick at its head.

In consequence, this:

I carried the morning coffee into the main house in time to hear a clamour from the front room; the tom had upset the cage of the two love birds and was crouched before it where it lay on its side, tail lashing at the creatures flapping within. Madam was on the cat in two movements and it dangling from her fist by its neck skin. She flung it from the front door, beyond the veranda.

That afternoon it returned and this time it had its teeth in one of them before Madam could act. The tom fled into Madam's room and there was trapped. Jansie entered the front room to hear the cat scream as Madam beat it, and she ran to shield it with her body and so drew from Madam a year's worth of bated fury.

I know not for how long it had been going by the time Meerem and I ran in to Madam's room. This is what I saw and this told the Fiscal when he came again to Vogelzang: in the near corner Madam leaned one hand on the wall and one on a stick to keep her balance as she swung her booted foot into the mass tucked there. She panted with the effort but kept a rhythm and counted each kick on her exhaled breath – two and twenty … three and twenty …

Meerem and I took her by the arms and pulled at her but she was heavy with anger and we could barely move her; then Le Voir ran in from the front room and thrust his shoulder at her and tipped her away but it did no good. Our girl was gone where she was, in the corner. When we lifted her to carry her to the kitchen we found beneath her the unbreathing tom with blood come from its mouth and ears.

We laid her on the table. Le Voir came after us and said we were not to wash her head because it was proof of the crime. He spoke in a pinched voice and seemed not to catch breath, but Derde Susann just nudged him out of her way and set down a bowl of water and began to wash Jansie's feet. The disgrace to the estate was already in the shadows of the gable; it needed no blood left to crust over to prove it. We all felt it but he.

Next young mistress stood in the kitchen door way. She closed her eyes and drew a breath then could look at Jansie but could not move to cross to us nor find words. Le Voir caught her up and sent her ahead of him as he left for the inner house. Meerem and I joined Derde Susann at her work, wringing our cloths in water and wiping her to clear the blood and dust. We fetched pure grease and smoothed it on her skin until it gave back light.

Derde Susann worked at the poor head where it was bloodied on one side. A head is a heavy thing and difficult to break unless it is of wax and dropped, but Madam kept a knob stick by her bed and had used it upon Jansie's, and broken it.

We worked in silence with the click of the water and shuffle of our skirts as a back ground, and the sounds that we made to keep our tears in our heads and not let them fall on her. Then she was ready and the men came in and stood at the table or moved past it. They left but went no further than the bottom of the steps where they made a close group, shifting with stopping and starting, and wanting someone to fight.

In the house Madam keened over the bird on her lap; its mate panted in its cage. Calcoen was at the window in the front room, his fist to his mouth, looking down towards the gates as though expecting the Fiscal at that moment. Le Voir and the young mistress shared a bench and murmured to one another. I set down a tray; Derde Susann had sent me with it saying they would lock the doors within the hour and would need food. As I turned to leave them Calcoen called to me and bade me tell the knecht he was wanted. I would find him at the hut in the grove, he said, and I all but gaped that he should not know that I knew where the knecht would be.

Well before nightfall doors were locked front and back. Without, there was talk among those come more lately to the place of setting Vogelzang to the torch, but the talk of most ran to scaring themselves with speculation about what would befall Madam, that the estate and they must now be seized or sold, in that line of prediction. Derde Susann lit candles and closed the door on them and we sat with Jansie until one by one we slipped into sleep.

The disgrace was in the gables of Vogelzang; it was the gravest matter to murder a slave. But I cannot say I saw remorse in the days that came after, days filled with the sound of carriage wheels, low voices and voices raised – filled with these sounds, but I watched Madam for any sign of shame and I would say she did not feel it. Rather there was this: a whine for her own lot, and when she spoke to Derde Susann and Meerem and even to me it was to seek our love. The more our manner showed we had no inclination to comfort her, the more she sought it to the point that she twisted matters to force an illusion of our regard – saying, when I carried in her tray, something of this sort: 'O, you are looking after your own Mother who needs you.' In my mind I would answer, It is but coffee on a tray and that by the order of Derde Susann. I would rather have had her spite than this.

But I cannot give too much to the after math of the day Jansie died. I had left the estate in my mind and it remained only to use this new sorrow and this new indifference to carry me to a point that imagination and courage had not, and leave in fact. The day after the day that Jansie was killed the estate could be likened to a hen cage when the jackal is by, and there was no profit in attempting any plans on a day when you could not predict what would meet you at each corner. The day after that the Fiscal came and Madam was ordered confined as a mad creature for Jansie's killing, and then we could bury our yellow girl, then one more night passed and some sort of order returned and the men gathered tools and spent the day at the grind wheel or scouring vats, but I yet stayed – to gather my courage, I would say; to await a sign, my mother would have countered. On the fifth day I knew it as I rose; it could not be dodged.

I fetched my bundle of hatchet and such and added to it a loaf and bribed the boy at the pen for a crock of donkey milk and hid these near the road. There would be no question of taking leave of those I had lived among this year – not Le Voir, particularly none of the people in the house – but I could leave a sign for three and so tucked a red kerchief in Meerem's bedding and some ribbands beneath the pillow on Derde Susann's cot, and in the workshop left a green feather I hoped was from a sugar bird. The purpose and intrigue acted on my humour in the same way that the guitar boys produced a truer note when they tightened their strings: I was so sharp of mind that my senses told me when, in the still part of the afternoon, the knecht had coaxed his lady to a sugar bush – told it as though a boy had been sent to say so. And then I was in the cool shell and with the babe. I laid her cloths upon the bed and her upon them and swaddled her as I had seen my mother do 'til the infant was tight as a barley sack.

I drew from my apron a piece of indigo cloth and arranged it on her face to save eyes that had not yet seen sunlight, and I held her to my breast and covered both with my shawl and moved in a blind bolt past the buildings of Vogelzang, and together and unremarked we left that unsafe laboratory and set ourselves for the road home.

24

IN SLAGTERSKOP, FRANK WALKS FROM THE CAMPSITE, CROSSES the bare ground, crosses a road. He pushes past a man at the door to the café. There is a bustle – bottles of soft drink are being delivered – and the proprietress (the woman who had predicted servitude for Jacob all those years before, though Frank could not know that) is quite pink. In one hand she holds a sheaf of papers; she brings the back of the other against these with an arid Crack! Something to do with the number of crates of Hubbly Bubbly cola not according with the previous month's invoice.

On the counter, a small dog is shrilly outraged at the Native delivery boy being almost through the front door of the café. The woman grows pinker and turns her back on him, snapping: 'Ag man, I haven't got a photogenic memory!'

Frank concludes, turning the excellent phrase over in his mind, that his is of bareheaded Vergilius as the light from a hurricane lamp reflected off the shiny trailer side and lit her face. The first time he saw her without her veil. After she stopped by his trailer – and returned to the convent to be chastised in code by St Augustine's letter – Frank had remained sitting out under the deeper dark of the acacia and trailed through his mind the eddies and ripples from Vergilius's visit. He turned to his books, but after an hour or so gave up trying to figure out a manual on metalled roads and walked away from the mission, more to leave the human clutter than to escape the light that hid the stars; only the odd hurricane lamp still burned at that time of night.

He gained the Great North Road and walked along its centre line, his hands in his pockets, his gaze on the sky ahead of and above him, narrowing his eyes and playing with perspective to bring the stars within arm's length. In the non-light, the strip of sooty road seemed to be a chasm through the soft landscape, with the stars the chief reality.

He noticed a darker shape ahead, on the road, hunched, denser than a plant, something about it suggesting an animal. He slowed his pace. With no warning it flared to twice its size, as though it had sprung on to its hind legs, and for a moment terror seized his brain. He must have made a sound, because the creature spun around, and in the same instant Frank and Vergilius recognised one another. They stood quite still on the dark road in the warm night, then she beckoned to him and he moved again. She was standing over the body of a night jar. It had mottled feathers and a pretty face, with huge eyes and what seemed to be whiskers near its beak. It seemed perfect and whole, but was quite dead.

'They lie on the road at night for the warmth, and the trucks don't see them … I'm always finding them out here.'

Frank knelt by the bird and felt its body – limp, the warmth ebbing, it would have been alive even ten minutes before. He lifted it and its wings and heavy head moved loosely as he took a few steps into the verge and laid the dead bird in the grass. When he turned back to her, Vergilius had her back to him, her head to one side. She turned at his step and spoke:

'I have a place … I know another place where they like to go, off the main road. If you like, there is a special kind we may see … with long ribbons that trail off …'

Her hand fluttered about her opposite elbow, her arm showing a soft sheen where the sleeve fell back, and who knows but that was when her wanton heart gave the secret signal, and his heard it.

Now he lets the café door close with a pneumatic click and brings his list to the woman at the counter. He is packing up his trailer and truck, securing cans and spare tyres. He chafes to be gone. The ease of being a stranger – of being excused from being oneself, and spared the judgment of peers, the unexpected boons of travel that he has come to rely on, well, many of them have been missing since the caravan stopped at Mannamead. Jacob has judged him with the eyes of a son, Vergilius as a woman, and the point of his exoticism is to place him beyond judgment. As for the Africans of Africa, he has moved between them as between trees in fruit, useful trees, with only Jacob real to him. People whose every word ends in a vowel – as only baby words and Italian words have done in his life till now – you would expect vagueness from speakers of such a language. He wants the click and closure of words that end with consonants. Stay too long in a place, take a midnight swim with a woman, teach her boy the knuckle start on a track, laugh with them – barriers are breached. He needs to shake his head at these strange ways, throw up a screen of tolerance for the ways of these people between him and them.

'To Sister Vergilius!'

The caravaners have gathered at Bandolier for a farewell picnic that has the air of a coming-out party for Vergilius. Frank is on his way to being drunk. The Buffmires gulp as the etiquette of the toast evades them – how to congratulate a Roman Catholic nun on leaving the order? Whether to? She is seated on a blanket among the roots of a wild fig. She wears one of her Gupta dresses. Her neck and shoulders are gilded, her hair tousled, catching light from the setting sun. The Badineaux sisters treat the day like an important birthday – sixteenth, or twenty-first. Orie Badineaux asks her: 'You going to keep your name, honey? That's a man's name, isn't it? Almost Vergil, when you think about it. What were you called uh before?'

'I was Catherine. It will be strange to be her again.'

'And what are your plans, darlin'?'

As Pie asks the question to which the farmer longs to know the answer, he feels he is watching the world claim her. Her time in limbo after Mannamead, with him on the farm, is almost up. She must decide to go, or to stay.

Mr Buffmire finds his feet. He winks at her:

'Pretty girl like you, some man will come along with plans enough for both of you. Am I wrong, Mother?'

Mrs Buffmire, who has been nodding in agreement at his predictions for the young woman, shakes her head. She says: 'Soon enough you'll be welcoming a little stranger and looking after a home of your own. Your hands will be so full, you won't have time to think about plans.'

Catherine/Vergilius looks at the Buffmires in amazement. Watching her, Shone thinks the world has not quite won her yet. He steps into the group to hold her attention, attempt to hold it, one more time.

They feel like they are welcoming a new tribe member, with delicacy – how can they discuss sex or, worse, money, in mixed company? What is her strongest urge now that she has left the order? The picnic group answers this secretly for themselves. Does she crave money to buy pretty things? Is it sex she wants most (they all, even Mrs Buffmire, assume that impure thoughts are a strong contender)? Is she itching to be disobedient?

What she wants most is privacy – not to have her thoughts guessed at, her sins known, her faults policed. But where can she go, what can she do? The rest of the group sees the world before her as limitless, full of choices. The guidance they are trying to give her – on how to be like them – amounts to a safe way to inhabit such a world. The proper way to be. What they have arrived at by custom and inheritance and habit they expect her to adopt as a clear-eyed choice, though they might as well be asking her to decide on the right field in which to stand and chew the cud. Shone wonders, watching her hold herself still amid the restless gestures of the other women, how the world will change her. He does not expect her to be like him; his is not any kind of life to emulate. He would like to teach her, if that were possible, to be unlike him. If she stays at Bandolier, he will tend her like one of his improbable orchids, ease her through her first season. But of course this never-to-be-spoken offer to teach is just the acceptable face of a need to learn. He flinches at his longing, reminds himself that once Teichert hears back from Pretoria, Bandolier will be a prison.

Handsome men, florid and moustachioed in pressed khakis, strong teeth clenched on briar pipes, confident loins, the Badineaux women deferential but not quite, holding themselves separate through a veil of humour – this she sees as she watches the Americans and the farmer. They cannot know it, but she has already made her plans, made a deal, agreed to a last duty to death before she steps out into her own new life: she and Jacob decided it in the course of a walk from the homestead to the end of the sisal road. As they passed the spiked ranks that day he limped, but she told herself he walked more easily each day, and might even run again in a year or two. She hoped so but it had lost significance, whether he did or not. He was being handed on to a new school – after a night crossing into Southern Rhodesia, thence by Frank's truck to Addis, thence with Shone's money to Rome – one where running for its own sake might not matter. He would carry a letter of introduction in case, she said, he overtook the letter Mother Rose sent from Mannamead. She thought, He is so young, yet she was not much older when she left her parent's home and went to the convent, went to war. She is relying on the Jesuits' disdain for grubbing around for vocations to keep Jacob safe from any rash decision as he completes his education and makes his way in the world. Mariah Kobe, who packed him off to the nuns when he was a little boy, approved this new plan.

Talking it over, Jacob was animated for the first time since he and Prakash Gupta climbed Motor Car Koppie at dawn on Republic Wednesday and rearranged the painted rocks so that they no longer read '1961' but displayed instead his time for the 100-yard dash, a time that he knew would not be bettered that afternoon by the sons of the new citizens running on the track that he had helped to make and been locked out of. It was, of course, pepper flung in their eyes, in retaliation for which he had almost lost one of his.

As Jacob wondered aloud about Rome, a figure in the distance swayed over the cattle grid at the farm gate. Amos had taken the letter from behind the radiogram in his room behind the mission building and placed it, as planned, in his shoe, and made it as far as Bandolier. Now he greeted the boy and the sister that caused all the trouble and eased himself onto a rock by the roadside, removed his shoe and slid out the pages. He handed them to her and she read them. That was when, after days of auditing unlikely scenarios as they occurred to her amid a growing feeling of being adrift, she made her own decision about her immediate future.

Jacob crossed last night in accordance with arrangements he asked her not to enquire into, leaving her and his grandmother after crushing each in the embrace of a much younger child. It is almost her turn.

The picnic is breaking up. The Buffmires shake hands and are forgotten. The Badineaux have brought gifts: a pair of hand towels fit for a trousseau from Orie and a silvery hair slide from Pie. She flushes as the twins press these into her hands. Frank shares a few words about Jacob with the farmer, then faces her with an air of ceremony, but she just smiles into his face and shakes his hand.

Mrs Kobe sets a dish of spinach on the table and turns to the side-board to fetch the rest of the meal, then heads back to the kitchen, thinking about her grandson. The light above the dining table surges and settles into a greenish glow. In these last days Vergilius and Shone have told one another their stories; now they eat in silence. He notices how her skin gleams where it stretches over bone: at her wrist, jaw line, collarbone; how it holds a softer light where it swells into her lips, her rounded forearm, the upper edge of her breasts. She steals glances at his hands, their pleasant mottling, their heft and hair.

Cutlery sounds and swallowing, until at last the meal ends and he stands up and reaches for her. She gives him her hand, her cool, smooth skin sliding against his hand twice the size of hers.

'Come.'

He could be leading her to his bed, but it's the study door he stops at, then steps back and guides her into the room with a hand at the small of her back.

The windows are open, the curtains pulled wide. The room is lit only by moonlight. In front of the windows, a cage of fine mesh sits on a small table. The farmer takes hold of her elbows from behind and uses the length of his body to walk her past the edge of the faint light, to where darkness hides a padded bench. He lowers her to it and unfolds a blanket on her lap and legs, then leaves her for the other end of the room, where he fumbles at the desk.

He steps over to the cage with a glass collecting jar in his hands. He opens the cage door and takes off the jar lid, using his fingers to ease a large moth from jar to cage, then shuts her in again.

He sits down next to her and says, 'This is what I wanted you to see.'

He tucks the blanket in around both of their bodies, then leans even closer and says in her ear, 'That's Gonimbrasia belina in the cage, a female Saturniidae – an emperor moth. You probably know her better in her caterpillar stage. That lovely creature is what happens to a mopane worm if you don't eat her first.'

His breath tickles her ear and she shivers. He lifts the blanket to her shoulders and tucks the edge behind her.

'Watch,' he whispers.

There's little to see. The female, her tawny wings hard to make out in this light, is quite still in the far corner of the cage.

'Wait.'

She presses the side of her body into his warmth. He shifts in his seat, breathes out. Now she can make out the moth more clearly: her large eyes take up most of her face, the feathery antennae above them swivelling to sense the air. She seems to be waiting for something.

'You can't see it, but she is calling for a mate. Ah … here we go.'

A shadow at the window resolves into a large moth bumping into the room and up to the cage, where it alights on the mesh nearest the female, its abdomen pulsing against the wire.

The female turns her back to him and begins to tremble her wings. The male beats his.

Then another tiny thump, and he is joined on the mesh by one just like him. Then two more, then a stream of them, clustering against the mesh, trembling and pulsing, straining to reach the female.

The farmer's mouth brushes her hair.

'She called them, with a sort of scent, a sex pheromone, letting them know she is ready to mate. They've come from miles and miles away. They can't help themselves.'

Her body is both taut and warmly aswim.

The farmer moves apart from her.

'Who was first, can you remember? The chap in the corner?'

He eases himself from under the blanket and crosses to the cage. He reaches for the male moth that may have been first to scent the female, pinches its abdomen between thumb and forefinger and, opening the door with the other hand, inserts it into the cage.

'Now watch.'

He returns to the bench, his body tense.

In the cage, the male moth traces a wavering path to where the female is sitting, pulsing and shivering. Trembling, he steps onto her body as though she were a twig, and lowers his abdomen as she raises hers, and they connect. Their furred, joined bodies create a sense of privacy, of engaging in a secret matter.

And as though a switch had been thrown, the dozen male moths clinging to the mesh cease their agitated movement and peel off, in ones and twos, and head out into the night.

'The moment she mates, the others leave. Quite amazing,' the farmer says. 'I'll let these two out tomorrow morning.'

He is using his normal voice again, and she can feel her own body returning to normal too. The feeling that had been dense in her moments before is thinning. Its cool ebbing leaves her feeling faintly nauseated.

She stands, and he places his big hands on her shoulders and looks her full in the face.

'I wanted you to see that,' he says. 'To understand that it's a chemical thing. They come because it's her time. They can't help themselves. They lose interest fast.'

She understands the warning. She does not understand how much he wants her to read the promise of a haven in his warning.

But she never has heard any man above the demands of the course she sets herself. At dawn the next day when he goes to the study to release the moth lovers, Shone finds her note on the desk. She is gone, has taken with her some few small things, among them *A Wig-Maker at the Cape: The story of Katrijn van de Caab and the child Eva*. As he reads her note, she, alone on an empty Great North

Road, somewhat south of Slagterskop, is breaking the rules again. Her back is turned to the village, her arm extended towards the white line in the road, her thumb pointed skywards. Presently she takes a small towel from the bundle she carries, twists it into a tight doughnut the right size for the crown of her skull and places it and then the bundle on her head. Female and hitchhiking while balancing her load aloft, as though she imagined herself to be a strong African woman (a woman whose arm would be the circumference of this one's thigh) – on this road, in this place, with her paleness, her height and audacity, among the waxy green menorahs of the young naboom trees and the unlikely boulders of the plateau …

She continues along on the dust of the roadside, self-conscious about keeping the bundle steady without lifting her arms, conscious of the roll of her own hips, of how this ancient balancing act has calmed her arrhythmic, wide-flung stride to a regular pace where each step connects fully with the ground. She comes abreast of the butchery. The flame-haired women who live there round the corner of the building. One of them, a few steps ahead of her twin, stops short; her sister bumps gently against her and they stand bosom to shoulder, blank-faced at the sight of the woman in the man's khaki trousers and shirt, a bundle on her head. She lifts a hand in greeting, at which the sisters dip their orange heads and unsure smiles and turn away.

The odd passing car shifts into lower gear and slows but she is not looking for such a ruly ride with its assumptions and questions. She hopes that, in order not to attract the cars she does not want, she passes for male. After some minutes, though, she hears the wheeze of her target making heavy work of it on the far side of a hill. She pulls back her shoulders and flags down the pantechnicon, and stands in the hot armpit of the idling truck, in its warm diesel stink, and shouts the name of a city up to the man in the cab. He closes his eyes and lifts his chin, forearms resting on the almost horizontal steering wheel as he watches her clamber up, then he ducks his head to check the side mirror and swings back to the road.

He speeds up. At this rate she will reach Johannesburg before nightfall, and be on the road to New Brighton tomorrow to bring the letter to the dead man's mother, and the awful news that is better than no news.

There is movement behind her seat. On a padded bench that runs the width of the cab, the relief driver stirs awake and looks at her. He is a slim, tanned man with a humorous face.

'Hello lady,' he says.

'Hello,' she says.

They look at one another, almost smiling.

She turns back to face the road. He continues to look at her neck, the plane of her jaw, the slight curls. The rocking of the cab sets him dozing again and as his mind slips towards sleep he thinks of the passenger that she is so fresh, she could have been born this morning.

25

THERE WAS NO ROAD BUT THE ROAD WE WERE ON AND IT offered dangers along with ease of passage. My ears were held ready for any sound of another traveller, not just one from Vogelzang in pursuit of us two, for I was without a travel pass and without shoes and carrying a pale babe; adrift of the estate we were anyone's to seize.

While she slept I made time and kept to the smoother way until I heard a wagon or cart, then stepped behind a hummock and once down to a dry stream bed. In this way the journey had a fair pace for part of the afternoon. I was making such good time that I began to wonder for how much longer she could sleep tied under my breast, when she obliged with a waking cluck and then a full cry and I had us off the road and in a green hollow, shushing and hushing while I got a cloth in the milk and in her mouth, but she spat it out and cried all the louder 'til my knuckle was offered and accepted, then the knuckle covered over with milk-wet cloth and at last the milk cloth alone, and in this way she drank a meal.

While she sucked I kept the dark cloth as well as I could by her eyes but it was all ways slipping and though it was the gentler part of the day, on the brink of evening, she blinked and squinted at the light. Then she was done with the milk rag and in need of clean linens and I formed a tent with my shawl over us both and stripped and wiped her. No doubt there was something amiss with her limbs but it was still a pretty babe that lay on the skirts between my legs.

I eased back the shawl and let the sun fall on her lower body, recalling Le Voir on warmth for growing creatures; the light lent gilding to her pale skin.

When we were done I had us up again and kept going until it was all but dark. I feared the night out there and had a notion to spend it in a tree, though I could not decide how to give effect to the idea; as it happened our road at that time ran close by a crop of rocks and among the nooks it offered was a grotto well above the road. There she took the milk cloth without ado and I ate bread and lay her by my side and she slept. I watched her and the stars, listening to an owl make his wind-blown sounds.

She awoke in the night and I fumbled to feed her, then she woke again before the sun tipped the horizon but this time with cries that cracked my ears and I in a cold panic at the sound and with all the unadmitted fear that I could not do this thing. I held her, offered the milk cloth, made mothering sounds, cried myself and rocked her with wild swings as though to shake the sound from her, but the crying ran on 'til it sang in my brain. She tired at last but still sorrowed with hiccoughs of upset.

The sun was about to break past the edge of the world and I had an idea of letting her eyes and body learn light in the way other creatures do, with the day's coming, and so I made a bed of my shawl at the opening of the little cave and laid her there, unwrapping more of her as our part of the world turned its face fully to the light, 'til she was naked, and then in horror I saw that a thorn was in her thigh and in a rush of guilt and relief, but the most part guilt, I had it out and the place of it healed with kissing. I had undertaken to save this babe but could not protect her even for a night! She was sighing and her breath shaking and I, sick in my stomach with the fright of it, began to learn how terrible is love, in those moments as the sun warmed us and I needed her forgiveness though she could have no thought of blame.

A wagon was come around the bend in the road way, drawn by eight. I bundled the babe and shushed her, keeping still myself among the rocks, but first the lead beasts showed themselves as familiar and then the driver, and I was up and waving with my free arm and he about stopping the train and stepping down to the road.

Melt held the babe until I was on the driver's bench then handed her to me with a lifted brow and a word: 'Cargo?'

'Jansie's babe that they said died,' was my introduction and that struck him silent, looking from my face to hers, 'til he shrugged with mouth and brows and walked to the head of the span and started them off, and when the wagon came abreast of him climbed aboard and took the whip. He said: 'We will out span at the river like before. Then tomorrow for town. And now I will hear your news.'

From his words I reasoned that though we two were runaways we were not sought by them at the estate and this he said was so when my tale was done, and how could we be chased after all, one of us free and one never admitted as being born? Calcoen must be in a fury at his experiment escaped, the estate gone to young mistress, Le Voir in his place, but he seemed so little like a real man to me by then, I could not enjoy his fall.

Even before noon we stopped for the day. As well as the tables lashed to the wagon bed Melt had food and a can of milk from the goat; he could not have known the babe was along but she could take goat near so well as the other milk, and water and pappy bread if it came to that, so her feeding joined our safety as problems I could leave by the way.

He made a camp from carpet and cloth and a fire in a circle of stones. I laid the babe in the wagon 'til we had out spanned the team and hobbled them, then brought her to the carpet beneath a tree. We had the rest of the day before us, and the night. I fed her from Melt's provisions and she and I slept while he watched out for us, then she slept and I woke to be with him, and afterwards took a better rest. When we woke in the morning he set a meal and I felt a tug of envy while he laid open a crock of butter with a bay leaf pressed in it; I had fled that place but yet resented that others belonged to it, and I own for all my grand words that without the babe giving me an impulsion I may not have left it at all.

We ate and Melt had the story from me again and we tried to guess the project Calcoen was about in the outbuilding. Melt thought it was to raise a babe with the milk of a white woman in a white place in order to watch if it might turn white; I thought it was that same thing but with the test of keeping a babe from light being the essential trial. Had he meant her to never be seen by the sun? Or only until her first teeth, or when her courses began? I did not doubt he had set a goal, and ruled columns to meet it, though what he hoped to gain by this alchemy if it succeeded escaped my understanding. Did he want all of us to keep from the sun and be other than we were made to be? Or merely make some law that said we chose to be thus and must expect what came our way? The hidden logic of his science made me grind my teeth until Melt, to divert me towards good humour, drew back the covers on the babe.

And after all ...

And after all we were beside a river and oxen sighing near by, and the babe awoke and could not keep her eyes from the shifting leaves. In the next tree a pair of birds squabbled in song. Melt leaned on one elbow and smiled full at me and I had the thought that this could be my family. He handed me a slice of melon; I reached for it and our hands met above the naked babe and I thought, I have seen these colours in a sparrow's fledging, opened a nut and found them, and in a cut tree. The world was made of our colours. Calcoen's science frightened me but was suddenly risible as well; I saw how blind and broken a thing he was for working to change others in a project to fix the flaw in himself.

My daughter, at that moment you laughed out loud, and the birds in the branches above you stopped in startlement at it. To my mind in that instant you completed the journey that a babe must make from first breath to a place in the family and in the world. You had come along from 'it' to 'her' while you lay in that maze hut and only your mother believed in you; now you were you.

Melt brought us to your grandmama's house, where another babe was all ways welcome, and is. She said you were the end of it, the sign that a curse was lifted from our family, but I did not credit such things and never will. And we are making a life, you and I. Melt comes six times between New Years and each time brings a pot of conserve and one of pure white lard with the leaf pressed thereon; once there was a note from the master of the place, the wigmaker who married the next mistress of Vogelzang and won the estate – tortoise, flower trees, crazed mother and all. While Melt is by me I breathe easier, surprise myself with a smile. Between his visits I some times summon him to my mind as he was on that first harvest day, laughing.

And as for you, my darling girl, you are as pretty as your mother was; all who see you mark it.

And as for why your legs are not grown so straight as they might have, and why you sway when you walk, and when you try to run sway more, we will go on telling those who ask that it was a runaway wagon that did this, for who would believe the truth?

And when they say, Thanks be her life was spared, I smile and I agree.

But I do not forget the story of my rickety babe.

AFTER

HE NEVER SAW HER AGAIN. HE SAID TO HIMSELF, IN THE FIRST years, that she may have written, but knew this was unlikely; she would be aware that what she wrote would be read by others before he saw it, and she had had her fill of censorship.

The sweet, stupid blonde sixties of bloated Herrenvolk and Crimplene and the slamming of prison doors; the seventies: a sere deck without any colourful royals; the punch-drunk eighties ... the decades unfold with no pattern he can see until, in another autumn, Shone puts on his good dark suit and orders up a taxi to fetch him for a tour of polling stations. Because it defies a voters' roll or any system at all, this tumbling confluence of citizenry and those just now released from the lesser classifications, today he may choose where he will vote.

He had no thought of doing so near to the place where he now lives, having left it too late to pick up the knack of community. He selects a polling station on the outskirts of the city, to the north, where waves of townhouse complexes break against less uniform settlements, each eating up the raw veld in an almost visible flow and where voting will take place in the classroom of a yellow-brick primary school, a new building among hectares of new buildings.

He pays off the taxi driver and joins the line. Forty minutes pass, an hour, another hour. The enfranchisees are a few young whites and at least one old one, and many, many black people of all ages, who arrive on foot, in groups or alone, from the settlements over the hill.

Marshals are checking documents, leading people to tables to fill out forms, ducking their heads to answer questions, to explain about the ballot, about the invisible dye that will mark people's hands so that each votes only once in this, the first election; for days they will go around with thumbnails that bear a yellow cast as though they had been caught by a hammer some time before.

It is growing hotter, throats are dry. He is close enough now to the polling station to make out those who have voted – the proud grins, as of an achievement, the odd prance and cackle and cheers of Ahe! and Buwe! from those still waiting. Not many can keep up any pretence of detachment, although the men are less demonstrative than the women, who more keenly claim the day. Men like Francis Shone, old and pale, confine themselves to hitching their trousers, perhaps stretching neck from collar, craning around with a shy look at their neighbours, diffident about showing their craving to belong. They're almost ready to join in, to join.

A high, silvered bakkie moves down the line from the polling station end, driven by a tan white man in his late thirties. He has, thinks Shone, the slack jaw and calculating gaze of a livestock farmer as he looks them over, those in line. Shone thinks: Afrikaner. He stiffens, feels some of those around him notice the man, notice how he holds himself apart from their lines, how he studies them.

Shone looks at his watch, tells himself to remember the time. They exploded a car bomb at the airport this morning; there have been explosions in Transvaal streets for weeks now, a mounting crisis of threats against this, the next new South Africa. Shone allows himself the thrill of pretending to think the man in the bakkie means them harm; what he actually fears is that he may sneer, or shout something to steal the day from the people here.

The bakkie moves slowly, its tyres crackling on the gravel lying in drifts along the tarred road. It traces the long line and as it passes Shone's knot of people the old man sees again the driver's scowl and the loose set of his mouth. Marshals further up the line point him out to one another with lifted chins, and tension in the facial skin that says, Keep an eye on this one. The driver gets to the end of the line and accelerates away. They can hear his engine whining through the new roads of the suburb, fading to nothing. They breathe out, crane towards the head of the line.

Behind him in the line is a young couple, white, wrapped up in one another. Ahead, the packed, bright parcel of a Shangaan rump. He clears his throat and addresses this woman in BaVenda. He has to greet her twice before she registers that these words are coming from this white man, and she answers sweetly enough but is too distracted to provide the pleasure and praise that usually reward his formal baby talk with its vocabulary of twenty words, and she turns back to her friend.

They shuffle forward.

Odd that he should have placed the man in the bakkie as a farmer, and of animals. He has not been one himself for two decades and has concluded that it is something he, they, need to get out of their systems, this childish clinging to the brute fact of a place to be, or to have been, as if that conferred the sort of legitimacy that the surely less-controvertible fact of mere being could not. Boys in a sandpit, fighting over who got here first. Now all he has to deal with is the legacy of having once had a farm, which he fears may be in his system as its defining fact for all the days he has. In the tradition of his time, he knows, he is expected to remember it with nostalgia, but he can only see Bandolier (the name tightens his chest) as a place that people left, until he was able to leave it, too.

Jacob made it to the New World, where, Shone understands, he picked up, and soon lost, the habit of writing to the farmer, possibly because he never received his letters and so never wrote back. Shone has heard he is American now, like the man who taught him to drive on Mannamead's track and with whom the farmer did exchange letters – his, asking after Vergilius, Shone's telling him nothing. Jacob's grandmother died in service six years after he left Bandolier for the last time. Shone conspired with her cousins to bury Mariah Kobe illegally, on the farm, with her ancestors; one of those cousins, Bettina Kobe by name, replaced her in caring for him, a hardship post when no one came to them from year to year.

After Teichert was promoted to Pretoria, Shone slipped off the list and escaped to Johannesburg, where he picked up some of the forgotten tricks of conversation. That and laughter and shared anger helped to build a padding of context around what felt like the theft of his life.

He misses the insects – if he meets with five decent Scarabidiae in a year it is a lot – but the birds were not long in following him to the city: grunting louries and ibises patrolling the lawn in constabulary pairs, and stocky, painted barbets.

When he is asleep his thoughts escape him and he dreams of Bandolier; the best dreams are when he sees it and the village and convent from a godlike perspective, drifting overhead, knowing he will discern the pattern in it—

A silvery flash at the corner of his vision. The bakkie has returned. This time it clambers off the road and parks on the grass verge across from the patient line, which does not exactly cower but certainly shifts, and they bump against each other like cattle. This time the marshals fix their scowls and make straight for the vehicle but they are fifty metres away and the man is out of the cab and flicking aside a tarpaulin covering the bed. Now those in the line can see that two young children have followed him out of the bakkie, and see, too, that on the truck bed is a plastic drum fitted with a tap. Without looking around him, the man fills cups from the drum and hands them to the children. The girl takes her brother's hand and performs a careful mime of looking both ways and left again before they cross. Concentrating on not spilling any, they reach the line to hand the cups of water to the waiting voters, watching while they drink, and take them, empty, back to their father. He keeps his head down, filling cups, lining them up on the open tailgate of the high truck. When he finally eases his shoulders and looks over to the line Shone catches his eye. The man's glance slides sideways, he is blushing. He lifts a hand in a gesture that takes in the line, the marshals, the mamas. He calls to Shone in Afrikaans-accented English: 'I just wanted my kids to be part of it.'

The marshals who had started towards the bakkie are returning to their station, joking and jostling against one another. Shone hears African women down the line, bending to the blonde children, saying, Thanks for you, my baby, as they accept the cups, sharing with one another approving sounds about the man and his water and his respectful children.

They were wrong about him but they are not ashamed of themselves for having feared his silver bakkie, his narrowed eyes. Among the sentiments they feel at his actions, the strongest is surprise. They are surprised at his kindness.

But the line is shuffling a few steps forward again, and now someone outside the hall is kicking the ground in a contained jig, giving the thumbs-up high over her head, her thumbnail wearing its fine new, old bruise.

He thinks that tonight he will dream of Bandolier and beyond, and he does, flying over a night-time, waterless place like a swimmer carried past reefs and lurking fishes. It is a village below – barely that: a scratchling lane clinging to the straight black Great North Road has gathered accretions of a filling station, a grimy café, a hotel and police station. Plots cling to these and to one another, and bonewhite pumpkins hold down the roofs of houses. A flag has caught a night swell of air and set a lanyard clinking on a pole. It interrupts a police sergeant's dream; he swallows his snore and shifts against his abundant wife. In a room in the hotel another policeman lies alone, cringing like a mollusc in his narrow bed. Moonlight catches the oily nacre on his empty boots.

Behind the butchery and abattoir with their blue porch light, the butcher slumbers in his bed, his wife in hers, and in the next room, kept from her by a wall but lying nearer to her sister, a twin of the butcher's wife. Each sister's orange head with its black net lies in the centre of its pillow. Each sleeper's right hand rests upon a mounded stomach, the left just touching a collarbone. As one, they mutter something and sink deeper.

There are more sisters if you take three godlike strokes and skim beyond the village to where they lie in rows of cells. An alarm clock sounds as you watch, and a slow ripple runs through the honeycomb, touched off by whispers like wind across the veld: Sister … Sister, and at the summons each sleeper slips from her cot and kneels.

And you, from where you watch above them, see that in a moment the earth will have turned to the sun again, and soon it will be too light to fly.

END

ACKNOWLEDGEMENTS

The enthralling and exhaustive *Children of Bondage, A social history of the slave society of the Cape of Good Hope, 1652–1838*, by Robert C H Shell, inspired the stories of Trijn van de Caab and of Jansie. I also consulted *Human Biodiversity: Genes, Race, and History (Foundations of Human Behaviour)* by Jonathan Marks, wherein Carolus Linnaeus's categories of human types as used by Calcoen are to be found in a history of the absurdity of race. In *Travels in the Cape 1772–1776, A Voyage to the Cape of Good Hope towards the Antarctic Polar Circle Round the World and to the Country of the Hottentots and the Caffres* Volumes I and II, by Anders Sparrman, published by the Van Riebeeck Society, the dashing Swede, a disciple of Linnaeus, makes good company, spicing his account with gossip about the locals. Also useful were the first English translation of Prosper Montagné's *Larousse Gastronomique*; *Briefwisseling van Hendrik Swellengrebel Jr Oor Kaapse Sake 1778–1792*; *Cape Town to Cairo* by Lillie B Douglass (an account of a journey by forty-one American families in Airstream trailers travelling the length of Africa in 1959); *Through the Narrow Gate*, by Karen Armstrong (a memoir of life in a Catholic convent in the 1960s); and *African Insect Life*, by S H Skaife. The sentence on p. 229 which reads "the observer is part of the society he observes, truth can only be judged, imprisoned or bribed" comes from the writing of French mathematician and social theorist the Marquis de Condorcet, writing in 1782; see *The French Encounter with Africans: White Response to Blacks 1530–1880* by William B Cohen.

Many, many thanks to the siblings, daughters, cousins, friends and colleagues who were the first readers and the constant encouragers of this book before it was this book, in particular James Robertson, Lucy Neal, Helen Sullivan, Julia Sullivan, Aubrey Paton, Gabriella Bekes, Peta Scop, Julie Reid Stevenson, Jennifer Cohen, Jane-Anne Hobbs and Jenny Hobbs. For her crucial help, thank you to Michele Magwood. Fourie Botha and Fanie Naudé, two kind, diplomatic, funny and brilliant men, are my first publisher and editor, so I have no way of knowing whether all such are as great to work with as they, but I suspect they are better than most.

Claire Robertson lives in Simon's Town. She has spent the past 30 years as a journalist, reporting from South Africa, the US and USSR. She has worked in newspapers, magazines, radio and television, and now works as a senior copy editor on the *Sunday Times*. She has won awards for her reporting and her work is carried in several anthologies. *The Spiral House* is her first work of fiction.